MORGUE DRAWER CLINK OR COOLER?

Also by Jutta Profijt:
Morgue Drawer Four
Morgue Drawer Next Door
Morgue Drawer for Rent
Morgue Drawer: Do Not Enter!
Dust Angel

MORGUE DRAWER CLINK OR COOLER?

Jutta Profijt

TRANSLATED BY Erik J. Macki

amazoncrossing

Text copyright © 2014 Jutta Profijt
Translation copyright © 2015 Erik J. Macki
All rights reserved.

Previously published as *Knast oder Kühlfach* by Deutscher Taschenbuch Verlag, Germany, in 2014. Translated from German by Erik J. Macki. First published in English by AmazonCrossing in 2015.

Published by AmazonCrossing, Seattle
www.apub.com

Amazon, the Amazon logo, and AmazonCrossing are trademarks of Amazon.com, Inc., or its affiliates.

ISBN-13: 9781503944473
ISBN-10: 1503944476

Cover design by Scott Barrie

Printed in the United States of America

PROLOGUE

Article published on April 3:

Cologne City Observer
COLOGNE'S NEWSPAPER
INDEPENDENT - SINCE 1802 - NONPARTISAN

Robbery: Pharmacist Dies

DOWNTOWN – The Cologne police today reported the death of Stefan Groscheck, the owner of Asterix Pharmacy in Old Town, who died from a neck fracture police say was caused by a fall after struggling with a burglar during a break-in. Groscheck had closed the pharmacy for the night but was still onsite at the time of the alleged crime. The press release indicated that a silent alarm went off at the pharmacy at 10 p.m. Officers arriving on the scene found evidence of a break-in and discovered Groscheck's body in the back of the premises. Officers later arrested a known drug addict, who had multiple packages of narcotics on him, in the vicinity of the pharmacy.

On Wednesday, another pharmacist confirmed that these were missing from Asterix's inventory. The suspect is currently in custody pending charges.

Groscheck, 51, was well known in Cologne for his active involvement in the city's massive annual Carnival celebration. He was also known for the nonprofit cancer research organization he founded with his brother-in-law, pharmaceutical executive Bastian Weiz. The partners started Cologne versus Cancer five years ago after the death from colon cancer of Weiz's wife, Melina Groscheck Weiz.

ONE

June 27

There was no advance warning, no alarm, not even a tiny hint that Detective Sergeant Gregor Kreidler was about to be arrested. On the contrary. Everything was totally chill. Gregor was sitting with his girlfriend Katrin, his best friend Martin, and Martin's girlfriend Birgit in a Chinese restaurant that met the whole group's requirements: Katrin loved food as spicy as she was, Martin lived primarily on vegetable matter he rescued from the compost bin, and Birgit was pregnant. And if all of that wasn't enough, Birgit had now developed a strange appetite for disgusting things like slimy mushroom salads and gristly pigs' ears—seriously: actual ears from actual pigs—which were available locally only in this restaurant. As usual Gregor had gone along with what everyone else wanted because there was only one thing that Gregor ever needed from food: it had to fill him up.

Since I had been dead for over a year and couldn't join in on the fress fest, my objections went unheard. Even when I was alive I hated vegetarian fodder, but I also hated the noise of human teeth biting through pork cartilage, so it would never have occurred to me to make my diet dependent on wok wielders.

I don't want you to think I'd willingly hang out with these four whenever they got a snack flash. It's just that today they had brought a baby name book along and were going to finally give the bonsai in Birgit's belly his stamp of individuality, three weeks and a day before the due date. The main goal was to avoid Brittneyitis—the technical term for the disease suffered by countless modern parents who can't give their babies a normal name—and to take prophylactic action to avoid hideous playground nicknames. That's why I was tagging along now—for whatever input I could offer through Martin.

They had just finished their appetizer and were on the letter G.

"Gregor is a thoroughly heroic name, even for a little girl," the expectant godfather was saying, which earned him a thwack to the back of the head from Katrin, a shake of the head from Martin, and a belch from Birgit. "The etymology is Greek and means 'vigilant.'"

"And the related Latin word *egregius* means standing out from the herd," Martin added.

"See?" Gregor said, turning to Katrin. "No reason for physical abuse. I expect an apology the second we get home." Katrin gave him a dirty grin.

"A very thorough apology," Gregor added softly.

Birgit hiccupped.

"Gregoria would be the feminine form," Gregor explained in a feigned schoolmarm's voice, which earned him rolled eyes from Katrin, a sigh from Martin, and a giggle from Birgit. Gregor's cell phone rang, interrupting the expressions of general annoyance.

He answered, listened for about three seconds, furrowed his brow, and growled, "Hey, what's that supposed to mean?" The other caller hung up, leaving only the *beep-beep-beep* of a German dial tone coming from the phone.

"What was that?" Katrin asked with alarm as Gregor pressed the red button on the screen. As the main squeeze of a police detective, she was always braced for the worst.

"No ide—" Gregor began, but stopped when two men suddenly appeared on either side of the table.

"Gregor Kreidler, you are a suspect in the murder of Susanne Hauschild. We have to ask you to come with us."

In the subsequent silence all we could hear were Birgit's burps, a sign of nervousness that had increasingly been torturing her—and me—since she had been five months along.

"This is bullshit!" Katrin burst out. "Who are you jokers anyway?"

I thought Katrin knew everyone Gregor worked with at the police department, but apparently not these two. I didn't either.

"Criminal Investigations, Düsseldorf Police Department, ma'am," the taller joker said. "Detectives Keller and Stein. And, no, this isn't bullshit. Mr. Kreidler?"

Normally other detectives would have first addressed him as *Detective* Kreidler if they talked to him during an investigation, quickly switching to more collegial first names. Yeah, I know what you're thinking. Even the uptight asshole types from Düsseldorf.

But in this situation there wasn't a trace of collegial solidarity. Gregor's complexion had run through the color chart from dark red to ghost white, and now it was settling into a creepy gray. He opened his mouth and closed it again without saying a word and then pushed his chair back and stood up.

"I'm ready," Gregor told the cops. He didn't look back, avoiding the stares of his dining companions.

"Gregor!" Katrin whispered harshly as she stood.

"B-but . . ." Martin stammered.

Birgit hiccupped.

And with that, the two Düssel-dweebs were off with Gregor in tow.

Katrin fell back into her chair, Martin and Birgit still had their shit traps gaping open, and even I was frozen for a few seconds in a state of shock. Then Martin and I reacted at the same time. "Pascha, after him!" he brainwaved me, but I was already on my way.

My physical condition, by which I mean my lack of a physical condition, was a benefit in this case, because I could tail Gregor and the two Düsseldorf detectives unnoticed. Duh. I'm dead, after all. Well, not entirely, of course. Otherwise I wouldn't be around in any form. See, when I got murdered a year and four months ago, my soul never found the tunnel with the light, and so I've been moldering around here ever since, stuck between the realms of the quick and the dead. My body is long buried, but my soul is way livelier now than when I was alive. By which I mean: I can't booze it anymore so I'm constantly sober. I can't sleep anymore so I'm constantly awake. And I've learned tons from Gregor, the only cop I've ever thought was a cool dude, and from Martin, the only person I can communicate with. Martin and I discovered our special relationship on the occasion of my autopsy, when Dr. Martin Gänsewein, doctor of bodysnatchery at the Institute for Forensic Medicine at the University of Cologne, sliced me up from neck to balls, gutted me, and very crudely sewed me back together.

I can hear and smell the world of the earthbound, even though I don't have ears or a nose anymore. I can feel electromagnetic waves and even control them sometimes, since I'm an electromagnetic wave myself. So there's tons I can still do, but communication only works with Martin. Which seriously cramps my social interactions in both quantity and quality. In other words, being stuck with one and only one role model is bad enough, but I'm sure Martin is also some kind of punishment for me, like an afterlife of soapbox derbies for a Formula One driver. You'll learn more about the special relationship between Martin "the Meticulologist" Gänsewein and the coolest ghost this side of heaven and hell over the course of the story—maybe more than you want to.

For now, in any case, it's all about Gregor.

Düsseldorf and Cologne have a lot in common. They're major cities on the Rhine, about forty minutes away from each other if you take the A57 at one a.m. to avoid autobahn traffic. Düsseldorf has half a million people, Cologne a solid mil. They're major rivals in sports and everything else. Think of it this way: Düsseldorf is like Mercedes, and Cologne is like BMW. Each thinks it's better than the other. Which is bullshit. Apart from the historic fuckup—back when the powers that be made Düsseldorf the state capital—that hicksville on the tailwater of the Rhine has nothing on Cologne. Which is why Düsseldorfers just *love* dumping on people from here. But in the end, people in Cologne know that Cologne's *Kölsch* and Düsseldorf's *Altbier* are brewed in the same way, so the reason why our beer is light in color and the beer down the Rhine looks like it's from the tank on the back of a liquid-manure spreader is one you can mull over yourself.

Even in terms of the cop shop itself, Cologne is way ahead. The Criminal Investigations department at the Cologne Police Department is housed in sleek, glass-and-tile new construction over in the Kalk neighborhood, whereas Düsseldorf CI is stuck in an ugly hundred-year-old brick bunker. And that's where they hauled Gregor off to.

Of the two plainclothes who had picked Gregor up, the one who looked like a choirboy did all the talking, while the other one just kept digging the dirt out from under his fingernails. A lot of dirt. Maybe he was actually a gardener and just helped the cops out once in a while. No idea how Düsseldorf handles its staffing.

"I'll be recording our conversation," the choirboy said, pushing "Play" on his handheld recorder. "Could you state your name for the record?" he asked.

Gregor said nothing.

"What were you doing last Friday night at six o'clock?"

Gregor said nothing.

He said nothing in response to that question or to any of the subsequent questions about his daily activities over the past week, about his relationship to Susanne Hauschild, or the reason why they had met the previous Friday. He just stared for a solid hour at the tabletop in front of him until he finally raised his head and opened his mouth.

"May I have some coffee?" he asked.

Detective Keller—or was it Stein?—sighed, got up, and went to get coffee for all three of them. Then the questions continued. But Gregor separated his upper and lower lips only to gulp down the disgusting, acrid-smelling brew. They couldn't even make a proper pot of coffee up in Düsseldorf.

Since Gregor continued not contributing to the conversation and since I still didn't have the foggiest what was actually going on here, I made my way back to Cologne. Martin, Katrin, and Birgit had left the restaurant and were now hunkered down in Martin and Birgit's place. Katrin's red patent-leather pumps were set neatly beside Martin's orthopedic comfort shoes and Birgit's sneakers by the front door. A fourth pair of shoes clued me in on who had joined the trio before I even went into the living room: Gregor's partner, Jenny.

"I cannot believe that he just went with them like that," Jenny said.

Katrin exploded without saying a word, leaping up and going into the kitchen to pour herself a glass of wine.

"Jenny, honey," she hissed when she returned to the living room, "could you please drop the incredulous child's routine and put on your I'm-a-police-detective face? I get that it's hard to believe. I also get that it has to be a mistake. But we're not getting anywhere with the endless I-can't-believe-it crap."

Normally I would have been way into Katrin's tantrum, because when her eyeballs shoot out laser beams, her cheeks glow, and her lips tremble—that's when she looks her hottest. But these circumstances had spoiled even my mood, so I couldn't really enjoy the sight of her.

Jenny made a face and sipped her herbal tea, which Martin had brewed to calm the nondrinkers' nerves. Birgit was munching on a carrot and staring into space. She didn't seem to notice the tears that were slowly and evenly trickling down her face. Katrin took a couple of deep breaths, dropped into the armchair next to Jenny, and laid her hand on Jenny's arm.

"I'm sorry."

Jenny gulped and nodded. Then she straightened her shoulders and pulled a notepad out of her bag. "OK, let's start from the top."

"Hey, Martin!" I said, interjecting my thoughts into his. "They asked Gregor about any alibi for last Friday night."

Martin mentally waved me off.

"This might help get your stupid debate here going," I said, pushing back.

"And how do you propose that I explain my sudden awareness of that information?" Martin asked me. Then he pulled his mental blinds shut.

Oh, great. Once again he had sidelined me with his classic argument, which is always a version of *How am I supposed to explain the things I suddenly know that I can't actually know?* It wouldn't have been so tragic in this case, tossing what he knew out into the world, because Katrin at least knows that I exist—as does Gregor, by the way. Martin had told Birgit that he occasionally gets "clues from the dead," and Jenny-Bunny was once witness to a situation where certain things might have occurred to her if that were in her nature. Well, that's unfair—Jenny isn't actually stupid. She's just young, green, and a little naïve, although her bulb clearly shines less brightly than Katrin's—or the brilliant Birgit's.

But Martin was totally ignoring me, serving up a summary of events for Jenny in his best professional tone, which he loves trotting out in court or in meetings with his boss.

"Does anyone know who Susanne Hauschild is?" Jenny asked after Martin had finished.

Martin blew on his tea and squinted over at Katrin.

Katrin noticed and raised her eyebrows. "You know her?"

Martin nodded. Slowly. Hesitantly. And clearly exceedingly unhappily.

"And who is she?" Jenny asked, clearly impatient.

"Gregor's wife," Martin mumbled.

And that even drove me out of my lane.

After Martin's dirty bomb, the silence in the room was so intense that for a few seconds I thought I had sudden-onset hearing loss. But I couldn't imagine how that could happen, so I calmed back down. Birgit had stopped chewing her carrot midbite, Jenny's pen hovered motionless over the paper, and Katrin's mouth was opening and closing without any sound coming out.

"Maybe they're divorced by now," Martin whispered after what felt like eons. "I'm not entirely certain . . ."

Just a refresher: Martin is Gregor's best friend. They know each other from high school. And here Martin didn't know whether Gregor was married or divorced? Or widowed or whatever? But no matter. We were all shocked in any case.

"Wh-why haven't I ever heard of her?" Katrin finally stammered.

Martin shrugged.

Birgit resumed her nibbling.

Jenny jotted something down. I flew around her shoulder and read: *Susanne Hauschild—Gregor's secret (!) (ex?) wife!?!*

This revelation had obviously exceeded the drama barometer, because most violent crimes are perpetrated by people in the immediate social circle of the victim. And spouses are at the top of that particular list.

One more reason never to get married.

"What did the detectives in Düsseldorf s—" Birgit started.

"Assholes!" Katrin bellowed.

"Katrin!" said Martin, who normally stays all earnest and friendly even if a carjacker were ordering him to hand over his wallet before jumping off the overpass over the A1. Which isn't as risky as it sounds, by the way, because the Cologne Beltway is always backed up. So there's no way you could get run over; at most, you'd land on the roof of some stopped vehicle and break your leg.

"She's right," I interrupted with a yell. "Assholes!"

"They didn't say anything," Birgit mumbled. Those were the first words she'd uttered since I rejoined their conversation.

Birgit's a real firecracker, actually. She is amazingly hot with her endless legs, long blonde hair, and slightly upward-curved smiley mouth, and she doesn't just have something going on her blouse but also in her braincase. She worked at a bank until her maternity leave kicked in, which in Germany starts six weeks before the due date *and* is required, even if you're not lazy. Birgit's not lazy, and working in a bank sounds worse than it is—at least, it hasn't screwed up her character or anything. Actually Birgit has always been pretty relaxed and cheerful. But that changed abruptly once she was flooded with mommy hormones. And the bigger her belly has gotten as the bonsai balloon has swelled up, the quieter she's gotten. "Pensive" is what Martin calls it. And then for a while whenever she'd say anything, she was a bit on the bitchy side, which wasn't at all like her and which I did not like. But that phase was over, thank God, and she was starting to resemble a sluggish East German Trabant more than a zippy West German BMW convertible. The latter of which was the car Birgit had saved and saved for but which now stood parked and unused despite the weeks of awesome weather we'd been having. "Pregnant women shouldn't drive convertibles," Martin had opined. *Yawn.*

"Those two guys are detectives from Düsseldorf," Birgit said. "Their names are Keller and Stein, and they said Gregor had to come with them because he's suspected of murdering Susanne Hauschild. That was everything."

I beamed. Was that a glimpse of the good old Birgit I loved? Who could think and banter with the same precision and excellent grammar as Martin but who—unlike him—never sounded like a high school teacher? Who sometimes clued in on connections that even I was slow to realize? Hey, I said *some-times*! Rarely, in other words. Or, actually, never.

"Did they say when the murder happened?" Jenny asked.

They all shook their heads.

"Friday night," I roared, but Martin didn't react.

"And Gregor—"

"Stood up and went with them. Without a word," Katrin said, still stunned and interrupting Jenny.

"I'll see what I can find out," Jenny said as she stood and fled. Well, at least that's how her departure came across to me.

Katrin got up right after Jenny left, muttered something about needing to be alone, and disappeared. Martin and Birgit stayed put, as though they had been blast-frozen to the sofa. But Martin asked me mentally to serve up my latest findings for him now. *Bah!* As though I were a genie in a bottle he could let out only when needed and cork up the rest of the time? I'm not a genie! Since Martin had so rudely given me the cold shoulder, I wanted to pout for a while, but instead I flew back to Düsseldorf.

Gregor wasn't technically under arrest, because for that the court would need to issue an arrest warrant. And German judges don't shoot out a piece of paper like that just because someone thinks, statistically speaking, the husband is always the murderer. For an arrest warrant, a German judge needs a solid reason.

Of course, the cops can still hold a suspect, but only for one day. And then they either need to officially arrest you or let you go. So it wasn't exactly the worst sign when Keller—or was it Stein?—told Gregor, "Please stay here for now, Detective."

It had bummed me out he hadn't addressed Gregor as "detective" before, but now that he did, it sounded snide.

Gregor didn't react. He kept staring into his empty coffee cup, silent.

Something was not right here. I mean, apart from the fact that Gregor had allegedly offed his ex. Gregor could kill someone if he had to—just like anyone else. But we're talking about Gregor—the most hard-nosed detective this side of the Atlantic. We're talking about Katrin's boyfriend, and Martin's best friend. We're talking about a man with incredible intuition, a man who is a master of tedious deskwork and lightning-fast apprehensions and who is also always ready to dole out some cool line.

I did not believe that *that* Gregor had taken out his old ball and chain. But what I didn't understand was his silence. Why wouldn't he say he hadn't murdered her and be done with it?

Why wasn't he giving Keller and Stein a friendly suggestion they go continue their circle jerk in the basement of their crappy old HQ building instead of pissing on the legs of seasoned colleagues? Why didn't he just stand up and leave?

Well, fine, that wasn't possible now because he was being detained. But the only reason they were holding him was because he was acting all coy, like a groom getting his marriage license. Normally they say "don't talk, you walk," but that didn't seem to apply here.

I couldn't shake these thoughts as I accompanied Gregor into the transfer van, to the jail, through security and processing, and into his cell. The jail was fairly new, and at least the cell wasn't a holding cell for lots of people—but the ten square meters with a bed, table, chair, and toilet didn't come off as exactly cozy. Gregor didn't even look around. Instead he hurled himself onto the bed, put his hands behind his head, and lay there completely still. Unfortunately, since he didn't start talking to himself out loud, I had to bail on him after a while in frustration for lack of information. A silent sad sack like that wasn't going to get me anywhere, so I decided to start my own investigation immediately.

I left the big house and zoomed back to Martin and Birgit. They were in bed, where Martin was rubbing some kind of massage oil onto Birgit's big belly. Seriously. Now, of all times? But he wasn't massaging; he wasn't really even rubbing. He was just sort of gently pinching the stuff into her skin—supposedly to help minimize stretch marks and promote intimacy between the expecting parents. At least, that's what that old bag of a midwife claimed at their birth class. Call me crazy that I think a round of screwing is somehow more intimate, but Martin was working the lotion with passion—underneath his anti-electrosmog net. It looks like a metallic mosquito net, actually, and it keeps unwanted electromagnetic impulses away from the person sleeping inside—in other words, me. *Great!* So I wasn't going to be able to get any help from Martin right now. I apparently needed to get going on my investigation without him, because everyone knows the first few hours and days in a murder investigation are the most important, and this murder already happened forty-eight hours ago. If Gregor was the only suspect after that long, then the cops had been bobbing for two days in the wrong toilet bowl.

A murder investigation always begins with the victim, because that's all you've got at the start. So I zoomed up to the attic, where Martin had set up a computer for me in the cabinet, and I Googled "Susanne Hauschild." I came across a picture of her that sent off all the alarms in my head. I had just seen the chick, a couple of days ago. Alive. With Gregor.

I decided to reconstruct Gregor's activity in the week before Susanne Hauschild was murdered. I didn't think that would be too hard since Martin and Birgit were still busy talking over baby names, nursery décor, childrearing approaches, childhood diseases, puke, and related topics, and I felt like being around them less and less. Of course I still needed Martin as a conversation partner, but when it came to dawdling away my days, lately I'd been sticking closer to Gregor.

TWO

The morning Gregor was supposed to meet Susanne Hauschild, I got to Gregor's office around ten. It was a sunny, warm Friday, and I didn't have anything special up. On Friday mornings there's not much going on in hospitals and emergency rooms, where I like to hang out. I don't want you to think I'm blood-thirsty or that I like to revel in the suffering of people who got tangled up in a lamppost when they crashed their motorcycle or got an ax stuck in their shin while chopping wood. Not at all. I'm just waiting around for a kindred spirit. So far my existence has been a pretty lonely business. There aren't any other souls in my limbo world because, usually, here's how things go: at the moment of death, the soul leaves the body and maybe says "hi" quickly before disappearing into heaven or hell. No one ever stays behind. Sometimes as they pass me by I'll call out "Say hi to Marlene!" She was the pudgy little nun who's been the only one to keep me company for any length of time here on my middle plane so far. But eventually she said good-bye on her way into the light, too, but I'm pretty sure she occasionally looks in on me.

Other locales where I like to spend time don't have much going on Friday mornings either. That's when they air out the beds at the brothels and delouse the swinger clubs. So I stopped by to make sure Gregor was all right, because I knew he had a major appointment today. When nothing else is going on, I often tag along with him to court.

Gregor was putting on a tie. That's something he normally avoids, but today he was testifying in a case, so he bowed to the pressure of convention. He was so annoyed trying to tie it, he pulled down on it so hard I was worried he might cut off his air supply. Jenny was standing all-grins in the doorway to their office, which pissed Gregor off even more, but he finally managed to get the knot more or less tied. Maybe not good enough for Willie Windsor's wedding, but for court, it looked more than fine.

The court appearance of the great Detective Sergeant Kreidler was a complete success. He answered all questions accurately, he explained the evidence against the accused without any loose ends, and he didn't stammer once when he was asked how he had even come to notice the accused in the first place. It's not like he could say that his slasher best friend Martin had autopsied a car thief a while back and that Martin had since been getting fed hot tips from the realm of the dead by the ghost of the aforementioned thief—namely me. So Gregor did what he usually does in such cases and stretched the truth. The truth was already pretty stretched out at that point, but fortunately he was asked about how he had come to know certain things only in certain cases, namely, whenever the defense attorney was driving at some procedural error, which didn't work in today's case. Gregor left the witness stand upright and serious. He showed his spiteful grin only once he got back out into the hallway and Jenny asked how things had gone.

"Starting now, the only women he's going to be seeing will be on splotchy paper."

The satisfaction was all mine, though, because even though I had gotten in trouble with the law more than once when I was alive, there are still some kinds of criminals I cannot stand—and those are the guys who use their wieners as weapons to torment other people. And when those victims are kids or women . . . well, that is fucked up. The defendant who Gregor had just helped earn a lifelong career at Café Cubical was in that category. He was a rapist who had killed his most recent victim between (!) committing multiple other sexual assaults. Accidentally, he claimed. No idea how a guy "accidentally" gets a tear-proof plastic bag stuck over someone's head using a hundred ninety-seven centimeters of duct tape. With that much tape we used to repair whole production series of Opels. Anybody who reaches for that stuff knows exactly what he's doing.

Gregor was futzing with his tie again, this time to loosen it, when his cell phone rang. Someone had discovered a suicide in the attic of her house. Detectives have to go and check on reported suicides to make sure they really are suicides and not murders. So Gregor and Jenny got going, and I followed them.

There are way more ways to let it all hang out than the average citizen is aware, if that's how you want to go. Everyone knows the trapdoor-and-dead method from just about any western. That style is not merely swingy and dynamic, it's also pretty successful because the neck makes a loud click and—boom, it's over. No doubt, no extended suffering, just nice and quick. The most unpleasant version is hanging off the heating pipe or drainpipe under a sink. Yes, that's a real method. However, in these—let's call them near-earth suicides—the self-slaughterer usually dies on the slow side. The key thing is for the tension on the rope not to let up so the wannabe suicide can't just scramble back up the second it gets too tight. That method works only for the especially strong-willed.

The woman who Gregor and Jenny found in a multifamily prewar building had either not thought herself strong-willed enough or she had just made use of the available infrastructure, which happened to provide a top-notch neck snapping. She was hanging from an exposed roof beam. At first Gregor and Jenny studied her from the landing and through the attic door.

"Who discovered her?" Gregor asked right off.

The uniform guarding the attic door pointed at a small woman in a floral apron dress who was wailing into a soggy, brilliant-white pillowcase. She had apparently taken it out of the laundry basket she had brought to the attic, intending to hang some things up to dry. Three of the four clotheslines were still in place, but the fourth was wrapped around the body's neck.

"Everyone informed?" Gregor asked.

The uniform nodded. Sooner or later the slicers and number girls would be showing up.

Gregor turned to the wailing apron. "Do you know the woman?"

"She's Paulina Pleve," the apron sobbed, half suffocating in her pillowcase.

"Does she live in this building?"

"She's my neighbor."

"When did you last see her alive?"

The apron blew her nose loudly into the pillowcase and shrugged, uncertain. "Yesterday? Maybe it was the day before. I don't know . . ."

Gregor asked Jenny to take down the apron's contact information and accompany her to her apartment. He stayed at the door to the attic, looking around studiously.

The uniform cleared his throat. "I had to break in the door. It was locked from inside."

Gregor sighed. "The neighbor called the police because the door was locked from inside?"

"Of course not." The uniform carefully pulled the door shut. Although the ancient glass in the old mullioned door had a frost-and-snowflake pattern etched into it, Gregor could still make out the shape of the body, subtly swaying in the lukewarm draft.

"Tell Crime Scene Investigations exactly how you found the door and what you did to open it."

"Of course."

It took another ten minutes for the slicer to arrive from the Institute for Forensic Medicine—in the person of Katrin. She gave Gregor a fleeting peck on the mouth, pulled on her shoe protectors and coverall thingies, stuffed her beautiful long hair under the hood, and went inside. It was about as hot in the attic as Death Valley in August.

Katrin is pretty loud when it comes to complaining about working conditions in those hideous full-body getups, but she never deviates from her professionalism. She will never be the one standing before a judge, confessing that the scene of the crime was contaminated by her or her colleagues because it's too hot to wear the coveralls in summer, or too cold in winter. Too cold in winter because there isn't room for a sensible jacket underneath those coveralls, let alone Katrin's down coat. On this cardinal rule she and Martin agree absolutely—presumably the only thing the two of them have in common.

Katrin read the thermometer in her kit and noted the ambient temperature as thirty-five degrees Celsius; she measured the openings of both attic windows and determined the compass directions in which the windows were pointing and took a couple of pictures as memory aids. Coroners need all that information to determine the time of death, because a corpse doesn't cool down as fast in a hot attic as it does in a dank basement—obviously, right? But if drafts from open windows came into play, Katrin would even research overnight temperatures to calculate as precise a time of death as possible. Katrin isn't merely the hottest chick on the slicer team. She's also one of the best.

From my perspective, by which I mean two meters above the floor and just as far from the mope on a rope, Katrin and Paulina Pleve looked amazingly similar to each other, since Paulina was also dressed all in white. White T-shirt, white jeans, and white tennis socks. But she didn't seem like she had gone with the all-white angel's raiment just for the occasion. More likely she spent her days holding suction nozzles for a dentist or syringes for a family doctor. Or maybe she was the tooth fairy herself, or a pediatrician, or an orthopedist . . . I couldn't tell based solely on the quality of her tennis socks.

Katrin didn't pay much attention to the body at first. She was way more focused on the old wooden ladder lying under the feet of the hanging body. Katrin measured the height of the ladder and the distance from the dangling feet to the floor. A match.

The CSI number girls—most of whom were actually men today—started bustling into the attic, also wearing white coveralls. They shooed Katrin out briefly and scanned the slightly dusty floor for footprints, putting their number cards in front of the prints and the ladder and the clothesline on the floor. They measured distances, took pictures, and then called Katrin back in.

"She was still alive when she was hanged," one of the number girls rumbled in his deepest bass.

"Tell me, Mr. Expert, how you know that?" Katrin asked.

"Take a look at how the tongue is hanging out of the mouth."

"The tongue can come out postmortem," Katrin replied with audible *Schadenfreude*. "But the excess flow of saliva is evidence she was still alive."

Another number girl gave a friendly tap to his temple with his index finger, and several of them rumbled with greater or lesser spite, but not one of them was distracted even for a second from his work. They were all hunched over studying the floor, some holding magnifying glasses up to their eyeballs. The whole scene looked a modern-art performance with faceless dudes swarming among themselves attempting to articulate important-like questions of humanity and such. I saw that on TV once. But actually they reminded me more of a team of auto-body painters all looking for someone's contact lens.

After they had scoured everything, the CSI folks helped Katrin remove the body. Katrin secured all the evidence from the body while the number girls continued investigating the scene. They had the uniform explain how the old door used an old-style key that had locked the door from the inside and how he had slid a rug under the door and then tried to shake the key out of the lock, but it hadn't landed on the rug. Then he had taken a saber, which the apron had brought him from downstairs, and slid it between the door and jamb and finagled the door open with force. "A saber?" Gregor asked, who had overhead that part of the conversation.

"Heirloom," the uniform explained, pointing at a jagged piece of metal decorated with panaches of tassels now lying out on the landing of the stairwell.

The number girls measured the door and frame, and they confirmed that a potato-peeler-thin knife would have been enough to break through, since the whole thing was so old and warped.

Finally everyone had seen enough, Paulina Pleve was transported away, and Katrin nodded at Gregor.

"A suicide, in all likelihood. Everything adds up: the height of the ladder for her feet, the type and position of the knot—"

"The locked door," Gregor added.

"Then I hope we'll be seeing each other tonight for once, before I'm forced to dump you." Katrin started unpeeling her white plastic skin, and Gregor wasn't the only one staring. Sweat had made her gauzy blouse transparent and the hair at the nape of her neck curly. The temperature in that attic seemed to shoot up by several degrees.

Katrin drove to the Institute for Forensic Medicine and performed the autopsy with Martin. Martin snipped while Katrin chattered everything they learned into her voice recorder.

"If I wanted to kill myself, I wouldn't use a squeaky-green plastic laundry line that the neighbors had been hanging their underpants on for years and years," I told Martin, who was just pulling the rope out of the swollen neck tissue. "I'd buy myself a nice, new rope. Something that lies nicely on the skin. So, no hemp, sisal, or jute. I'd need it to be soft, like—"

"You would encounter no objections from me if you decided to finally kill yourself properly," Martin countered in his thoughts. "But unfortunately a rope won't help in your present situation."

"But don't you think it's strange?" I asked. "A laundry line? It's too unwieldy!"

Martin resisted the observation, but he secretly admitted I was right, as far as I could make out from his unprotected swirl of thoughts.

Katrin obviously wasn't in on our conversation, and instead she was droning the findings into the recorder. "The knot in the ligature is crude but expedient. It is positioned laterally on the neck, and the ligature mark presents as a furrow with yellowish discoloration from drying of the skin. The ligature mark rises in a V shape at the position of the knot . . ."

When the ligature, or rope, mark around the neck forms a V shape where the knot was on the neck, it means the person was hanging when the noose went tight. If the person had been lying down first or if someone had been standing behind her and tied the noose around her neck, the ligature mark would have been consistent and higher on the neck. Yes, I've learned a lot from the slicers.

It also came as no surprise that they found the usual congestive bleeding, which they documented dispassionately but no less meticulously. "There is talcum powder residue on the hands."

"Talcum?" I asked.

"The powder you find dusted inside single-use rubber gloves so they don't stick when you pull them on," Martin explained to me.

"So she didn't wash her hands before hanging herself," I said.

Martin stopped short. "No."

Katrin switched off her recorder and said, "I don't recall seeing any rubber gloves lying around at the discovery site. There weren't any in her clothes, either—so where did the gloves end up?"

"Your significant other is responsible for that," Martin said abruptly.

Oh, my little Martinmas goose. Ever since I've been butting in on his investigations, he's developed an aversion to any thought that lies within even one millimeter inside the area of his professional expertise.

Katrin turned the recorder back on. "The hands show no signs of attempts at self-rescue, nor does the skin of the hands present any evidence to that effect."

"So she was unusually relaxed," I noted.

"I note facts; Criminal Investigations draws conclusions," Martin said stoically.

"Where is Criminal Investigations, by the way?"

No answer is still an answer. Usually at least the investigator on the case, sometimes even the public prosecutor, would be present at the autopsy so he could find out everything firsthand and as fast as possible. But in this case, Batman and Robin— Gregor and Jenny—evidently had no doubt from the get-go that this was a suicide.

Here's the digest version to keep things moving along: at the end of the autopsy, it turned out that the traces of talcum powder on the hands and the lack of signs of attempts at self-rescue were thought unusual but not a clear indication of third-party negligence or foul play.

The corpse was barely back in its morgue drawer when Katrin glanced nervously at her watch.

"I'll do the rest," Martin offered. "Have a nice vacation."

THREE

June 19, eight days before Gregor's arrest

The next morning, Martin and Birgit had breakfast around nine. Technically speaking, Birgit was having breakfast for the third time. She had already been up at half past four and a quarter past six, each time availing herself of the opportunity to get a bite to eat. The first time it was six slices of toast with butter and orange marmalade; the second time it was just some fruit: two bananas and a honeydew. A *whole* honeydew. The constant fidgeting and getting up, lying down, getting up, lying down is an entirely normal side effect of pregnancy, Martin had explained to me, but it was still driving me ca-razy. One second the bonsai balloon would be pressing into Birgit's bladder, the next into her spine from the inside; then she'd get all hot or cold, or her legs would get restless, or the bonsai would get in some kickboxing practice or . . . there was always something. *Not pleasant.*

It used to be Birgit was all relaxed most of the time and could easily go megachill. Eat breakfast in bed, pull the covers up over her head after finishing her coffee, and go back to sleep. But since she's started ballooning up, she's let Martin talk her out of the coffee, and now they eat breakfast together at the table—müsli, like Martin. And since Germany forces maternity leave on you six weeks before the due date whether you want it or not, she can't even go to work. So she's gotten totally sluggish. Martin keeps talking her out of any reasonable activity because he thinks Birgit needs to be taking care of herself. He hardly ever lets her out of the apartment alone anymore for fear something might happen to her. I keep hoping the good old Birgit might put in another appearance once the bonsai makes it into this world, because I didn't like this Valium version of her one bit.

"I think we should consider Liam some more," Martin said, some kind of dark kernel or grain from the müsli stuck between his teeth. "And I think Roger is nice too."

He naturally pronounced both names German-style: *Lee-aaam* and *Rrrow-chuh*. "He thinks those are shitty names," I informed Martin.

The *he* in question had been my key to Martin's full attention the past few months, since by "he" I meant Martin's son. I could speak with the progeny, see. Well, I had *asserted* I could do this, at least, although the scientist in Martin naturally didn't want to believe it. But Martin also hadn't believed a person's ghost could continue broadcasting to other people after death, and that was something Martin now knew was possible from personal experience. So Martin believed I could talk with his unborn offspring. Well, *sometimes* he believed it. And in those moments I was the most important person in Martin's world, because I could tell him if the progeny was feeling all right even though Birgit kept puking out her soul every time she ate. I would tell him what the baby thought about stuff based on my own mood and needs, and in exchange for this information I had won certain concessions. For example, unlimited access to my computer, which I've already mentioned. But more on that later.

The due date was July 19, exactly one week after my own birthday. I seriously hoped Birgit and the bonsai would both stick to that plan and not abuse my birthday for their own purposes.

It was hard enough to celebrate my birthday now that I was dead because, apart from Martin, no one *could* celebrate with me. Plus, Martin's and my notions about what constitutes an appropriate piss-up were not exactly congruent. All this gave me less reason to want to spend my B-day in the future with a horde of whining milk-tooth terrorists.

"You say that for every name we've shortlisted so far," Martin replied, annoyed.

"Because you two keep coming up with such lame names, like Linus, Titus, or Jörgen-Malte. They just make me want to barf."

"Oh, shut up for once," Martin moaned.

"I think I'm about to explode," Birgit moaned, herself, before unleashing a loud belch.

I floored it out of there. There were way too many bad vibrations.

I found Gregor and Jenny at the cop shop. They had just finished downing a few cups of coffee while going through the forensics report, and they were about to head out to the old folks' home where Paulina had worked.

I was surprised, because the slicers hadn't given any indication of foul play. On the contrary, everything matched up. Strangulation characteristics, ladder height, the angle she had fallen, the force with which her neck had been caught in the plastic laundry line. Even the door being locked from the inside was a pretty good indication of a suicide. So I was looking for some kind of explanation about why the gumshoes were on their way to Paulina's workplace—and on a Saturday, no less. Jenny solved the riddle for me by dissing the old lady in the apron.

"I can't believe that old bag actually came in to file an official report of suspected murder," Jenny said as they were getting back into the car. "She claimed Paulina would 'never, ever, ever hang herself.' It would 'break one of the good Lord's commandments.'"

"Good Lord," Gregor grumbled with a grin.

"Amen," Jenny said with feigned enthusiasm.

"So what's got you so cranky today?" Gregor asked after a while.

Jenny blushed. "I had a date planned, actually, but then it took me so long to take down that stupid cow's statement . . ."

Whenever Jenny blushes, she looks way more like a schoolgirl than usual. She's a hair shorter than an average fourteen-year-old boy, and she doesn't fill her blouse any better either. Her skin is pale, her hair nothing special, and she has Cindy-Lou-Who eyes. Actually, she doesn't look half bad, but usually she comes across as boring because she wears staid, respectable clothes to seem older than she is. Jenny graduated from cop college as a full detective at *only* twenty-two, which is unheard of, but like all the other CI clowns, she had to get her feet wet on the mobile squad first, the one that gets the crappy jobs like political demonstrations and soccer hooligans. I didn't know Jenny back then, but it's hard to imagine her in a serious street brawl. She more than survived that break-in period, obviously, because after two years on the frontlines, she was hired by the Cologne police to be a detective—the youngest on the force by far at only twenty-four.

"So who's the lucky guy?" Gregor asked.

Jenny and Gregor got along great as a team, even though they didn't spend any time together outside work. Probably they got along great *because* they didn't spend time together outside work. And Gregor wasn't much of gossip, so he presumably didn't know that much about Jenny's personal life. I could have told him there wasn't anything worth knowing, because Jenny lived like a nun. Besides, what seminormal guy takes a badge bunny as his bride? That's what I'm saying. But I was starting to wonder if Jenny's bed had recently come to life.

"God, and then Andy stopped by the office while I was taking down her report. I had my hands full with the woman because she kept going on and on with stories of Paulina's childhood, Paulina in elementary school, Paulina in the Nativity play. So poor Andy ended up wasting a solid chunk of time listening to that woman drone on and on about what she knows about the suicide."

"And what does she know?"

"*Nothing.* Except for the good Lord's commandment bit."

"Good Lord," Gregor grumbled again. "So who was your date?"

"Well, Andy." Jenny rolled her eyes at Gregor for being slow on the uptake. "We were going to go out to dinner together."

"We're talking about *Andy*? Detective Offermann?" If Gregor was wondering why Detective Andy would stop in on a weekend just to help Jenny-Bunny out with a difficult witness, I couldn't hear it in his voice.

Jenny blushed again. "Exactly. But it started getting pretty late with the witness, and Andy had to go to his best friend's bachelor party at ten, so we couldn't go out."

Gregor shook his head. Maybe he was wondering. Or maybe he was thinking a bachelor party might be better than a round of screwing. Or was he wondering why he hadn't noticed Andy's interest in Jenny . . . or had he noticed and was wondering why Andy had taken so long to show it? Or maybe Gregor just had a stiff neck, which he was trying to loosen up by shaking his head. Remember: I can't read Gregor's thoughts. Unfortunately.

At the Sonnenschein Home, the director told Gregor and Jenny that Paulina had been a highly reliable employee. The shift leader explained through tears that she had rarely had such a good, prudent nurse working for her. In the break room, where all the other employees had been summoned, everyone confirmed those comments. The detectives emptied out Paulina's locker, but just as they were about to leave, they were halted by a loud voice.

"Gregor? Is that you?"

That was the first time I had seen Susanne Hauschild.

She walked toward Gregor in hesitant little steps but stopped an arm's length in front of him. "If this isn't the biggest coincidence—I've been thinking of you a lot the past few days."

Gregor acknowledged her with a nod.

"I, uh . . . you look great," Susanne stammered. At the time I obviously didn't know that she was Gregor's ringdove. Or had been, rather. Or that she had ever played a role in Gregor's life. She wasn't at all Gregor's type. Susanne Hauschild was petite, plump, and blonde. Her light blue eyes disappeared under long feathery bangs, which she pushed out of her face every few seconds. She wore an old pair of jeans, a plaid shirt, and sneakers. At first glance I pegged her for late forties, but I later found out that was almost ten years older than the truth.

Susanne pushed her hair out of her face again, peered up at Gregor, and abruptly asked, "Do you have time for a coffee?"

Gregor smiled. "Hi, Zuzubee. Unfortunately I can't. We're in the middle of an investigation."

Susanne a.k.a. Zuzubee got all wide-eyed. "A murder investigation? Here? Is it . . ."

Gregor shook his head. "A nurse. Likely suicide. A mere formality."

Susanne frowned and started fiddling with her bangs frantically. "Could you please give me a call later? I need to talk with you."

"Does it have to do with our investigation?" Jenny said, interrupting them.

Susanne seemed to notice Jenny only at that point, looking
her up and down and then forcing a smile. "Uh, no. It's more of
a . . . personal matter." She rummaged around in the pocket of
her jeans for a business card, which she handed to Gregor.

"I'll be in touch," Gregor said about to turn to the door.

Then he stopped again. "What are *you* doing here?" he asked.

"My father lives here now. When you've got time, stop by and
visit. He'd love to see you."

If you ask me, this encounter between Gregor and his ex
seemed completely unspectacular. And even in retrospect I'm
not sure if there was any spark between them, or if there was a
hidden message in what they said, or if there was some kind of
sign that predicted Gregor would land in jail six days later for the
murder of his little Zuzubee.

June 28, one day after Gregor's arrest

Overnight I had checked in on Gregor several times in his cell,
but it was pretty boring watching him toss and turn, occasionally falling asleep only to wake up again soon after and lie there,
staring into the darkness. I'd never wished I could read Gregor's
thoughts as much as I did during those hours. But, sadly, no such
luck. And Gregor wasn't the kind of guy who talked to himself
out loud.

If I had been interested in the verbal diarrhea that some of the guys in the other cells suffered from, I'd have had more luck. Several of them delivered entire discourses on why they had, say, recommended a fraudulent investment to the little old retired lady, why they had sawed the branch off the apple tree at exactly the moment their neighbor had fallen asleep on his hammock underneath it, or how they were victims of their childhood/circumstances/one of Germany's political parties and thus could not be held responsible for the tax evasion/manslaughter/rape in question. If those losers jabbered like this all night, I didn't even want to think about what went on here by day.

In addition to all the bullshit, which couldn't be heard much through the solid doors of the cells and thus mercifully remained private, the one thing that bugged me most about this deluxe jailhouse was the *stench*. The joint was actually on the new side, but the funk from sweat, steamed vegetables, and disinfectants already permeated the walls. Meanwhile, clouds of pomade, sock stink, and foul farts billowed through the night. I had never been all that squeamish, but this place was revolting even to me. Probably because everything that made a place *gemütlich* for me was missing here: cigarette smoke, beer vapor, and motor oil. Or the scent of greasy French fries and currywurst.

But in a place like this, once again I was bummed not to have nose plugs or ear plugs anymore. I took off and enjoyed a bit of R&R for my senses at an illegal body shop where they put new paint on stolen cars.

I felt more or less restored after an hour or so. I might have stayed and watched some more since nighttime offers few opportunities for eavesdropping or people watching, but I needed to do some thinking.

We had a victim. Good. And a suspect. Bad. Bad, because I was presuming our suspect was not the perpetrator. So I needed another suspect. It was a problem that I didn't know anything about the victim. I would have to change that, but first I needed to know why in hell the police were so sure Gregor was guilty. Maybe Martin knew more than he had let on so far. So I zoomed back home.

Of course I don't actually have a home—because I don't need one. When my body was still lying at the Institute for Forensic Medicine, I considered the morgue drawer labeled "No. 4" to be my home for a short while, but then one day I found an unsightly hamburger corpse in there, and my own physical husk—whose appearance had been spoiled by Martin's seam sewing—was buried. Since that day I really haven't had somewhere I belonged. Apart from the place where the only person who I can talk to lives. My first haunt was Martin's old bachelor pad, but then he moved into a beautiful, hundred-year-old building and the nice apartment that Birgit had found so the expectant parents could move in together.

Initially the apartment was all right since Birgit has more or less normal taste as far as furniture and stuff go. But not long after they moved in, THE ROOM came to be. By which I mean the kid's room, which had been fully renovated and furnished to be child-friendly. It featured wallpaper in alternating stripes of pastel yellow, pink, and blue; it was equipped with mobiles of grinning whales and cross-eyed octopuses; and it was filled with ecofashion clothes made of cotton so fully pesticide-free and compostable that you could presumably eat them. Stuffed animals, picture books to cut his teeth on (literally), music boxes, and thousands of little trinkets were now stuffed in every corner of the closets and dresser drawers, long before the little dwarf was even close to making an appearance. One of the music boxes already tootled all the time because Martin had read somewhere that babies can hear quite well even in the womb. So whenever he thought the offspring happened to be in a peaceful mood, he would play one of the music boxes. He hoped that the association would work later on both to reinforce calmness and to help him calm down. That kind of preconditioning might work on the Mini Martin in Birgit's belly, but the whining tones had preconditioned *me* to hurl.

At six in the morning on the day after his best friend was arrested, Martin was sitting in the kid's room listening to the calming music box. I watched the expectant father start to doze off the second the first notes sounded while the bonsai grew more and more aggressive with each beat, wanting to jam the stuffed animal down its daddy's throat by the end of the first verse. Then again, maybe that was me, projecting my own negative emotions. That's what that psychologist lady on TV had called it, anyway.

"Nonsense." Martin brainwaved me sluggishly.

"What do you know about Gregor's relationship with Susanne Hauschild the past few years?" I asked.

"*Nothing.* There wasn't anything."

"What do you mean?" I asked. "There wasn't anything you knew, or there wasn't any relationship?"

"Gregor never mentioned her. He hasn't mentioned her for years. So, there wasn't any relationship."

I could have explained to Martin that it can be a healthy self-defense mechanism to avoid mentioning certain names, but Martin doesn't believe in the goodness of a person until that person's evil side has been fully proved. Which means that general clues such as not mentioning your ex-wife don't necessarily raise Martin's red flags.

"Didn't he mention that he'd recently run into her again?" I asked.

Martin froze. "When?"

"Last week."

He shook his head in slow motion. "Not a word."

That might mean Gregor thought running into her was a major thing he wanted to keep to himself, or it could mean it was so *not* a big deal that he forgot to mention it.

"Can you think of any relevant clues or tips to give me?" I asked, slightly annoyed.

Martin was holding up the music box again, hypnotizing himself with it.

I took that as a no. I looked around quickly for Birgit, who was standing in front of the mirror, giving her belly dirty looks. "Come on," she said. "I'm tired of this. I want to stop feeling like an elephant and start feeling like a human being again."

A friendly invitation would sound different, I thought and bailed.

Jenny-Bunny scrambled into the office at seven and called Düsseldorf. She couldn't reach Keller or Stein or their lieutenant. They were totally blowing her off. It was also typical Jenny-Bunny. Gregor wouldn't have let them get away with blowing him off, but Jenny just hung up the phone, sighed, and walked over to see her lieutenant.

"I heard," her boss mumbled as she stepped into his office. "Our colleague from Düsseldorf called me already."

"And what exactly did he say?" Jenny asked.

"That Detective Kreidler is a suspect in the murder of his ex-wife. And that there's compelling evidence. Circumstantial evidence but also witness statements. And the suspect isn't talking."

Jenny slumped. "I don't believe that."

The lieutenant gave her an unhappy look. "At this point in my career, I've seen everything . . ." he began.

Jenny blinked at him in disbelief.

"But I don't believe it either. Every person should be treated as innocent until proven guilty, and that's particularly so in this case."

Jenny nodded. "I'm going to—"

"You're not going to do anything, Detective Gerstenmüller," the lieutenant said sharply. "We're going to make sure our colleagues in Düsseldorf get every bit of help that they ask for from us, but otherwise we're not going to lift a finger. I don't want anyone to say later on that he or she compromised or manipulated an investigation to help our colleague."

Jenny straightened up and quietly said, "Of course." She left the office and ran into Andy Offermann in the corridor.

Offermannequin wasn't a side dish, even though he looked that way. "Side dish" is what I call detectives who don't lead investigations but usually just stand beside a more experienced one. Jenny is a side dish.

But Offermannequin was an experienced cop. He was in his midthirties, so about the same age as Gregor, but he looked way younger. He somehow seemed harmless, kind of like Columbo. But his shtick wasn't playing dumb so much as acting like investigations really annoyed him because he always had something better planned. All kinds of people had already fallen for it, since he looked like a surfer with his beach-bleached long hair, bright

T-shirts, and ratty old jeans—a surfer who was annoyed to be kept from the next big wave by a pesky murder investigation.

"What'd he say?" Andy asked impatiently.

"That we should support our colleagues in Düsseldorf if they ask us to do something, but otherwise to stay completely out of their murder investigation of Gregor."

Offermann snorted like he was blowing ocean water out of his brain.

"But . . ." Jenny began, tears welling in her eyes. Bawling women are bad enough, but bawling police detectives are a disgrace.

Offermann put his hand under her chin and looked deep into her eyes. "If I can do anything for you, Jenny, let me know."

The way Jenny sank into him, leaning her head on his chest and her fingers clinging to his T-shirt, left me no doubt she'd be knocking on his door in the near future.

FOUR

About sixty hours had passed since Susanne Hauschild was murdered, and twelve had passed since Gregor had been arrested. Which meant our pig partners, as Katrin so aptly termed the boys, should have a few results to show for themselves by now. So I zoomed off to Düsseldorf police HQ.

". . . about a colleague from Cologne PD, we need to proceed with the utmost care. Of all cases, this is the one where we cannot make a single mistake."

The guy prattling on so pompously was standing there in suit and tie in front of a heap of half-asleep detectives in a big conference room with a gigantic table in the middle. The table was covered in the chaos of various coffee cups, empty cookie boxes, crumpled bakery bags, and bottles of water. The condition of the room made me suspect that Desperately Seeking Susanne, which is how I thought of the disheveled special investigations team, had already been on the clock for a few hours. Either that, or the janitors had refused to do their job surrounded by bloody crime-scene photos.

I struck that last possibility from my brain, though, because there wasn't any blood in this case. The photos on the walls featured multiple angles of Susanne, who had apparently been strangled, and of the crime scene itself. There were also a couple of close-ups of objects lying on the floor. A couple of tipped-over houseplants, one woman's shoe, and—I stopped breathing. The next photo was something I immediately recognized: the fob from Gregor's keychain. Anyone who knew Gregor knew that fob because he cherished that thing like life itself, which was perfectly understandable because it was one of a kind.

The beat-up metal fob that hung from his keychain was the original VIN plate off a 1982 Kreidler Mustang 80 motorcycle. That bad boy had been Gregor's first set of wheels, which he had bought himself with his own money at the tender age of sixteen. It was a bright-red Enduro, and the last—and I mean *literally* the last—bike that the original Kreidler Werke GmbH sold before it went under. They drew a big black line across the page and that was the end of it. The hot rod was already eight years old and well used when Gregor bought it, but it was still in pretty good mechanical condition. Gregor was a man possessed when he worked on it and restored it. He drove it until he was thirty. Well, OK. He hadn't tinkered with it much in those last few years he rode it, but he told the story of his first True Love with such spirit that no one really griped when he recited it time and time again.

The separation came in the form of a Polish semi. The trucker, who must have learned his trade in a Kazakh gravel pit, had been driving for seventeen hours straight when he dozed off and plowed through and flattened every vintage bike parked in the lot outside the annual convention of the Historic Motorbike Association. The driver was lucky the owners of the various Kreidlers, BMWs, BSAs, and Zündapps didn't slaughter him on the spot. It was a dark day for the insurance companies, and it was a dark day for Gregor. The only thing that he still had from his beloved 1982 Kreidler Mustang 80 was its VIN plate—a thin black-painted aluminum placard about half the size of a playing card, with two screw holes on either side to mount it on the bike. It was bent and all scratched up, but you could still read "Kreidler Werke GmbH" and "West Germany" across the top as well as the serial number, model year, and total road weight in kilograms. Sigh.

Well, that VIN plate was not in a lost-and-found box somewhere; it was lying right beside the corpse of Gregor's ex-wife. Now I got why the Düsseldorf detectives were so damned sure they had ID'd the murderer.

I wanted to yell, but since it was impossible to butt into their conversation, I tried to focus on what they were talking about.

". . . had been divorced for a while," a chick with hair dyed blazing red was saying. She couldn't have marked herself more clearly as an emancipated woman if "Men are pigs" was tattooed across her forehead. "To the extent he isn't even someone within her immediate circle of family and friends."

Detective Keller—or was it Stein?— sighed in irritation. "Well, we should take that point with a pinch of salt."

"Her current boyfriend Agathangelídis has an alibi in any case," the other of the two detectives added.

"It's a pretty dubious one," the man-hating color catastrophe said dismissively. "He closed his pub at one. He actually had plenty of time to drive to her place and kill her."

"But none of the neighbors heard or saw anything at that hour," a suit said calmly. "Which is why it's important for us to focus on Kreidler right now. To say nothing of the fact that he's clammed up."

"And why is he being so stubborn about saying anything?" a pretty boy asked. "Is he withholding an exonerating statement just to take the wind out of our quick success? Or does he just not have anything to raise in his defense?"

"Plus, Kreidler left his trademark at the scene of the crime," one of the Keller-Stein duo added.

"Exactly," the hair dye said. "I really don't want to be a party pooper, but I don't think a professional detective with so much experience would be so stupid to—"

"Even a colleague with the reputation of Gregor Kreidler might make a minor mistake in a situation of extraordinary strain," the pretty boy said. "Assuming he isn't habituated to committing murder."

So, there *had* been another suspect who was demoted from number one on the list of suspects for exceedingly questionable reasons. We were going to have to get to work on that guy. Plus, I had to follow up on the path that the Kreidler VIN plate took from Gregor's keychain to the apartment of the victim, because—presuming Gregor's innocence—the VIN plate did not get into the apartment on the occasion of the murder.

I tried to remember when I had last seen the VIN plate. It was surely the Monday Gregor and Jenny went to investigate the suicide of the nurse from the old folks' home.

June 21, four days before Susanne's murder

Gregor and Jenny had only briefly inspected the apartment of Paulina, the attic pendulum, the day her body was found, and then they had sealed it. The hope that they'd be able to quickly close the file as a confirmed suicide was dashed by the wailing apron lady, so now they were back, three days after Paulina Pleve died, in the building where she would henceforth be haunting the attic—if the wailing apron, who was raising a hue and cry that Criminal Investigations wasn't doing its work properly, was to be believed.

"What exactly are we looking for?" Jenny asked as she pulled on some plastic gloves.

"The usual," Gregor replied. "Reasons for a suicide, or reasons for a murder."

It was a one-bed, one-bath apartment with a tiny balcony and kitchenette, about the size of an old-style yellow Deutsche Post telephone booth. In this case, however, the prehistoric tiles were clean, all the floors were swept and mopped, the carpets were lint-free, and every little thing was in its place—down to the single teacup and spoon in the dish rack and an empty sugar bowl on the kitchen table. That made Gregor and Jenny's work easier, and they found what they were looking for in only half an hour. They were staring at the empty blister packs that Jenny had plucked from the trash can.

"What was in them?" Gregor asked.

"Sedatives," Jenny said. "A strong one, actually. Same as Valium, but produced by another company. If she swallowed all of these at once . . ." They both stared at the packs of pills.

"We're going to need a tox screen," Gregor said. "And I want to know where she got these."

A few minutes later when Gregor was unlocking his car, the Kreidler VIN plate was still dangling from his keychain.

June 28, one day after Gregor's arrest

"What's the latest about Gregor?" Martin asked before he had even hung his closed checkered umbrella on the coat stand. The blue sky was filled with sun, but the forecast had mentioned showers. No human being of any temperamentally normal constitution would react to something like that. Yet more proof: Martin wasn't normal.

Katrin was wearing jeans and a translucent white blouse that was just loose enough that I could fly in to check out the color of her flopper stopper. Mint green. Not as good as her red one, which Gregor and I both liked best, but still not bad.

"Nothing."

Martin froze. "Nothing?"

"He hasn't been in touch." Katrin's voice sounded bitchy, insulted, irritated . . . something along those lines. I knew that tone, but I'd never heard it applied to Gregor before.

I freed myself from the spell of the green lace and turned to Martin. "I *would* have mentioned that Gregor hasn't graced those Düssel-bustles with the sound of his voice yet, but you shut yourself off in your pretty little world and put your best friend out of your mind." Martin frowned in annoyance.

Katrin snorted. "It's been fourteen hours since those two losers hauled him off, and he apparently hasn't yet found it necessary to call me."

"Maybe . . ." Images were popping up in Martin's braincase that would not be good advertising for the German criminal justice system. Gregor sitting in an interrogation room with those two cops, a lamp pointed right into his eyes. Gregor nearly falling from his chair with exhaustion, the two cops mercilessly firing off their questions as they sneered down at him. "Maybe he can't," Martin mumbled.

"Have you been huffing car paint?" I asked. "Gregor spent the night all cozy on a tax-financed bunk in a cell that's as clean and tidy as the medicine cabinet in your bathroom."

Martin shook the scene from his brain and wondered how someone like him, who had unconditional faith in law and order, could have such ridiculous pictures going through his mind. He naturally blamed me for manipulating his thoughts, but in this case I was totally innocent. Maybe somewhere deep in Martin's subconscious lurked a tiny spark of doubt in the infallibility of the existing system.

"He's entitled to a phone call," Katrin said, her sulking tone reminding me of battery acid.

Martin cowered and shrugged. He can't deal with conflict. By contrast, Katrin is the living embodiment of conflict, with occasional moments of peace. OK, fine. Her harmonious phases are more frequent than that, but even the slightest provocation is enough to get her blood boiling. She rebels against superiors, picks fights with prosecutors, and generally doesn't shut up. I am constantly amazed that Martin and Katrin not only really like each other but also always stick together, even though they often have conflicting views on the correct solution to a problem. Martin prefers to stick to the facts; Katrin prefers banging her head against the wall.

I was generally more in line with Katrin, myself. In the current situation it obviously made perfect sense that she was upset. But she didn't even know the half of what I knew.

"CI found the fob off Gregor's keychain at the crime scene," I reported to Martin. He turned pale.

Katrin was so infuriated that she didn't notice Martin's horror.

"How did it get there?" Martin asked me.

Score one for loyalty.

"The murderer lost the placard at the crime scene?" I suggested.

"Gregor is innocent," Martin said—aloud.

"Why's he acting so weirdly then?" Katrin snapped back.

That was the million-euro question, wasn't it, and none of us knew the answer.

By eleven o'clock, Martin couldn't stand it anymore. He powered down his computer and announced he was driving to Düsseldorf.

Katrin blinked at him in disbelief. "What do you want to do?"

"I don't know," Martin said. "But I can't sit around here doing nothing while my best—and to be honest, only—friend is being held unjustly for murder."

Katrin stared at her screen, her lips pinched together.

"You're still angry because you didn't know anything about Susanne, correct?" Martin asked softly.

Katrin nodded.

"I'll see what I can find out. You can be sure there will be an explanation for everything," Martin said. And then he left the office.

Martin harbors an inexplicable love for the butt-ugliest and most ridiculous form of locomotion in human history: he drives a Duck. By which I mean a Citroën 2CV. In Germany it's called a Duck, as in "The Ugly Duckling." If you've ever seen how a Duck handles tight curves, you know why I call it a swaying trash can on wheels. And it took Martin all squeezed inside his swaying can a solid eternity to make it to Düsseldorf. So I had plenty of time to scout ahead and pilot him to the right spot, namely, the command center for the Desperately Seeking Susanne team.

"I'm a friend of Detective Sergeant Kreidler's, and I'd like to know with what you're charging him," Martin said to the pretty boy, who had been sent out to handle the annoying visitor.

"Unfortunately I'm not able to disclose any information to you," the guy said, all snotty-like. He clearly looked like one of those vampire gigolos from the movies. Which in and of itself was reason enough for him to be on my shit list.

"Where can I find Detective Sergeant Kreidler?" Martin asked.

"He's in custody pending charges."

Martin turned pale. "You have an arrest warrant against him? On what grounds?"

"We have circumstantial evidence and witness statements that incriminate him."

"But that doesn't justify holding him in custody," Martin replied, thinking.

"The severity of the crime alone is sufficient for police detention until his court appearance."

"No," Martin said, adopting a schoolmarm's tone. "Without further grounds for arrest, you would never—"

The snot raised his right hand and counted off Gregor's issues finger by finger: "Risk of suppression of evidence—he knows exactly what to do. Flight risk—he lacks strong family ties." The snot winked at Martin fraternally. "He strangled his most recent family tie the night before last."

"Y-you're making an enormous mistake," Martin stammered.

"He's practically confessed," the snot announced condescendingly.

Martin wobbled. "Confessed?"

The snot shrugged. "He hasn't denied anything at least. How would you interpret that?"

Martin looked like a punching bag at a boxing club after an intensive training weekend and beat his retreat. But he didn't drive back down to Cologne. Instead, he drove straight to jail.

"Do you seriously think you can just stroll in there?" I asked.

Although I had earned my living by stealing pricey cars, I had been so good at it that I'd never landed in the clink. I hadn't even once been a suspect in a case. I had practically been a phantom even when I was alive, at least when it came to the cops. Which is why I was also unfamiliar with conventions of the German penal system.

Martin didn't find it necessary to answer me and instead proved a half hour later that prisoners in pretrial detention are in fact allowed to have visitors. Although only during visiting hours. The clerk handed him a list of visiting hours, and Martin turned on his heels and drove back to the Institute for Forensic Medicine. On the way, he had trouble not bursting out in tears. I bailed because I'd met my measure of misery for the day.

Instead, I wondered what was really going down here. There were actually only two possibilities: first, Gregor had zeroed out his Zuzubee and was keeping his trap shut so as not to incriminate himself. Second, he had not killed her. Why then was his motorcycle VIN plate found at the scene of the crime? Where did the circumstantial evidence and witness statements come from? How could an innocent man look so guilty?

The most likely answer was Gregor was being set up. But then why wasn't he defending himself?

I continued to assume Gregor was not the perpetrator. But the question remained who was trying to frame him for the murder. And above all *why*? And how was I supposed to find that out if Gregor hadn't breathed a single word to the cops? And why for the love of turbochargers wasn't he saying anything? My thoughts were swirling around in whirlpools, and I just couldn't find a hook to hang them on. I was going to have to dig way back down into my own memories.

I could only hope the answer would be found in the events the few days before the murder. My memory wasn't that great even when I was alive, and my death hadn't improved the situation at all. But if I sat still and really focused, I could force myself to come up with plenty of details. But dammit, I needed to find something out. This was *Gregor*, after all.

FIVE

June 23, two days before Susanne's murder

Gregor and Jenny hung up simultaneously.

"You first," Gregor ordered.

"They confirmed Paulina had diazepam in her blood," Jenny said.

Gregor raised an eyebrow at her.

"Diazepam is the active ingredient in the sedatives that we found the empty blister packs for in her apartment. However, she had taken only one or two of the pills."

"And what does her doctor say?"

"He never prescribed those or any other medication, and he wouldn't know what she would need them for. She was fit as a fiddle. No physical or psychiatric conditions."

"Why was she even seeing her family doctor then?" Gregor asked.

"Successful allergen desensitization the year before last, regular flu shots," Jenny read from her notepad. "Now you."

"Paulina's fingerprints were found on only two of the blister thingies in the blister packs in the trash can, and even those two were pretty smeared up. None of the other pill pockets had prints on them."

"You mean they didn't have *her* prints on them."

Gregor shook his head. "They didn't have *any* prints on them."

"What does that mean?" Jenny asked.

"That the blister pack wasn't hers."

Jenny stared uncomprehendingly. "How can that be?"

"Take a look at the blister packs you have in your medicine cabinet, Jenny. They'll be covered in your fingerprints. Every time you press a pill out of one of the cavities, you leave a fingerprint behind. Unless you are in the habit of putting on rubber gloves every time you pop an aspirin."

The two of them stared into space for a moment until Gregor sighed. "OK, first the issue of where she got the pills from. The easiest way to get them is probably at work. Come on, let's head out into the sunshine."

For the second time, the detectives drove over to the old folks' home where Paulina had worked, and they checked in with the director of the facility, Ms. Sonnenschein. Sunshine, Sonnenschein—get it? They told her they were looking for the source of the pills and watched as the blood drained from her face.

"Paulina? You think she stole sedatives to commit suicide? I can't believe it."

The chick with buffalo hips, whose massive seat cushions started vibrating dangerously when she walked, accompanied Gregor and Jenny to the in-house pharmacy, explained to the white coat on duty what the situation was, and left the detectives alone with him.

After five minutes of pharmaceutical chatter, I understood, first, that the pill apportioner would always wear plastic gloves when administering pills for hygienic reasons and, second, that reinventorying the pharmaceutical stock using prescription lists, packing slips, daily dose planners, and other documentation would take the rest of the day—if not the rest of the week. I made myself scarce.

On my way out the door, I noticed Gregor's ex sitting in the café area with an old man, drinking coffee that a teenybopper with ultrashort platinum-blonde hair had served them both. At the time I didn't know that all three of them would yet play a decisive role in this tragedy; otherwise, I would have all too gladly kept them company for a few minutes.

June 28, one day after Gregor's arrest

Gregor and Katrin didn't live together, which was primarily because Gregor thought Katrin's condo was too cramped and Katrin thought Gregor's rental was in a crappy neighborhood. The Monday after Gregor was arrested, Katrin came home from work around six to find Keller and Stein perched on the flight of stairs up to her condo, like latchkey kids without keys.

"You might have called," Katrin said coldly.

"We could have," said the bald fat one. I still didn't know if he was Keller or Stein.

"What do you want?"

"To come in and have coffee and a nice conversation."

Katrin made no bones about her aversion, but she let the detectives in. They looked around with curiosity, which quite obviously displeased Katrin.

"Don't touch anything," she barked as one of them was about to pick up a photo of Katrin, Gregor, and a moose. The photo was from a vacation in Sweden, and the moose was stuffed. Katrin had explained that at one point to Martin because he had practically had a coronary seeing the giant beast directly behind them. I'll say it again: Martin is a serious sissy.

One of the detectives held his hands behind him and the other kept his hands in his pockets as they continued studying Katrin's realm. It was a one-bedroom condo, and the great room that served as living room, dining room, and kitchen in one had a ceiling that was almost four meters high. One wall consisted almost entirely of a ginormous all-glass dormer with an incredible view that even included Cologne Cathedral. Well, you actually could only see one tiny corner of one of the towers, but it was still way better than the alley view from Gregor's pad.

Katrin's place really was pretty nice. Cabinet and shelves in red and black varnish, a wooden dining table about the same size and weight as a small Italian car, a mishmash of wooden chairs from a flea market, and a nicely padded leather couch that Gregor and Katrin used for far more than just watching TV, if you get what I mean.

The hardwood floor looked like it had spent a previous life as part of the hull of the *Niña*, *Pinta*, or *Santa María*, and the lampshades were actually all sorts of repurposed things like a megaphone, a zinc mop bucket, and a conical Vietnamese sedge hat. The detectives didn't go into the bedroom and bathroom, which were both tiny, although I was familiar with both rooms and found the stainless-steel-and-walnut bedframe and the *Psycho*-themed shower curtain pretty freaky. Not the biggest place, but ultracool.

Katrin filled the coffee machine and switched it on, then she sat with the two detectives at the dining table. "Now which of you is Keller and which is Stein?" she asked, holding out her hand.

The cops correctly interpreted what she meant and starting digging in their pockets, pulling out their badges and IDs and setting them on the table in front of Katrin.

Thorsten Keller was the fat bald one. No taller than the average woman, midfifties, straggly residual hairs around his ears and the back of his head, stubbly face, bulgy lips. Coffee stains on his button-down shirt, which kept coming untucked, and grease stains on his suit jacket. He reeked like an ashtray that hadn't been emptied in a week.

Next to him sat Michael Stein, who looked like a choirboy at the cathedral downtown. Clean black jeans, light blue button-down shirt, linen sports coat. Clean-shaven and freshly showered. He either used an overpowering aftershave or had just slicked a similar-smelling gel into his "Stepmother's Darling" haircut. I kept my distance from the guy because I was worried that the cloud of solvent might decompose whatever it was I was made out of.

"We're investigating the murder of Susanne Hauschild."

Katrin didn't react.

"Ms. Hauschild was the ex-wife of Gregor Kreidler."

Katrin folded her arms in front of her and leaned back.

"That is, the ex-wife of your boyfriend."

Stein had been talking while Keller unwrapped a lozenge and pushed it through his rubbery lips into his mouth. Now Keller leaned forward.

"Are you doing the silent routine now, like Kreidler?"

"If there's something you want to hear, you should try asking questions," Katrin said with a candy-sweet smile.

"Where were you last Friday night?"

"In Renesse," she said. That's a resort area about an hour southwest of Rotterdam on the North Sea in the Netherlands.

"Alone?"

"With three girlfriends."

"Names?" Keller mumbled past his lozenge as he opened his notepad. The notepad had coffee stains on it, and two pages were stuck together. He pulled them apart roughly and tore one of the pages. Keller grunted angrily and flipped to the next page.

Katrin gave him the names.

"May we check your closet?" Stein asked politely.

"What do my clothes—"

"Actually I mean those," he said pointing to the hooks next to the front door. The hooks were made of gnarled tree branches hung artfully on the wall. It looked way too eco for me, but Katrin thought it was all that. Which made sense, since she had gone out into the woods, sawed off the branches, and sanded and oiled them herself. The part where she oiled and polished the thick limbs sounded hot, leaving me once again to miss my erectile tissue.

Katrin shrugged.

"Is the coffee done?" Keller asked.

"Go see for yourself."

Katrin followed Stein to the hooks, keeping an eye on Keller as he took a mug from the cupboard and served himself.

"We'll be taking this with us," Stein announced after a few seconds. In his hand he was holding Gregor's jean jacket, which he always wore when it wasn't too cold. "If you will permit us, of course."

Katrin shook her head. "I'm not allowing anything."

Stein hung his head and looked disappointed. "If you're withholding evidence, you'll find yourself in trouble too. Is he worth it?"

He could hear the volcano within Katrin seething.

"Out," she hissed, and it was surely beneficial to her relationship with law enforcement that only that one word passed her lips. Because Katrin is so good at swearing that she can make even me blush.

"You're making a mistake," Stein said as he walked out the door Katrin was holding open for him.

"Thank you for the coffee," Keller mumbled. He had added a fresh stain to his shirt.

I stayed with Katrin and watched her pick up the jacket, hang it back up, pour herself some coffee, and stand in front of the coat hooks holding her coffee, staring at the jacket for a few minutes. Then she called Martin.

"The cops from Düsseldorf were just here and wanted to take Gregor's jean jacket. Did he wear it last week?"

Martin and Gregor didn't hang out just in their free time; they also constantly ran into each other professionally, so Martin was able to answer her with an unambiguous yes.

"Including Friday?"

Martin didn't know that detail for sure. I did, however. The answer was yes!

"And then he left it at my place so the cops wouldn't find it at his apartment?" Katrin asked, a little rattled.

I was pissed. I had expected more loyalty from Katrin. I left her alone and zoomed over to Martin. It was high time he did something to save his best buddy's ass. Especially since nobody else was trying—not even Gregor himself.

Martin and Birgit were sitting at their dinner table as if everything were peachy even though Gregor had been in the slammer for almost twenty-four hours.

"Susanne's dad is living in the old folks' home where Gregor ran into her. Maybe he can tell us a little about his daughter!" I bellowed at Martin.

Martin had laid out a few ridiculous rules when the three of us were together, and I had had to solemnly swear I would follow them. Number one: I was not allowed to be in the apartment alone with Birgit. That had something to do with Birgit's privacy. Since neither Martin nor Birgit could check up on that, I had sworn on my own grave to follow that rule. But naturally I had not followed it. Why should I? Since Birgit didn't even know about me, it couldn't bother her if I took a shower with her.

Rule number two was that I was not allowed to bother Martin and Birgit when they were screwing and that I couldn't interrupt important conversations. And rule number three: I wasn't allowed to use either Martin's or Birgit's computers. In return, he set up my own computer for me, complete with Internet access. I had negotiated hard for that. By regularly hosing the operating system on Martin's computer so it would crash. Sometimes he just needs a little pressure, you see.

While they were eating dinner, I kept feeding Martin the details of the encounter between Gregor and Zuzubee, and I repeated my suggestion of chatting with her dad. Martin broadcast a brief reminder to me about his "no interrupting" rule, so I shut up. Martin devoutly *chewed* his mashed carrots, even though they were so mushy he could have sucked them in through the gaps in his teeth. Was he already sampling baby-food recipes for his progeny? I couldn't imagine Martin buying ready-to-eat fodder in glass jars in a million years.

"Some friend you are," I said. "Peacefully spooning up mush matters more to you than saving Gregor."

"Birgit needs consideration and reliable rituals in her condition," Martin condescendingly explained to me.

"What Birgit needs more than anything is stimulation for that bright brain of hers, variety in life, and a guy with balls in his pants."

Martin blushed.

"We should do something to help Gregor," Birgit suddenly said, her mouth full of food. She was eating an open-face cheese sandwich.

I yodeled in happiness. Gregor's arrest seemed to have woken her up, and she was taking an interest in the life around her.

Martin looked at her, stunned.

"I can't think about baby names or the color of the curtains in the nursery as long as Gregor is sitting in a jail cell," she said.

What? The nursery *still* wasn't done? They still had to pick out curtains? Madness!

Martin looked embarrassed. "Well, what do you have in mind?" he asked.

"I don't have the first clue about police work," Birgit said with a little burp. "And the police will surely not appreciate it if unauthorized people get involved in an investigation."

Martin nodded emphatically, mentally hurling a "Quite right!" in my direction.

"But I need to do something. Otherwise, I'm going to go crazy here. Maybe I can go ask around and talk to the people who knew his ex-wife and hear what they have to say about how things stood with Gregor and her."

I could have kissed Birgit. She was back to her old self. Well, she was twice the size, waddling on splayed feet, and constantly belching. But her brain had resumed operations.

"Susanne's father lives in a retirement home here in Cologne . . ." Martin mumbled.

Aha, now he was able to show off the information that I had served him.

Birgit struggled up out of her chair.

"What are we waiting for?" she said.

It was seven thirty when Martin and Birgit parked the swaying trash can in front of the Sonnenschein Home. They got out, and Birgit looked around with interest as Martin fished her jacket from the backseat and hermetically sealed and locked the tin can. Since it was practically beach-going weather, Birgit wasn't going to want her jacket, and there's no such person as a "thief of a 2CV"—even if all the windows were wide open and the key was in the ignition. But Martin was resistant to advice on either matter.

I had already been here with Gregor and Jenny, but since Birgit and Martin were studying the building, I did so for the first time myself. The Sonnenschein Home lived up to its namesake as the setting sun reflected in the windows of the main entrance. The building consisted of three wings in a U formation open toward the back. Its three stories, gigantically tall windows, stucco moldings and decorations on the façade, and little towers along the roofline all showed that the architect wasn't from our era, but the place didn't come off as old and crumbly like lots of prewar buildings do. Instead it was pristinely renovated, from plinth to parapet. The plantings were way more varied than the standard greenery that you normally see around hospitals, nursing homes, or government agencies. I can't give more detail on the plants since botany isn't exactly my hobby, but I had seen the banana trees standing astride the main entrance in an ad before. Any semi-attentive observer would realize that the residents of this facility weren't exactly the ones whose breakfast purée was being paid for by the social security office.

"I'd like to see Mr. Hauschild," Martin said at reception, which would have fit right in at a four-star hotel with its marble counter and the slick chick behind it.

"He is likely in the park. Please just walk straight through this way," she said, gesturing in the direction with her manicured hand.

I followed Martin and Birgit through the lobby, past the Café Sonnenschein and the newspaper stand, through the glassed-in winter garden where more banana trees and other exotic stuff was growing, out the back door into the park. There were lots of trees here too, as well as fountains, benches, chess tables, with mowed lawns and flowerbeds everywhere in between. And between the decorations, quite a number of old people.

"Which one is Susanne's father?" Martin asked me.

"How should I know? I've never seen him before."

Martin sighed, but Birgit had become fast friends with two Muppets sitting nearby. They were asking about her belly.

"No," she answered their question, "I don't know if it's going to be a boy or girl. Yes, the due date is coming up—about three weeks. Yes, it's my first baby. By the way," she then added. "Do you know where I can find Mr. Hauschild?"

As it turned out, Mr. Hauschild was the man a few meters off, standing and drawing at an easel.

Martin and Birgit approached him and introduced themselves. "We're friends of Gregor's. Your son-in-law."

"Gregor, yes. The boy with moped."

Hauschild had icy gray, shaggy hair. He was shorter than most guys but not tiny, and very thin. He swayed as he drew, which made him look a little like an orchestra conductor with his shoes glued to the ground. If his balance wasn't on the fritz, his eyes seemed to be good still because he was drawing a bird he had spied about twenty meters away perched on a branch of a tree in incredible detail.

"The bird is a woodpecker," Martin silently smart-assed my way.

"Peckers being your hobby?" I asked.

Martin blushed.

"Have you seen Gregor recently?" Birgit asked.

"Of course. But it was strange, somehow. He looked old."

Hauschild folded over the page of his drawing pad and then started a quick portrait of a man's face. Martin and Birgit stared first at the paper and then at each other, impressed. He had perfectly rendered Gregor with only twelve bold strokes of charcoal.

"Does he still have the moped?" Hauschild asked as he flipped to another fresh sheet. Then he drew a portrait of Birgit, which left even my chops agape. He had perfectly represented Birgit's eyebrows and nose with just a single continuous line, and had put just the right upward curve into her lips.

The man was a genuine artist.

"He had it until he was thirty," Martin said.

"Thirty? What drivel are you spewing there, my friend? Susanne would never marry a man so much older than her!"

June 29, two days after Gregor's arrest

They hadn't gotten one sensible word out of Hauschild. But Birgit had whined all night they needed to do something for Gregor, so Martin was forcibly dispatched back to jail on Tuesday morning to talk to Gregor. Martin recited his spiel but was informed in return that the inmate didn't want any visitors.

"That must be an error," Martin said confused. "I'm his best friend, and—"

"We've been instructed by Detective Kreidler not to allow any visitors. We cannot force him to receive visitors if he doesn't want them. Good day."

"This is a matter of life and death pertaining to his unborn child," Martin said. He thought *godchild*, but said *child*.

"You're lying!" I shouted—enthusiastically. *Martin lied!* I was going to have to mark this date on the calendar in red and have it declared an international holiday.

"If you do not immediately produce Detective Kreidler in the visiting room, I shall hold you personally liable," Martin continued.

"Martin, Martin!" I chortled. "You're going to burn in hell for that one."

"Nonsense," the gatekeeper declared, but his voice didn't sound as certain as it did before.

"Do you want to risk it?" Martin asked.

I hardly recognized my sweet little goose. Never in his life had Martin acted so brazenly without even remotely flushing or stammering or hyperventilating or falling off his chair.

The guard turned away from Martin and picked up his phone. He hung up quickly. After a moment, the phone rang, and he picked up and listened. Then he buzzed the door open.

Martin stepped through the door with a mixture of elation over his coup and excitement about seeing Gregor again. A plain-clothes was waiting for Martin in the room where I presumed they normally ID'd and searched visitors. He asked for Martin's ID, jotted down the information, and handed it back to him.

"So, Dr. Gänsewein. Could you please explain to me what you meant to achieve by appearing here today?"

Martin turned pale.

"Surely you didn't really believe you would get away with it."

Martin looked at the floor.

"If you want to help Detective Kreidler out, please don't annoy the employees at this facility by making threats or inventing wild stories. Are we clear?"

Martin nodded with tears in his eyes.

"The situation is a burden on any friend or family member, but the sooner you resign yourself to the obvious, the better it will be for all parties involved. *Auf Wiedersehen.*"

The man set his hand on Martin's shoulder and escorted him to the door. Martin slinked like a beaten dog past the grinning enforcer and hurried to leave the building. Back in his trash can, he rested his head on the steering wheel. I couldn't watch his suffering, so instead I zoomed over to check in on the Desperately Seeking Susanne team to see how their investigation was going. Maybe those boys were having more luck with their endeavors.

"We've got Kreidler's VIN plate in the apartment of the deceased, we have statements from witnesses that his car was parked directly in front of the main door to the building on the night of the murder and that it was seen again afterward on a side street, and we've got Kreidler's DNA on the body," Stein recited.

As usual, he looked fresh out of the pages of a fashion magazine, while Keller might as well have spent the night under a bridge.

On the subject of witnesses, the detectives had probably spent the past forty-eight hours going door to door chatting with hundreds of talkative, feeble-minded, megalomaniacal, exhibitionistic, criminal, boring, pushy, and cracked-up people—the typical kinds of neighbors you find on any middle-class street in Düsseldorf. In Cologne, half of the neighbors would have been gay, and the other half would have been working in television, whereas in Düsseldorf they all work either in banking or high fashion. In Cologne, at least twenty percent of the neighbors would have opened their doors and been willing to help the police—despite the strong foreign accents—whereas in Düsseldorf people would have called the cops on the cops knocking on the door for bothering them. At least, I think they would. Wouldn't surprise me at all.

But I didn't give a shit about any of that, because what it came down to was the single and solitary fact that things were getting down to the wire for Gregor. Circumstantial evidence and witness statements are one thing—but DNA on the body is a different story. Unfortunately the detectives didn't say what type of DNA they found—whether it was a hair on Zuzubee's shoulder or bodily fluids from regions one doesn't reach when shaking hands. As long as this source wasn't giving me any clues about the nature of the two exes last meeting, then I was going to have to call on my own memory to think about the mood when I was watching them. I zoomed up the 240 meters to the tip of the Rhine Tower, past the observation deck and rotating restaurant, and perched on the tip of its telecommunications antenna. I tried to block out everything around me and remember Thursday of last week.

SIX

June 24, three days before Gregor's arrest

Gregor and Jenny were about to leave their office and check on the results of the pill inventory at the old folks' home when the front desk called up to say they had a visitor.

"A Ms. Sieger? She says she has information about the murder of Paulina Pleve," the voice from the handset said.

Gregor furrowed his brow for a moment and then remembered Ms. Sieger was the awkward apron who had saddled them with the whole investigation in the first place. He grabbed his jean jacket and pushed his chair back to stand. "I'll head over to Sonnenschein myself, and you can take down the 'important' information Ms. Sieger has. Have fun."

Gregor whistled his way out the back exit while Jenny went down to escort the overzealous neighbor back to the office.

"Now, what would you like to share with me?" she asked.

"Could I trouble you for a glass of water?" Ms. Sieger asked. "It's so hot out today." She was fanning her face with a crisply ironed floral-print handkerchief as she looked around Jenny's realm with curiosity.

Jenny ran into Offermann on her way to the break room for the glass of water. I got the impression he had started stalking Jenny-Bunny the second Gregor had taken off. He actually seemed to be interested in our sweet little kindercop.

"Did I just see that old gossip in the building again?" he asked Jenny with a grin. "She just won't give up, huh?"

What was this guy blathering on for if all he wanted was to get horizontal with her? Why didn't he stop talking her to death and just hit on her already? Didn't Offermannequin get women at all? I sighed. If even the cop shop was full of softies, then there wasn't much hope for this world.

"She doesn't have anything better to do," Jenny sighed.

"Do you want me to take over?" Offermann offered. "I can get her out of your office in about three minutes."

Jenny grinned. "No, thanks. I can handle her."

"If you need me, you know where to find me."

Offermann took his hand and tucked a strand of Jenny's hair behind her ear, turned around, and ambled off. Bewildered, Jenny started walking the wrong direction until she remembered the glass of water. By the time she was sitting at her desk again a few minutes later, the color of her face had normalized.

"Well?" Jenny asked.

Ms. Sieger took a tiny sip of water, set the glass down, and took a deep breath. "Have you already spoken with Paulina's boyfriend?"

Jenny looked up in surprise. "She had a boyfriend?"

The apron triumphantly stretched her chin upward. "Aha. Now you're surprised. Shouldn't the police have found that out on their own by now?"

I was just as flabbergasted as Jenny because no one had turned up any evidence of a stallion when they had frisked the apartment. It doesn't need to be a used jimmy cap or something, but normally in the apartment of a woman who has a boyfriend you do find a second toothbrush, a razor, maybe a men's T-shirt, or at least a picture or something. Women need that, while men are happy when chicks don't leave anything around their place, like tampons or face cream or leg wax. So I started listening expectantly only to be disappointed—yet again.

Paulina's boyfriend was a nice, young man. At least, Ms. Sieger thought so. Unfortunately she had seen him only once. In the stairwell. More or less in the dark. And she didn't know his name either. But she said she was pretty sure he was a doctor, since that's what Paulina had told her when she asked about him.

"By any chance did you notice a license plate on his car when he brought Paulina home?"

"No."

"And she never mentioned him by name?"

"No."

"How long had they been together?"

"Six months, maybe."

Jenny couldn't get anything else out of Ms. Sieger, even though she didn't seem to want to leave the office. I left the two of them and tailed Gregor to the Sonnenschein Home. He had lost his head start by getting stuck in traffic, so we actually arrived at the same time.

Gregor checked in at reception but didn't ask for the director; instead, he headed straight to the pharmacy.

"The director's office can provide you with all that information," Till Krämpel said in response to Gregor's question about what the inventory had turned up.

"I prefer to get information firsthand."

The pharmacist added a worry line to the existing worry lines on his forehead. I counted seven, all of them greasy and glistening.

"The inventory didn't turn up any missing stock," Krämpel said. My God, the guy was lisping like he had a napkin ring around his tongue.

"Why did it take so long to determine that?"

"It's a complex system." *People with speech impediments should really avoid expressions like "complex system,"* I thought as Gregor discreetly wiped droplets of the guy's spit off his face.

Krämpel licked some sweat off his upper lip. "Every resident gets his or her own specific medication, which we store separately for each individual. Look here."

He opened the door to a huge cabinet with about two hundred narrow little drawers inside, each labeled with a name.

"The medications are the property of the residents. If a doctor has a resident discontinue a medication, we remove it from the drawer only after consulting with the resident. If he or she wants to keep it for some reason, it stays here. If we have another resident taking the same medication, we can pass on unused medication to that person, but in that case we also would need the consent of the owner. When someone dies, the same thing applies. Now, in addition to all of that, we have to follow expiration dates, and sometimes expired medication has to be disposed of while the patient continues on his or her prescription with fresh pills. Then that has to be corrected in the inventory, because pills are technically present but considered missing. Do you follow?"

"Of course," Gregor replied. "And you've audited all these incoming and outgoing pills and have found absolutely no anomalies?"

Krämpel nodded.

People who claim they've mastered a complex system without any error or anomalies are liars. The experience of any human being shows that errors are just a part of complex systems. Which is why space shuttles explode, which is why a Formula One car will lose a wheel on occasion, which is why buildings collapse into subway tunnels. Apparently, the only exception was Mr. Worry-Wrinkle's complex system, which was completely error-free. Ridiculous.

Gregor didn't seem to be convinced either because he asked to see a few pages of documentation, inspected the drawers with the names, and inquired how Krämpel put together the residents' daily rations. He tried to check the trash for medication that had expired or was no longer needed, but the special pharmaceutical disposal bin was sealed as tight as a ballot box. Krämpel said the bin was picked up by a waste removal contractor, and no one onsite actually had a key.

"As you can see, no one can get a medication out of the bin once it's in there," he explained.

Gregor nodded, said thank you, and left. I couldn't read Gregor's thoughts, but *I* was thinking that the path a blister pack might take in the pharmacist's hand from drawer to trash can passed damned close to the pocket of the pharmacist's white lab coat. And if someone were to *not* put medication into the trash can at all but rather into his coat pocket, it wouldn't matter one bit that pills thrown into the trash can couldn't be gotten out again.

Gregor wasn't exactly in the best mood when he strolled through the lobby back toward the parking lot. He was lost in thought, but after a few steps he realized that every table in the café and lobby was occupied—by nearly as many teenagers as Muppets. Gregor stopped and looked around in disbelief.

At that moment, Susanne slinked up to him from behind and grabbed his shoulder. "Strange, huh?" she said. "I get the impression you still don't read the paper regularly."

Gregor turned toward her and shook his head. "Too much bullshit."

They gave each other knowing smiles. Must be an inside joke.

"Maybe you can tell me what's going on in here," he said, nodding toward the bustling tables.

"Well, I'm sort of the documentarian on this project," Susanne said. "It's a good example of how a single good idea can sometimes solve lots of complicated problems."

Gregor made a confused face. "You know I'm suspicious of anything that sounds too easy."

Susanne laughed. "Problem number one: old people in assisted living get bored because they're all in the same situation and don't have anything new to tell each other. Problem number two: lots of kids suffer from the phenomenon of daytime home-lessness because their parents work. Problem number three: lots of working parents can't afford childcare and don't have time to help their kids with homework. And problem number four: kids with bad grades can't even get an interview to try to land a spot in a vocational training program, since there are more applicants than available apprenticeships."

Gregor nodded.

"The solution: schoolkids come to the facility and spend a few hours a week with the seniors. The old people have some-one who will listen to them and explain things like how a smart-phone works or who will help them e-mail their grandkids. Some seniors give the kids extra help with German, history, math, and so on. The kids in this program have their participation noted with glowing praise on their report cards, and this increases

71

their chances of getting into vocational training, or any other job for that matter."

Gregor thought about it for a moment. "And that's it?"

Susanne grinned.

"What's the catch?" Gregor asked.

"Oh, you. You're an incorrigible pessimist!"

"I'm a realist. There may be kids who want to spend their time here with old folks for all the reasons you gave, but not *this* many."

He gestured at the room full of teens and younger kids. "So? What's the *actual* incentive here?"

"Caught me!" she said. "There's a sponsor. For every hour a kid spends here, Weiz Pharma AG will donate five euros to the school's PTA fund. As you know," she continued with a grin, "week-long class trips are important in certain grades, which is a huge motivation for those students."

Gregor grinned back. "So as usual, it's all about one thing— money. My pessimistic world view has been restored."

Susanne nodded.

"What did you want to talk to me about?"

Susanne looked around as though she was worried about eavesdroppers. "I'd prefer not to discuss it here."

Gregor groaned.

Susanne's face instantly flipped from friendly and relaxed to angry and annoyed. "Stop with the drama, Gregor. I'm not kidding. You can stop reminding me every time we see each other that my corruption investigation into your boss put you into 'an embarrassing situation.'"

Gregor made a pained face.

"You know after Mom died I wasn't all there," Zuzubee said.

Gregor nodded.

"OK. Then let's just talk with each other like normal people. I'd like to talk with you in private for a bit."

"Why?"

"Not here."

Gregor hesitated for an instant, but then he pulled himself together. "OK."

"When do you have time?"

"Tomorrow after work."

"Will you come to my place?"

Gregor nodded, and then he was gone.

Neither he nor Susanne had noticed the teenybopper with the super-short, platinum-blonde hair who had been listening in on their conversation from behind the folding partition separating the lobby from the café area with the tables.

SEVEN

My memory hadn't brought me any new information about whether Gregor's DNA had been found above or below Zuzubee's waistline. In other words: I had witnessed Gregor and Zuzubee agreeing to get together to talk—not for a hot screwing session. Although that didn't mean anything. Plans can change. Especially since Gregor is a Real Man and Katrin had been on vacation for a whole week already. It's only a problem when coitus is followed by exitus, and the cops pop up with all their annoying questions. But maybe nothing had happened, and Gregor's testosterone stayed at levels compatible with faithfulness to Katrin.

So I wasn't any more in the know than I was when I first overheard the Düsseldorf detectives discussing DNA.

I zoomed over to Martin to give him an update on the evidence that the Düsseldorf PD Criminal Investigations unit had on Gregor, and I found him in his cozy shared office with Katrin. They were both sitting at their desks in front of their computers, but neither of them was working.

"I had completely forgotten Susanne," Martin was saying. "It's been so long."

"Why did they get married so young?" Katrin asked. "Gregor isn't conventional like that at all, actually."

Martin thought for a moment and said, "It wasn't about convention or stuffiness for him. It was a chance to finally have a family." Katrin pressed her lips together.

"After his parents had died in the accident, Gregor lived with an aunt of his, who was unmarried. They never did hit it off."

"I know," Katrin mumbled. "He's told me all about his version of Mrs. Prysselius."

"Gregor met Susanne during their senior year in high school. She was completely different than all of the other girls. She was a hippie, wore floral skirts, went barefoot, and talked continuously about justice, love, and things like that."

Katrin laughed incredulously. Even I couldn't imagine Gregor falling for a free spirit, but apparently he was cut from different cloth in those days.

"He and her father got along well straight away. Gregor and Hans became fast friends. In fact, Gregor applied to the police academy because Susanne's father had been a detective. Gregor became a solid member of the family in short order, and I think he really wanted it to be official. He wanted to belong somewhere he felt comfortable and at ease. It was somehow logical that he and Susanne got married."

"How long were they married?"

Martin shrugged. "When I went to the university, we lost touch. But when we met again, it was over with Susanne."

"Why doesn't Gregor want to see either of us?" Katrin asked after a few minutes. She was close to tears. I'd never seen her this way.

"I have no idea."

"Maybe he did it . . ." she mumbled.

Martin gulped.

"Have you been huffing butane?" I bawled him out. "Gregor did not kill that chick."

"Then the detectives will find that out," he rebuked me mentally.

"I'm not so sure," I bellowed back. "Those cops are totally convinced they've got their murderer."

"Even so, we need to leave the investigation to the authorities," Martin replied. "Anything else will only make it worse for Gregor."

Then Martin sealed his brain bulkheads.

So once again Martin couldn't be expected to help. To quench my need for information, I zoomed back up to Düsseldorf. If the operating procedures are the same at the Düsseldorf PD as at the Cologne PD, then they probably were holding their end-of-day meeting, and I wanted to be there. I had to putz around for an hour until all the plainclothes had gathered, but then things got going.

"Kreidler was seen multiple times in recent days with the murder victim, specifically at the assisted-living facility where Susanne Hauschild's father is a resident."

"That is also where Agathangelídis's mother lives," the Ferrari-red redhead volunteered. "Maybe her current lover saw her throwing her arms around her ex-husband . . ."

All of the detectives groaned.

"Has anyone questioned the father?"

"He's operating on less than a full deck now."

"What about Kreidler's alibi?"

"He doesn't have one. On the contrary. Kreidler called the victim three times on Friday. Once in the afternoon, then at eight that night, and one more time around ten. The last two calls were made from the immediate vicinity of the crime scene."

"Was she already dead then?"

"We don't know."

"Why would he have killed her?" the redhead asked.

The team groaned at her again.

"What's the deal with all the macho crap?" she snapped back. "The issue of the motive is . . ."

"The last item on the list," Keller mumbled through his thick, bulging lips. "And naturally you're super sly—"

"Extortion," Stein interjected casually.

Everyone in the room fell silent, even the women's libber with the chromatic aberration for hair. But only for a second.

"Who supposedly extorted whom?" she asked.

"Susanne Hauschild's computer is missing," Stein explained softly. They all pricked up their ears like dogs to hear him. I flew in closer. "Why would the murderer steal a five-year-old laptop but leave all the other valuables alone? Because he wants to hide something she discovered. The victim was a journalist, if I recall correctly."

"Still," Agent Orange said. "What would she have been extorting him with? Is there something about Kreidler we should know?"

Stein took his time answering. I didn't know what the other folks in the room were thinking, but I for one wished I still had fingernails to bite, I was so tense.

And then he said it: "Karpi Glazunov. Susanne Hauschild called him the week before she died, and she was at his home on Wednesday, two days before she was murdered."

The Düsseldorf detectives looked at him all bug-eyed with confusion, but I knew what Stein was trying to say: Gregor was fucked.

"They've got a motive, Martin, and it makes Gregor look like an idiot," I started roaring even before I made it into his and Birgit's apartment.

Martin was drinking his late-afternoon tea. Today was raspberry leaf, to clarify the mind and spirit. That's what the package says. For the first time in my life, though, I hoped that that New Age junk would be authentically beneficial.

"The Düsseldorf PD has established a connection between Gregor's ex and Karpi Glazunov, and now they think Susanne was extorting Gregor, which is why he murdered her."

"Glazunov?" Martin asked as he wiped up the tea he had spilled on the table when I mentioned the name of Glazunov. He had turned pale and was trembling. Yes, Martin knew that name.

"That's what they said."

"But that case was closed . . ."

"Zuzubee met Glazunov, Martin. The Wednesday before she got murdered. And she had been in touch with Gregor and was waiting for him on Friday night at her place—right before she was murdered, or while she was being murdered. How do you think that looks to the Desperately Seeking Susanne crew up in Düsseldorf?"

Birgit came out of the bathroom and sat opposite Martin at the table. She wasn't drinking raspberry leaf tea but carrot juice. As she had been *for weeks*. The palms of her hands were already turning orange.

"We should think about what we can do for Gregor now," Birgit said.

"Uh, yes. Uh, something has been r-revealed . . ." Martin stammered.

Birgit raised her eyebrows at him to continue.

Martin explained that Gregor's ex had had some kind of contact with Karpi, and Birgit turned pale too. She instantly understood the conclusion we were supposed to draw.

"OK, then let's go find this Karpi guy and ask him what Susanne wanted from him," Birgit asked.

Martin started to squirm.

"Birgit's right," I said.

"I'll go alone," Martin decided. "You shouldn't be going to a nightclub in your condition."

Birgit rolled her eyes. "I'm not sick, Martin. And I want to help Gregor. Plus, they're not going to do anything to a woman who's nine months pregnant."

Martin shook his head. "You underestimate the seriousness of the situation, Birgit. It won't help Gregor if something happens to you."

"I'm coming along," Birgit said. "Don't argue with me."

To explain the significance of this new lead the Düssel-doofuses had, I need to tell the backstory of Karpi Glazunov. Not the whole story, of course. Just the part that had apparently gotten an incredibly stupid idea into the heads of the Desperately Seeking Susanne crew.

In late March earlier this year, Gregor was called to the discovery site of a dead body. Martin was already on scene securing evidence from a young woman whose nostrils were as white as the rim of a salt-slicked margarita glass. You couldn't make out the top of her face because the black wig she wore had slid forward and was covering her eyes. She was thin as a rail and dressed in a miniskirt and a halter top, the combination of which left her stomach exposed. As Martin instantly suspected onsite and later confirmed during the autopsy, she had died from blunt-force trauma to the larynx. The nightclub where she was found at the back exit was called Karpi Diem.

When Gregor showed up, he had a couple of extra uniforms in tow. He had them take down the ID information on the bobbleheads getting jiggy in the club, and then he locked Karpi in his office and Karpi's right-hand man in a broom closet and personally supervised the securing of the discovery site until the CSI crew arrived.

Then he went inside.

Alone.

He went into Karpi's office and chatted with the guy, who is the greatest living contradiction in Cologne's criminal underworld. He is originally from one of those republics that, after the fall of the Soviet Union, suddenly had no idea if it wanted to go the dictator or democracy route, and he arrived in Germany at the age of seventeen. He didn't speak a word of German and presumably would have gone downhill like other kids in his situation, if the eighty-two-year-old lady living next door hadn't just lost her husband. She was looking for something to do, and she found Karpi, who was shortish but all muscle. She taught him German, and he fell in love with the pun-ridden prewar poetry of Joachim Ringelnatz. He was built like an Olympic weightlifter and could carry her shopping bags home for her and he was polite enough to look at the pictures she would show him of her husband. When she died, Karpi stayed around for her funeral, and then he vanished. Three years later he returned in the form of a half-ton butterball with a suitcase bursting at the seams. No one had any idea where he had spent the intervening years.

Karpi still weighed half a ton, continuously stuffing pistachios, walnuts, or baklava into his face. Even though his voice sounded like the caterpillar track on a Leopard 2 battle tank, he had quotes from Ringelnatz's poetry ready for any occasion. People said you could buy literally any item from anywhere in the world from or through him, but he had never been caught doing anything illegal. While Gregor talked to him, Karpi shelled and ate a bag of pistachios as he expressed his regret over the death in the alley behind the club, saying people didn't snort coke in his joint—and if they did, he didn't know about it.

Gregor thanked him for the information and asked to use an office where he could interview Karpi's nervous assistant. Karpi granted him access to a small room whose normal purpose Gregor didn't need to ask about, given the green fabric stretched over the surface of the large round table. I'm certain if Gregor had asked Karpi about it, he'd have dished up an absolutely credible and watertight story about an allergy to wood polish he developed as a child that had recently been acting up. You just could not catch Karpi.

But Gregor then asked the fat slob's right hand into the poker room. When he tried to close the door behind him, Karpi squeezed in.

The assistant turned pale. He hid behind Gregor. Karpi didn't say a word, but he made a gesture that any underworldly person knows: he slowly drew his fat index finger under his fat chin and across his fat neck. When Gregor turned around to send Karpi out, the assistant put Gregor out of action by elbowing him hard in the ear, grabbing Gregor's duty weapon, and putting an end to his own botched-up life.

The juicy bit to the case was that the dead woman was actually the daughter of Gregor's cousin. But that was determined only later when Gregor, who had been pulled off the case because of the shooting, saw the file with the photo of the corpse lying open on Jenny's desk. He then puked into Jenny's lap, thereby answering the question of whether he wanted to immediately go and ID the body or wait a while first. The fact that they were related was like bags and bags of grist for the people who accused Gregor of shooting that slimy salamander "because he was to blame for Gregor's favorite niece." Never mind that she wasn't his niece.

Well, Karpi told the board of inquiry that his assistant frequently showed up to work with a runny or bloody nose and had left the basement of the nightclub multiple times during the presumed time of the murder—allegedly to smoke. Karpi confirmed that his assistant had committed suicide with Gregor's duty weapon, but the forensics report couldn't determine the progression of events unequivocally. The creep had stuck the pistol in his mouth and tilted his head back. If Gregor had rammed the thing between his teeth, the angle would have been similar. Another problem with the evidence was that Gregor had gunshot residue on his hands—because he had just come from shooting practice at the shooting range—and that the salamander always wore gloves because of the itchy case of scabies he suffered from. Thus, the circumstantial evidence didn't resolve into a clear picture of what happened, and the detectives on the case had to rely on two statements that, although identical, came from the person being investigated —Gregor—and from a corpulent nightclub owner with a dubious reputation. Apart from that, they never could prove beyond a reasonable doubt that the guy who had swallowed the greeting from Gregor's gun had also been the murderer of the young woman.

No wonder there were people who kept quietly gossiping about Gregor's vigilantism.

There're always folks like that.

At some point those voices fell silent.

Until the whole thing with Gregor's ex happened . . .

EIGHT

While Martin and Birgit got ready to leave the apartment, which for Birgit involved packing sizeable quantities of food, I zoomed back up to check in on the Desperately Seeking Susanne crew.

My interlude to update Martin hadn't taken that long, and the investigators were still in their meeting when I returned. Stein had just told the whole story of Gregor, Karpi, the slimy salamander, and the daughter of Gregor's cousin, apparently with relish because Agent Orange said, "If that case was solved at the time, what is the problem now?"

Stein replied with the line that had been whispered so many times in secret before: "What if Karpi lied?"

The room was silent for a moment.

"Are there reasons for him to do that?" the redhead asked. "Kreidler is still working homicide and not vice, fraud, or money laundering. What would Kreidler have offered this Karpi in exchange for lying on his behalf?"

She may have looked like crap, but inside the flaming cranium there was apparently a fully functional brain. Unlike the cluster of cells in the heads of Keller and Stein, whose mental GPS had only one destination, namely, to portray Gregor as the murderer no matter how.

"We'll find that out," Stein said. "And as soon as possible."

He didn't know it yet, but he was going to lose that race.

Karpi Diem was located in an old bunker from World War II. Although most of Cologne was flattened in the war, a bunch of these concrete blockhouses survived to become eyesores throughout the area, until someone came up with the idea not to tear them down but to put them to use in new ways. Some bunkers were converted into residential buildings; others housed archives or rehearsal rooms for musicians. Some were uglier than others, but none of those monstrosities could win a beauty pageant. Including Karpi's.

Karpi's bunker was half underground and in a surprisingly good location. It was an area where you didn't need to worry about getting raped, robbed, or rubbed out on your way to your Saturday night fun. Which is why the bobblehead bunker also offered a teenybopper disco on Saturday and Sunday afternoons. Even during years of undercover investigations, law enforcement never managed to find proof that Karpi had violated the Child Protection Act. And all of Cologne knew that no alcohol was served during the sock hops. Karpi's daycare competed with comparably soft-boiled offerings from the city's youth centers and parishes. But it was way, way cooler at Uncle Karpi's. It had the right atmosphere, and Karpi insisted on having his bouncers give the little shits the once-over at the door before they could head into the Pampers club. Karpi's reputation as a mysterious gangster was the cherry on the sundae. So his joint was always full.

Tuesday nights at eight, though, Karpi's bunker was dark and empty. There wasn't a bell at the steel front door, on which some jokester had painted the silhouette of a man and then dented the area around the heart by shooting bullets at it. Martin and Birgit stood in front of the shooting target, silently staring at it. Martin knocked. The sound his delicate finger bones made on the massive steel couldn't have been audible more than five centimeters away. Birgit pushed him aside energetically and hammered on the door with her fist. Much better audibility-wise, but still no reaction from inside.

I flew in and did a quick tour through the club. The bobblehead arena, the bar, and the lounge were all empty. The only action was in the storage room, where a few unshaven guys in black leather jackets and jeans with gold around their necks and in their mouths were unloading boxes from a truck and stacking them in a corner. The plates on the truck and the labels on the boxes were in Cyrillic letters. The boys finished the job and looked once more around the storage room, counted the boxes they had just stacked, nodded at each other, got back in the truck, and cleared out. I was sure the fine cloud of dust that spewed from the rust bucket as the ignition was turned would cause eyebrows to rise at the German Federal Environment Agency the next morning.

I finished my tour of the ground floor and zoomed down into the basement. Karpi's office was at the end of a long corridor, mostly dark except for an emergency light. That's where I found him. The boss was leaning back in his leather armchair snoozing. The stench coming out of his open mouth sent my flight path into a roll. Shit. Karpi had been dead for days and was moldering away down here. I was about to turn away when another sensory perception reached me through the nausea: his feet on the desk would occasionally twitch, and after taking a closer look I could see that his chest was rising and sinking. If he was dead, then things were fermenting so much in his bowels that the occasional leak of foul-smelling gasses were mimicking respiration. But what was making his feet twitch?

I decided that the guy was probably still alive, and I looked around in the office. The desk had three landline phones on it. Aha, that fat fish had also realized that good old telephone lines guarantee more security these days than an unencrypted cell phone signal. A visual inspection of the phones didn't help me much though, because the spot on the phone that was supposed to show the number you could dial to reach it was blank in each case.

There were papers all over the desk, some lists of phone numbers, some beverage delivery slips, a letter from the tax office about real estate assessments, a receipt for some pills whose name meant nothing to me, and a business card from Susanne Hauschild. Exactly like the one she had pressed into Gregor's hand. But that didn't help me much either.

I was about to give up when I found what I was looking for. Under the leg of the desk. One of Karpi's business cards folded up. Even shady figures have business cards, I guess. But the only information listed on his card was KARPI and a phone number. Unfortunately part of the number had been worn away under the desk leg, so I could only make out four digits. Which is a bummer because German phone numbers don't all have the same number of digits so there was no way of knowing how long the number was. But four digits was a start.

I hurried back to Martin and Birgit, who looked like Joseph and Mary on Christmas Eve. A man and a preggo on the verge of bursting, holding hands in front of a closed door. All they needed was a donkey.

"Call him on your cell. That'll likely wake him up," I said to Martin.

"The number is two, three, five, seven. It's a Cologne landline."

"Only four digits?"

He dialed the number into his cell phone, but it didn't go through.

"I couldn't make out the other numbers . . ." I said.

Martin scratched his head.

Birgit looked at the display. "Cologne numbers usually have six to eight digits, right?" she said. Martin nodded.

"Add one-one to the end," she suggested.

Martin dialed. No answer.

"OK, then add one-one and one-three," Birgit said with conviction.

Martin winced. "How can you be so sure?"

Birgit grinned. "Look at the pattern. All prime numbers. Two, three, five, seven, eleven, thirteen . . ."

Martin tried it that way. The call went through. I zoomed back down to Karpi's cave. The phone on the left rang. Amazing.

Karpi gurgled, gasped, coughed, snorted, and grunted, but he didn't budge. The ringing stopped.

I zoomed back up to Martin. "That was the right number, but he's asleep like the dead. Try again."

This time Karpi moved, his feet twitched again, then his legs, then an arm. He opened one eye a millimeter, then the other. It took him a solid fifty seconds to get his fat hand to the receiver. The ringing stopped. Karpi stared at the phone then pulled his massive figure upright and wobbled to his feet. He stretched, scratched his balls, and froze when the phone rang again.

"What time is it?" he growled into the phone.

I couldn't hear Martin's answer because I can't get into the old-style landline headsets such as the one stuck to Karpi's ear, but apparently Martin told him more than just the time because

Karpi grunted a couple times in response and then slapped a red button on the desk with his paw that buzzed the door upstairs.

I flew toward Martin and Birgit, met them at the door, and guided them in through the dark and empty nightclub to a door that didn't have a handle. It took a minute or two for that door to open. It was an elevator. It was empty. Martin stood there unsettled, but Birgit understood that it was an invitation. She quickly pulled Martin in with her.

The moment that Karpi and Birgit met was surely one Birgit would never forget her whole life long. She followed Martin out of the elevator and into the darkened corridor. Martin saw the light from under Karpi's office door. I confirmed for Martin that Karpi was waiting for them there as they felt their way over the uneven concrete floor. Once at the door, Martin pushed it open and stepped into the office. Birgit followed him over the threshold—and she saw a mountain of a man in a screaming-yellow satin suit and a Santa Claus–style hat on his head with a blinking tassel at the tip.

Martin isn't very responsive to that style of humor, whereas Birgit had a hard time closing her mouth again.

"You said you want to save your cop friend from the cops," Karpi told Martin. "With my help. So, you still believe in Santa Claus."

Birgit burst out in laughter.

Karpi gave her a dead serious look. "Are you laughing at me?"

Birgit shook her head but couldn't talk yet, and she kept chuckling.

"Please don't be angry with her. The h-hormones . . ." Martin stammered as he cautiously moved his pudgy body in front of Birgit to protect her from Karpi's potential blaze of anger.

"Your tassel is blinking SOS," she blurted out. "That's almost as good as the prime numbers."

Karpi brusquely brushed Martin to the side to get a better look at the puffed-up female half of these odd birds. Birgit flashed him a friendly smile.

"You recognized the prime numbers?" Karpi whispered. "What's your name?"

"Birgit. Pleased to meet you."

She held out her hand to Karpi, who stayed put and made no move to shake her hand.

"Oh, don't worry," Birgit said gesturing at her stomach. "It's not contagious."

"OK," Karpi said, finally shaking her hand.

Her arm disappeared nearly up to the elbow inside Karpi's massive mitt, but he shook her hand as gently as he would if he were holding a tiny songbird.

Martin and I watched speechlessly as Birgit cozied up to the king of Cologne's underworld, and I cleared my throat to get the conversation moving.

"We have a request," Martin began. Then he explained the whole situation to Karpi.

"Yes, that woman was here," Karpi whispered. He pulled a ginormous package of marshmallows shaped like little mice from his desk drawer and offered Birgit some. She took one of the wiggly white mice by the tail and bit its head off. Karpi nodded, satisfied.

"What did she want?" Birgit asked, mouth full.

Karpi didn't say anything.

Martin was fidgeting nervously.

"All right," Birgit said. She held up the rest of her headless marshmallow mouse by the tail. Karpi's eyes followed its every movement. He looked like a lazy cat mulling over whether to indulge in a game, even though he had a whole bag full of mice already. The guy really wasn't quite right in the head. "I'll pose the question differently. Was Susanne Hauschild here because she thought Gregor shot your assistant?"

Karpi shook his head, stirring about five kilograms of bacon fat under his chin to move back and forth as well.

"Did her visit have anything to do with Gregor Kreidler at all?"

Bacon fat wobbling.

"Let's assume that Susanne Hauschild came here because she wanted information about something that she thought you would be familiar with—and let's stipulate that you have no personal experience with that subject, OK?" Birgit squinted at Karpi. Karpi nodded. God, the woman had that freak completely wrapped around her little finger.

"What subject did it concern?"

Karpi set his fingertips on his various chins and started chewing his lip. Then he bent forward—to the extent his rolls of fat permitted. At that moment the phone in the middle rang. Karpi picked up the receiver with two fingers and held it to his ear. He listened and hung up without an answer.

"Get out," he whispered. "Through the door at the end of the corridor. Fast."

Birgit stepped back with a jolt as though she had gotten electrocuted, and Martin looked like he was about to burst out in tears. Once again, Birgit got it together first.

"Thanks for the mouse," she said, stuffing the rest of the white marshmallow rodent into her mouth so only its tail was hanging out, and she pulled Martin out with her.

In order to semisimultaneously tail Martin and Birgit to make sure they got home OK and be there when Keller and Stein visited Karpi, I resorted to racing Formula One–style between the two scenes, except at lightning speed. Karpi wasn't wearing his Santa Claus cap with blinking tassel anymore. He just sat behind his desk, and he didn't get up when one of his men escorted the two cops into his cellar lair.

They ran through their usual greeting script allowing the cops to decide if their conversation partner was willing or unwilling, and then Stein inquired about Susanne Hauschild's visit.

"Yeah, she was here," Karpi said.

"What did she want?"

"Nutritional advice."

Keller's face shifted from studying the room to Karpi himself. Stein's spine stiffened.

"Sorry?" Stein asked.

"Nutritional advice," Karpi repeated.

"Are you shitting us?" Keller muttered. Evidently he had something in his mouth triggering too much spit, because all of the sibilants in his question sounded like slobber.

"Why would I do that? By the way, you have a spot of something on your shirt." Karpi looked cool and relaxed.

"Are you a dietician?" Stein asked seriously.

"Neither trained or certified," Karpi replied. "But lots of people know that I know something about healthy eating."

The words seemed sort of, uh, surrealistic coming out of the mouth of the satin-suited jellyfish sitting there with his arms splayed behind his desk, his seams threatening to burst open at any moment. (I looked that word up in the dictionary, *surrealistic*.)

"Now . . ."

"For instance, I can tell you eat meat from the smell of you. That's not good," Karpi said. He shrugged. "But I'm sure you know this already. I don't force my advice upon people."

"But Ms. Hauschild came here expressly to ask you for exactly that advice," Stein said in the same tone he would use to inquire about details of a visit from little green men.

"Exactly. I'm vegan."

"What's that?" Keller asked. Drops of spit sprayed in Karpi's direction.

"I don't eat anything that comes from animals. No fish, no meat, no eggs, no milk, and so on."

"Pfff," Keller said.

"Why not?" Stein asked.

In Germany, even a salad has ham in it, you see, so I shared Stein's confusion. And I wondered what Karpi could have been eating as I thought back to the stench coming from his mouth earlier.

"It's more healthful," Karpi said. "Do you have any other questions?"

Keller and Stein kept asking the same question in various formulations, sometimes friendly, sometimes threatening, but Karpi stuck to his story that Susanne Hauschild had come to him looking for tips about a healthy diet. I circled overhead like a vulture in high spirits for a solid twenty minutes until the two Düssel-dweebs finally took to their heels. Unfortunately my mood didn't last because Gregor's predicament wasn't a step closer to being solved, even though those two detectives pulled out all the stops trying to catch Karpi up in his bullshit. Gregor was still the primary suspect. Ugh, what am I saying? He was the *only* suspect in the murder of Susanne Hauschild.

NINE

As I've already mentioned, Gregor is pretty much the only guy I absolutely one-hundred-percent like. I have wished many times for Gregor to be able to hear me. He and I would have been an awesome detective team. And Gregor definitely wouldn't make so much drama with stupid behavior rules and anti-electrosmog netting over his bed like pain-in-the-ass Martin. On the contrary. After screwing, Gregor would ask me, "Well, how was I?" And I could answer, "Today your form wasn't that great, but still better than James Bond."

I sighed. Gregor was on his way to hell, and he needed my help. Which is why I wasn't taking in the sights of the city in summer. Which is why I wasn't going to the movies anymore, I wasn't checking in on the whorehouse, and I wasn't zooming off to the emergency room—not even once to maybe catch another soul at the moment of death and get him to chat for a bit. No, I was spending all my time in the closet in the attic where Martin had put my laptop.

And that laptop was my access to the world. Using the same speech recognition software that Martin used at the Institute for Forensic Medicine, I was able to control the computer. I just thought a command, and the computer obeyed. All I needed was a wireless headset for it to work. The interface that connects the headset to the laptop was my secret doorway into the system.

Living computer nerds are, of course, totally lame. They sit at home chatting about making waves while they practice single-handed sailing under the desk. But it was different in my case. I didn't have any erectile tissue anymore, so I couldn't screw. I didn't have a body at all anymore, so I couldn't paw or rub anything or anyone. I couldn't take in a tongue tango or even blow into the ear of a hot babe. So I had every reason in the world to spend my nights in front of my online idiot box. But I didn't.

Well, fine. My first few months of being the proud owner of my own computer, I did spend a lot of time in the online world. I consumed the trash offered there, watched a Formula One race, took in stupid little movie clips on YouTube, or ogled babelicious bunnies playing with all sorts of toys. But even that eventually got tedious. I had looked around on Fluffbook, but there wasn't anything really interesting going on. There weren't any groups where people discussed pinching four-wheeled luxury toys. I could have contributed a fair bit there, but I understand that Facebook isn't the ideal spot for this particular type of technical conversation. Everything else there was basically a flavor of shit similar to what the boob tube spews out every afternoon.

So what really drew me to my computer up to now primarily had been writing out my experiences. Martin dug up some chick who calls herself a freelance author—I mean, is there such a thing as a non-freelance one? She has been putting out my autobiographical reports as her own "novels." And traveling the world as a celebrity earning wads of cash while I'm stuck out in the cold. But that's OK, because I don't need any money. And if I did, I'd have my own ways and means of coming by the necessary financing.

I actually didn't feel like writing up Gregor's story, because I didn't have a clue where the whole thing was going, but I did start keeping notes for myself. I wrote out the events from the days before Zuzubee was murdered, and I continued to mull over what possible reason there could have been to murder Gregor's ex. Find the motive, find the perp. That's how it usually goes, at least.

I kept coming back to the fact that the motive had to be somewhere in her circle of family and friends, or it had to be connected to some kind of story Zuzubee was chasing. All I knew about her private life was a boyfriend with an absolutely unpronounceable name that the Düssel-doofuses had mentioned. I was going to have to get kicking on finding out about him.

And the story that Susanne was working on was something else we needed to follow up on. But how? Her laptop had been stolen, and her cell phone was in the hands of those Düssel-doofuses. So that wouldn't be any help. Considering that I didn't have anything else to do, it might also be helpful to do some deep digging in my memory again and think back through the last few hours before Susanne's death. Because I had seen her, although briefly, on the Friday she was murdered.

June 25, two days before Gregor's arrest

The days at the old folks' home start even earlier than at your average doughnut shop. No idea why, though, since it's not like the shrunken heads are going to miss anything even if they sleep in till eleven or something. But no. Breakfast is served at seven thirty, and the dining hall is usually instantly at capacity. Lots of the residents are so impatient they'd beat their plates like drums except that there's at least one buzzkill sitting at each table who holds the others in check with electrolaser-sharp glares. Too bad. I'd seriously stay for the show if they'd start rioting here like we did that one time at summer camp.

I was there before breakfast, and I watched the preparations. The residents from the upper floors and the west wing were on the go, more or less independently. Some needed help getting dressed, but that was all done by the time I drifted in. The caravan of shuffling, rolling, and teetering old fogeys reminded me a little of an army of mummified zombies stumbling across the screen in some B horror flick. In this case though they were shuffling into the dining hall not to eat brains but to help porridge, soft-boiled eggs, and crustless white bread slide rapidly through their intestines.

Walking upstream were the white coats on their way to bring breakfast to the bed warmers who couldn't get up on their own anymore. Sometimes in the form of soups, purées, or white-bread cubes that looked like they had been prechewed; sometimes in the form of IV bags.

In the witch's kitchen, the in-house pharmacist Dr. Krämpel was busy filling pill cups. He was working through printed pages that listed the name of the dinosaurs followed by information about who needed to take how many pills and when.

What all the pills, drops, and ass bombs were supposed to do was not exactly clear to me, because I had no clue about the trade names of legal drugs. Except for the pills listed in the schedule table for ten p.m.—I guessed those were just sleeping pills.

One of the white coats came into the pharmacy, took the cart with the prepared pill doses, and distributed the chemical weapons throughout the building. It'd be funny to mix up the doses some time. Or at least mix up the times of day. Then we'd have sleepy gray-tops falling asleep and splatting their faces into their bowls of müsli while the hallways would be party town all night. But unfortunately the chick dispensing pill cups didn't look like she had much of a sense of humor. Grim-faced, with the corners of her mouth drooping down, she played the in-house drug dealer going from granny to gramps, slamming down each resident's ration of chemical happiness. The sun was shining in a cloudless sky—it wasn't even nine o'clock yet—and I was so depressed that I wished I could OD on sleeping pills myself. That was impossible, of course.

If I couldn't take in a blissful coma, then I was at least going to need a short break. So I flew out to the park. I spent a while racing squirrels and trying to annoy the ducks that had taken up residence in the brackish pond in the middle of the lawn. I flew swarms of mosquitos without getting bitten. My mood gradually rose from basement to ground floor, and then I moseyed my way back to the raisin ranch, which was unexpectedly in full pandemonium.

A garland reading "Welcome" had been hung up in the lobby. The letters looked like they had been fashioned by hand by the war blind. Wrapped like wreaths around the words were similarly hand-fashioned butterflies, whose wings were made of twisted wire covered with nylon stockings. Which meant some butterflies were old-lady beige and pigly pink, while the more exotic ones were polychrome.

The lobby was gradually filling up, especially with slightly less-sprightly seniors who shuffled in using a wide variety of means of locomotion. Visitors strolled in from the parking lot, and judging from their pads and pens and cameras or microphones hanging about their necks, they appeared to be representatives of the media. They were all making a beeline to the tray line in the cafeteria, where they dispensed themselves coffee.

Hands were hard at work hauling mic stands, and one shaggy-headed guy—who I could sooner imagine carrying a steel drum under his arm than a bedpan—was plugging in speakers mounted atop tripods. They weren't going to put out proper bass, though, that much was clear.

At ten o'clock sharp, a Stuttgart-built whip rolled up with a Cologne license plate. The driver parked it painstakingly and then emerged wearing a blue suit and tie. I reflexively yawn at blah faces on blah bodies in blah suits with blah ties.

The bore did the middle button on his jacket as he walked, stroked his hand over his neatly parted medium-brown hair, and straightened his frameless eyeglasses. He was greeted just outside the front door by the facility director with an ecstatic handshake.

A gong rang out through the whole building, and out of every corner more attendees came dragging along, this time including even the hard-working hands from the kitchen and two chicks from the administrative offices. And even Mr. Worry-Wrinkle from the in-house pharmacy helped greet the hordes. The director personally escorted the bore through the lobby and positioned him next to the mic. Then she waited until the shuffling of feet had finished, eagle-eyed the audience to make sure all of her subordinates were in compliance with her directive to attend, and cleared her throat before starting to speak.

Susanne Hauschild entered the large space during the boring salutations, stealing the limelight from the director until she pressed through to the back of the crowd, and then feigned interest as the suit stepped up to the mic. Shit, I'd missed the explanation of who the bore was.

"Good morning, my dear—" He stopped short.

Geezers, I thought, but even if that's what had been on the tip of his tongue, he swallowed his initial greeting and started again.

"Ladies and gentlemen, I'm so pleased to be with you again almost a year to the date after my first visit."

The scribblers in the audience scribbled, the shutterbugs shutterbugged, and the flacks from local radio kept covering their mouths to hide their yawns. They were going to jam their mics up to the guy's mouth after his official remarks.

"One year ago, Weiz Pharma AG launched a project intended to bring seniors and young people together for mutual benefit."

Aha, this was the guy who had put a wrench into the kids' after-school free time.

"Our success has exceeded our wildest expectations."

I couldn't follow the sleep-inducing jabbering without falling into a coma, so instead I checked out the onlookers. Half of them were asleep; the other half were fumbling with their hearing aids. I couldn't tell if they were turning the volume up or down, though.

I thought about zooming over to the closest funeral home, because things there had to be livelier than this scene, but a motion in the background caught my eye. Zuzubee was slowly and inconspicuously making her way toward the main staircase. I followed her up to the second floor and into the pharmacy. She grabbed the folder listing all the prescriptions, photocopied a whole stack of them, and carefully put the originals in order back into the folder, her hands trembling. She took another folder out of the cabinet, photocopied more pages that looked more or less like the first page, stuck all her copies into her bag, made sure the coast was clear, and then left the witch's kitchen.

If I'd been right behind her, I probably wouldn't have noticed that she was being watched. But I was curious what the label on the second folder said, so I had stayed back in the pharmacy for a second. Sadly the good woman had put the folder back into its spot in the cabinet and closed the door. It's as dark as an elephant's ass inside a closed cabinet, so I couldn't see anything in there. I hurried back out to catch up with Zuzubee, which is when I noticed the person stepping out from a shadowy old architectural alcove and looking down the corridor after Gregor's ex. I'd seen the platinum-blonde stubble head here before; it belonged to the girl who couldn't have been more than thirteen years old, the one I'd first seen serving coffee and who I'd taken at first for one of the helpful schoolgirls.

But no schoolkid would be traipsing around this place at this hour during summer vacation. No schoolkid in all of Cologne was even awake yet. Except for the towhead. Why? And why was she watching Susanne Hauschild, who herself was spying around?

June 30, three days after Gregor's arrest

Katrin had gone through the whole entry procedure at the front gate to the jail and was now sitting in the visitors' room, which did not have little facing cubicles separated by bulletproof glass like in American movies. It was just a normal room. Well, OK. Not exactly normal, since the surveillance cameras were suspended in plain sight in the corners. Their red lights were off, which didn't impress me. I had done so many wiring . . . *corrections* . . . to security systems that I knew a red light didn't have anything to do with whether a camera was recording or not.

Katrin also noticed the cameras but wasn't interested in them. She was pale, and she was chewing on the nail of her left thumb.

Then Gregor came in. A guard escorted him just outside the room and unlocked his handcuffs before Gregor stepped inside the way he been taught: always keep your distance from the guy with the keys. Wait in front of the door, walk through the door, take a step, wait some more. And in this case the distance he was keeping was a meter and a half, because the jailer can't do anything to the prisoner within that distance. Not from a standing position, at least.

Katrin leaped up.

Gregor took a step back and stood directly in the doorway. His face was impenetrable. Katrin took a hesitant step toward him. Gregor raised his hand. Katrin stopped as though she had hit a brick wall.

"Don't wait for me," Gregor said. His voice sounded like the final wheeze of a defective starter.

"Wh-what?" Katrin stammered.

"You'll have grown kids and be thinking about how to celebrate your silver wedding anniversary before I get out of here."

Katrin swayed. "Gregor, what the fuck?"

"I'm sorry." Gregor said, then turned around, submitted to handcuffs again, and stepped out of the room.

T E N

I was almost as shocked as Katrin. I hung around with her for a moment, but then I went to follow Gregor. He went straight back into his cell, sat down, rested his elbows on his knees and his forehead in his palms—and sobbed. The tears ran down his fore-arms and his shoulders heaved, but I didn't hear a sound. After ten minutes he wiped his nose, lay down, and dozed off. I had a bad feeling when I left him, but there wasn't anything I could find out there for now.

Despite my whistle-stop at the cell to see Gregor, I still made it to the Institute for Forensic Medicine before Katrin. Martin was blathering a report into his computer and naturally he was pissed when I tried to interrupt. He unloaded a bunch of hot air at me about the importance of generally accepted social rules and of compliance with the same, but when I told him what had just gone down in jail, he forgot his anger. He asked me three times if I was sure I'd understood everything correctly, if Gregor hadn't added something else that might qualify what he had said, if—

"Martin, he sent Katrin away. Forever. And he didn't say one thing about Zuzubee's murder. We seriously need to do something."

Martin sat at his desk and didn't budge.

"Martin! Wake up! We need to—"

"Gregor has his reasons," Martin whispered.

That left me speechless.

"We should wait to see what Düsseldorf Criminal Investigations finds out," he continued. "They are professionals. They know what they're doing. They will find out the truth."

It may be that my career as a car cracker negatively impacted my relationship with the authorities, or maybe that relationship had already gone rocky, which is why I switched to the other side the law, but in any case, my assessment of the situation was once again the total opposite of Martin's. The Düssel-dweebs were going to put Gregor away for life because he hadn't made any effort whatsoever to defend himself. We were his only chance. Or more specifically: I was his only chance. Except that without Martin as my mouthpiece I was gagged.

I was not unfamiliar with the problem; it's the great tragedy of my current existence, but experience has taught me I would eventually pull Martin off the fence and get him to help. The only issue was whether he would cooperate voluntarily or only under duress. I didn't care which. However, first I needed a plan as to how I was going to get Gregor out of jail, and that was the problem. I didn't have the foggiest idea how I could get a murder suspect—who wasn't making even the slightest effort to prove his innocence—sprung from the clutches of the most brainless cops since crime scenes were invented.

I bolted home and pondered the situation awhile in my cupboard, but despite my best efforts I couldn't come up with some brilliant strategy. I didn't even have a strategy at all. Out of sheer frustration, I caved on being alone to think and instead went to visit Birgit down in the apartment.

She looked exactly how I felt. Somehow driven but without a target. She was gnawing on a carrot and tugging on various mobiles in the nursery as she did a few physical therapy exercises to help her back pain, which was the latest thing she had been suffering from. I got the unambiguous feeling she couldn't take much more of being pregnant. And she was bored.

That's when an idea hit me. And an absolutely genius one at that.

I zoomed back up to my cupboard, turned on the laptop, and set up a free e-mail account under the name of Spirit of Truth. Then I entered the credit card number of a CPA who should have been in jail long ago but who I won't rat out so I can keep using his credit card, and I transferred a hefty sum to myself from his account.

Setting up financial transactions like this is pretty easy for me since I can watch over people's shoulders when they do their banking online. I read their account number off the screen and their PIN as they type it, and then I check their TANs, or "transaction authentication numbers," which are a type of two-factor authentication. After entering the account number and PIN, you have to enter a specific TAN to execute a financial transaction online. Nowadays these are often texted to people's smartphones, but the best ones are printed TAN lists some German banks mail to their customers. A lot of people leave these TAN lists out in the open on their desks. I could write a series of books on the topic of data security by now, but that would be stupid, obviously. Relaxed handling of sensitive data was fine by me because that's how I had access to multiple accounts.

And despite the weak economy, there were still tons of people with tons of money. Rich people make so many transfers to pay for all the crap they order online, they usually don't even bother checking on charges for less than a thousand euros that show up on their bank statements. I knew a lot of these people, and I had built up a pool of idiots whose accounts I could regularly use to go shopping or, as in this case, add money to an online checking account that I can use for any transactions that incur fees. Like sending text messages, for instance, which are never free in Germany. So I texted Birgit's phone: *Gregor needs help. Are you in?*

I read the message and considered it for a moment. If I was judging Birgit's state of mind correctly, maybe this would distract from her looming future and toward meaningful occupation. And what could be more meaningful than springing Gregor out of jail?

Martin would go berserk. But I didn't care. I thought "Send" and zoomed down into the apartment. Birgit's cell phone chimed to signal she had gotten a text message. It worked!

She set down her coffee mug, stared at her phone, and swallowed. Since when had she been drinking coffee again? Apparently not just her brain activity had returned to normal but also her noncompliance with Martin's nutritional program. ¡Viva la revolución! I yelled with gusto, but unfortunately Birgit couldn't hear me. As she started coughing and her homemade latte erupted through her nose and out the corners of her mouth, she ran into the bathroom to expel the rest under high pressure into the bathtub, and I congratulated myself on my awesome idea.

Birgit had covered all of the tiles on the surround over the bathtub with her coffee explosion, so she rinsed the brown brew off with cold water. Then she wiped the last few drops from her face and waddled back into the kitchen. She picked up her cell phone and stared at it again—this time in disbelief.

Then she responded to the message.

Who are you?

I'll give you the digest version of our conversation so you don't get too bored with me zooming back and forth between my cupboard to write messages and the kitchen to see Birgit's facial expressions:

Gregor's best friend.

Then I would know you.

We do know each other.

What's your name?

I hesitated. Should I give her my real name? What if she goes to Martin and asks who Pascha is? He would never talk to me again. On the other hand, it was super lame that he was still keeping his closest friend a secret from Birgit. So maybe the whole situation would have a silver lining if he finally had to spill the beans about me to her. So I told her my name.

Pascha.

I want to talk with you.

You can't. Only via text message.

NGH

Huh? What did that mean? I pondered for a second, but I couldn't remember. Obviously I'm aware that there are a gazillion lame abbreviations people use when texting each other. Some of which are used mainly by CHX, or chicks. But car thieves do not use girlie abbreviations, so I wasn't well versed in the dialect that uses *NGH*. I sent my response in plain German.

???????????

Not gonna happen.

Oh, duh. Why couldn't I figure that out?

You can't talk to me under the circumstances.

I sat in my cupboard and waited. No response. I zoomed down to the kitchen. Birgit was staring at my message.

She was reaching for the landline, presumably to call Martin, so I zoomed back up to my laptop.

Not a word to Martin, I wrote.

I zoomed down to Birgit and saw her hand hover a moment over the telephone, and then she pulled it back and texted her response to me instead.

What can I do?

Now we were talking.

I had to believe that Martin would punish me by ignoring me if he found out I had not only contacted Birgit but also roped her into helping set Gregor free, so I had to get Birgit to swear not say anything. No idea how long that would hold, but the main thing was that Gregor's rescue operation was finally rolling.

Find out about Susanne's personal life. Then I added more precise instructions.

Birgit changed clothes, which lately had turned into an athletic challenge since she needed to work around and over that giant bowling ball. She packed some cookies, apples, carrots, and a chocolate bar into her bag, went downstairs and got in her BMW convertible, and drove to the address I had given her. Zuzubee's apartment still had police tape outside it, but that didn't bother us. Birgit started looking for the neighbors who, according to the police report, had been nosy enough to see Gregor on the day of the crime standing outside the building's main entrance and even noted his license plate number.

It didn't take her long to find one. On my instructions, she started pressing buzzers for the apartments on the same floor as Susanne's. Almost immediately a window opened overhead.

An extended rearview mirror, like the kind mounted on the wings of a minivan towing camper, slid out through the window. Birgit looked up and found herself staring directly into the mirror and into the face of an old woman.

"Whom are you trying to reach?" the door guard asked.

"Susanne. We have an appointment. We haven't seen each other for years, but she's not answering her buzzer—"

"Oh my God, sweetheart. Haven't you heard?"

Birgit played blonde. I mean, dumb. She is blonde, yes, but don't be fooled.

"Ms. Hauschild is dead. Murdered!"

Birgit laid a hand on her stomach and put the other over her mouth and leaned against the door. Uh-oh, that didn't look good. Had she overdone it on my mission?

"Child, are you going to collapse? Wait—I'll open the door for you. Please come upstairs—I can't leave you alone in that condition!"

Birgit looked up at the mirror again and gave a weary nod. As soon as the mirror was retracted, she straightened her back and grinned with satisfaction.

Mrs. Berger, as we read on the buzzer's nameplate, took Birgit into her apartment and guided her by the arm to the sofa. As the old woman fluffed up a pillow and stuffed it behind her guest's back, Birgit looked around the room. Mrs. Berger flitted back into the kitchen, apparently to fetch a cold drink. With the pillow behind her, Birgit had maybe a quarter of the room she needed for her butt, so she pulled the pillow out and leaned all the way back into the sofa. This didn't interrupt her scan of the room, however.

The rug hung on the wall had to be about a hundred years old. The black-and-white photos next to it were only slightly more recent, and every horizontal surface had little porcelain figurines, collector's teacups, or silver-framed photographs on it. The arms of the sofa were covered in crocheted doilies, and more of these lacy rags adorned the coffee table, the dining room table, the windowsill, and even the television set. The TV doilies hung down so far over the picture that it would probably have made James Bond look like he was wearing a doily cap, but presumably folks with one foot in the grave only watched shows that went well with doilies. Songbirds on public television liked to wear crocheted crap like that while they tortured people with their warbling.

The lady of the house returned with a glass of water in her hand.

"Now please drink something. Would you like a little schnapps as well? To take the edge off?"

Birgit shook her head. "No alcohol, thank you. The water is perfect."

You could see the old woman's disappointment, but she smiled bravely as she retrieved a teensy doily from a drawer in her oak hutch and set it and the water on the coffee table in front of Birgit. She served herself a little schnapps.

"Well, then—" Mrs. Berger began. A tone from a cell phone interrupted her. "Won't you excuse me for a moment?"

Mrs. Berger set a gigantic pair of eyeglasses on her nose, fished last year's iPhone out of the baggy pocket of her violet knit cardigan, and read a text message, crinkling up her nose.

Naturally I was curious about the message the old bag had gotten, so I read along: *Cover me* is what it said. She typed €5, and the reply was *Highway robbery*. After a minute another message: *OK*. She smiled and put the phone away.

"My grandson," she said, pointing at one of the photos on the bookshelf. "I used to slip him money, but now that he's started taking on odd jobs, he supplements my pension. My daughter forbade him from working as long as his grades are bad, but the boy wants to earn money. So I give him an alibi, and he pays me for it. Everybody wins."

I'd have liked to know what kind of job the guy had where he earned so much money it was worth five euros to him for Gran not to rat him out to Mom.

Mrs. Berger raised her little schnapps glass: "And now: to Ms. Hauschild! May her soul rest in peace."

She downed the liqueur in one gulp and poured herself a second.

"Where did you know her from?" she asked.

"From school . . ." Birgit said. I had stressed that she needed to be vague with her answers and to ask a ton of questions so the old broad didn't have a moment to think. She was following my advice. "But, please, could you tell me what happened?"

"Ms. Hauschild was strangled to death. Last Friday night. The police were here, two gentlemen. One looked rather unkempt—he's likely not married. But the second one . . ."—she smacked her wrinkly lips—"he was handsome. The one with the smooth dark hair. He was just a little, now, how should I say it . . . cool." She tipped a second schnapps down her wrinkly throat. "Or arrogant."

"Were you able to help the police?" Birgit asked.

"I saw the murderer! Heavens, to think that it could have happened just as well to me." Whoosh—another glassful down the hatch.

"Someone buzzed at Ms. Hauschild's apartment; I remember that it was right before the national news came on. I can always hear her buzzer clearly because our bathrooms share the same air duct outside, and her bathroom is located right next to the buzzer. So then I looked out the window—it's always nice to know who is coming into the building. In any case, I saw the man standing there."

She gave a fairly accurate description of Gregor—at least, if you're checking him out via a mirror through a window from the second floor.

"When no one opened the door for him, he took his cell phone out of his pocket and dialed a number. Apparently no one answered. And then he went away."

"But then he can't have killed her," Birgit said.

"He came back. Later on, someone buzzed again, and it was him again. And then—and I told this to the police officers—then he walked around the building to the back."

"What could he have wanted there?"

"Maybe he wanted to yell up to her apartment. I don't know. My apartment doesn't have a window facing the back of the building."

"And could you hear anything from your apartment?" Birgit asked. "Given how poorly soundproofed the air ducts are . . ."

Mrs. Berger slumped. "Yes, that was the odd thing. I didn't hear anything from her apartment after she came home. Normally she turns the radio on first thing—a terrible station with dreadful music. But on Friday, she came home, slammed her apartment door shut as she usually does, which makes all the walls shake, and then . . ."

Birgit was sitting on the front edge of the couch. "Then?" she helped.

"Then, nothing."

"And you told the police that as well?" Birgit asked.

Mrs. Berger thought for a moment. She thought so long she had time to down another little glass of schnapps. Then she looked at Birgit with a cocked head. "I'm not certain anyone asked about it."

Birgit sank back and sipped her water.

"How awful," she mumbled. I got the impression she didn't really know how to turn to the conversation to Zuzubee's personal life, but then she pulled herself together and just blurted it out.

"Do you happen to know Ms. Hauschild's boyfriend? He supposedly owns a pub . . ."

I had fed Birgit that bit of info, even though I couldn't remember the name the Düssel-doofuses had mentioned. Something like Agatha. But wasn't that a woman's name? I must have been mistaken.

"He's Greek, but otherwise quite nice," Mrs. Berger said. "At least, he always said a friendly hello, and he carried my shopping bags upstairs for me a few times."

"Do you know what his name is? Or what his pub is called? I'd love to talk to him."

Mrs. Berger helped her memory along with another glass of schnapps, but then she shook her head. "I think the pub is in the Belgian Quarter, but unfortunately I don't know where exactly."

Well, Martin and I were going to have to go on a little pub crawl later, I thought. Our most recent booze cruise had been on my twenty-fifth birthday, almost exactly a year ago. Time for a refresher. Except this time we were going to need to check out a whole neighborhood. Martin would order chamomile tea or mineral water twelve times in a row, and I would spend the same time jonesing for a cold beer. To say nothing of harder fare and hot women . . .

"It's too bad that you just missed seeing her," Mrs. Berger said with slightly slurred speech as she raised another glass to the dearly departed.

I was amazed at the lovely wording to describe a rather unlovely murder, as well as at the hepatic hardiness of this tiny person.

"Ever since her father has been at the home, she's been spending quite a lot of time there. Apparently his clock is a little off now." Mrs. Berger circled her index finger around her temple. "Such a pity."

She drank another schnapps, presumably as preventive medicine for such a pity.

"What will happen with her apartment now?" Birgit asked. "Who will take care of it? Her boyfriend?"

Mrs. Berger put her clenched fist to her mouth to suppress a burp and then shrugged. "I don't think he even has a key. Whenever Ms. Hauschild was away, I took care of her plants. Her father is obviously out of the question as well. Honestly, child, I have no idea what people do in a case like this. I presume the landlord will throw everything away."

Remember your mission! I screamed at Birgit. *This is our chance!*

Birgit shook her head but obviously not in response to my demand—she couldn't hear me, of course. I hoped she was going to somehow express regret about the impending destruction of Susanne's personal belongings.

"Could I borrow a pen? I'd like to leave my phone number with you. When the police release the apartment, I'll take care of her things. It's the least I can do for Susanne." *ATTAGIRL!* No one had anything on Birgit, brainwise!

114

Mrs. Berger blinked as a single tear escaped the corner of her eye, and she laid a hand on Birgit's arm. Then she stood up—holding on to Birgit tightly for a second until she found her balance—and walked to the secretary desk for a pad of paper and a pen. Birgit wrote down her cell phone number. "If you think of anything else I can do, please call, all right?" Mrs. Berger nodded with a heavy head.

Birgit turned around once more in the doorway as she was about to leave.

"But what if Ms. Hauschild's murderer was already waiting inside the apartment?" Birgit asked. "Did you see anyone beforehand, by any chance?"

The boozehound, whose alcohol-laden breath now posed a hazard to Birgit's unborn child, nodded vigorously. "It was like Piccadilly Circus in the building the whole day. The young woman who rented the penthouse apartment moved in that Friday."

I had Birgit update me on her visit in minute detail—all via text message, which was of course very cumbersome. She wanted to just call me, but that wouldn't work, unfortunately. I praised her efforts and cleverness, and I would have loved to send her on to visit Susanne's father at the home, but it was already past visiting hours. Plus it was Wednesday, and Wednesdays had been marked out on the calendar for childbirth class.

At first I had gone along to support Martin, because aside from him there was only one other guy in the class. The other pregnant women either went alone or brought their best girlfriends with them. Martin's compatriot was a banker who kept running out of the room to take phone calls, which is why they kicked him out of class after the fourth week. Since then, Martin and I were the only guys.

"You have no business here," Martin had told me more than once, but the scene was so freaky I just *had* to come and see. The first few weeks my attendance was spotty, but today I came along again.

ELEVEN

At exactly seven o'clock, the gong in the lame-ass pastel-painted room rang out, calling the bowling-ball babes to order. They all held their breath for a moment before exhaling with a low buzz. This was how they unloaded all the pressure of the day and readied themselves for the latest episode of *German Idol: Pregnancy Edition*, in which contestants competed for most compelling infirmity.

"Liam-Wilhelm arrived into this world last week," announced the beaming childbirth instructor who wore a red velour tracksuit. "We're so happy for Jeanette and Michaela and send them our best wishes."

All of the women—and Martin—closed their eyes and sent their best wishes to the power lesbians, one of whom had taken on the challenge of having sex with a man to finally get pregnant. The guy was the brother of her partner, so at least everything was staying in the family.

"Now, let's hear how you all are doing."

"My doctor has been telling me for months that it would be a girl, and now suddenly it's a boy. After I painted everything pink already," Leonie whined.

"I seriously feel like having sex," Esther said. "It's driving me crazy, but how can I let loose in this condition and pick up a guy? Men freak out whenever they see my belly."

"Do it yourself," Leonie said softly. "That's the easiest way anyway."

"You obviously don't give a fuck," Esther whispered. "You have no idea what lust even is. To this day I've been wondering how you got into this condition in the first place."

Oy! Since when had these two bitches been at war? I could still recall them deep-tissuing each other's backs and kneading each other's bellies.

"Ladies, please," the velour vamp buzzed. "Everyone has a right to her own feelings, her personal opinion, and her wholly individual way of living."

"I've been so bored the past few weeks, but now . . ." Birgit said.

Uh-oh, uh-oh! Hopefully she wasn't going to go and blab what we'd been up to.

"I'm doing a lot better."

"We're glad to have a few more quiet weeks ahead, because after the delivery it will surely be stressful," Martin said quietly.

"Ugh, but I can hardly lie down anymore, and if I want to roll from one side to the other, it's so hard to get my belly to come along," Birgit said. She giggled. "It feels like it isn't even a part of me, like I need a giant shovel or something to carry it around."

"I'm sure you both know that prostaglandin has a labor-inducing effect, so sex can promote the start of labor. If you get much beyond the due date . . ."

Birgit smirked at Martin. Martin blushed. Esther purred like an alley cat.

"Don't be jealous please," Birgit said snidely in Esther's direction.

"My God, I'm not that desperate," Esther muttered back.

Martin stood up. "I'm sorry, but I'm no longer feeling at ease in this group."

Birgit struggled up from her mat first by lying on her back, then getting on all fours with Martin's help, and then up on one foot and one knee, then on two legs. "He's right. Everyone here has been really annoying lately. Which I can understand. But I'm not in the mood for it anymore."

The two of them left the room hand in hand, the other five beached whales and the velour vamp staring after them—enviously, I thought.

It wasn't even eight yet when Martin and Birgit made it home after their premature departure from class, and I thought it would be a good idea to check in on Katrin briefly. I wanted to see how she was coping since Gregor walked out on her earlier in the day. I expected to find her in front of the boob tube with a family-size carton of ice cream, but I was way wrong.

Katrin was just leaving her apartment in an outfit that instantly made me miss my erectile tissue again. A skintight pair of jeans, a low-cut shirt that the edges of her bra cups peeked out from, heels so high she looked like she was floating, dark eye makeup, and stoplight-red lipstick. Hot, naturally, and I of course loved how she looked, but I still wondered: who was she all gussied up for?

Even my worst fears were exceeded when Katrin set out on the road to Düsseldorf. She drove directly to police headquarters and had the front desk announce her. I didn't need to eavesdrop to know what her visit was about.

It took a few minutes for Stein to come down the lobby. He offered Katrin his hand. She held out the bag with Gregor's jacket inside.

"Oh, I—"

Katrin blushed. "Sorry."

She shifted the bag to her other hand and shook his. "I don't want to obstruct an investigation."

Stein cocked his head to the side. "Even if your boyfriend might—"

"He's not my boyfriend," Katrin said with ice in her voice.

"Katrin!" I bellowed in horror.

Stein raised his eyebrows.

"We had a fight just before I went on vacation. A big fight. I was glad to have some space. When I got back, I didn't actually want to try things with him again, but . . ."

Stein compassionately rested his free hand on her shoulder. His thumb lay on her collarbone. What a slime!

"You're doing the right thing. If he is guilty, I'll prove it. And if he isn't, then this jacket can't hurt him."

I could have puked. At this slime-ridden asshole for feeling Katrin up, and at Katrin for being an unfaithful slut. She was practically throwing herself on this guy. At least, she didn't wince when he put his mitt on her. Instead she put her mitt over his and gazed at him, her eyes narrowed slightly.

"Thank you," she breathed. "And for waiting for me to come by tonight."

Stein swallowed. I'm not a pervert and thus didn't go investigate the goings-on in his pants, but it would have surprised me if nothing was going on there . . .

"There's no quitting time during an investigation, I'm sure you know," Stein said.

Katrin nodded.

"But at some point a person needs to eat something. Do you think you might be interested in keeping me company over a pizza?"

Katrin hesitated for a second, and then she nodded.

"Be right back."

Stein raced up the stairs, dropped Gregor's jean jacket off with the nosy colleague who was going to lead the forensic investigation of the evidence, grabbed his keys, and returned to Katrin in the lobby and walked out with her.

If I could have, I would have dispatched a kit of pigeons to swoop down and shit on those two, but unfortunately those brainless flying rats were beyond my control. I was helpless. The only thing I could do for Gregor was to tail our new dream couple and keep my ears perked.

Stein was enough of a pro not to let the conversation shift to the current case. Instead, they told each other anecdotes from their insanely interesting professional lives. When they finally parted ways at ten thirty with a kiss to the left and kiss to the right, I needed some way to vent my anger. So I flew right into the middle of a power substation and cut off the lights in Düsseldorf. The spraying sparks prickled, and I was satisfied with the success of the operation—but not even that was enough to cheer me up. Something needed to happen, and whatever it was had to help Gregor.

I zoomed to Martin and found him—with his city maps. In the midst of the many things a guy has to do to get ready for life as a threesome, Martin had neglected his favorite pastime the last few months. But after winning back half an evening from the hasty departure from childbirth class, he finally had some time to dedicate himself again to his super exciting, extraordinarily spellbinding, and fascinating hobby: collecting city maps. Historical and modern. Now, if you should ever run into Martin and want to make friends with him, just bring a city map with you. He's got one of Cologne already, of course. More specifically, Martin possesses seventeen maps of Cologne *alone*, starting with a flimsy piece of fabric on which Cologne is not called Cologne and doesn't look like Cologne, although it *is* Cologne at some earlier stage with a massive construction project on the bank of the Rhine where Cologne Cathedral now stands. In addition, he has eighty-seven current and approximately two hundred old maps of a variety of places. Anyway, Martin was in the process of neatly cataloguing the street names of some dump or other on the Lower Rhine in the seventeenth century when I notified him that he was done surfing city maps for the time being.

"I wouldn't know why that should be the case," he mumbled at me in his thoughts.

"Because you and I are going on a pub crawl right now in the Belgian Quarter."

"Under no circumstances."

"We are visiting Susanne's boyfriend. He owns a pub. The guy is a suspect," I explained.

"Düsseldorf Criminal Investiga—" he began, but I didn't need to continue listening to know he was blathering nonsense.

"Düsseldorf CI is certain they have their perp, and Gregor isn't doing a thing to make them consider anyone else," I yelled at Martin to remind him. "In addition, we are not getting involved in an investigation. We are just going out for something to drink. The way two old buddies do."

Martin sent a cloud of rather unfriendly sentiments on the topic of "two old buddies" my way, which I heroically ignored. He turned back to his map.

"Enough with the street alphabet! Get your ass up and on the move!" I yelled.

"I'm staying with Birgit."

I went into the bedroom, where Birgit was blissfully snoozing.

"She doesn't need you."

"But when she wakes up—"

"She'll seduce the sixteen-year-old who's babysitting her, snarf down the entire contents of the fridge, and watch a horror flick on TV," I said.

Martin stopped short.

"Ridiculous, right?" I said with a virtual smirk. "Birgit's not a kid and doesn't need a babysitter, and she doesn't voluntarily watch horror flicks. If she wakes up and even notices your absence at all, she'll only think you're at a crime scene."

"I'm tired, and I would prefer not to get involved in the investigation," Martin said, but I could tell his resistance was weakening.

"You can come with me; otherwise, I'll come with you."

This threat almost always works, including in this case. The threat pertains to the anti-electrosmog netting that keeps me from bothering Martin at night. But if I slip through the opening *with* him, I can't get back out. We have more than a few of these pissing matches behind us, and Martin didn't want to spend another night with me under his protective netting. You see, I genuinely enjoy waiting until the split second he slides off into sleep, the moment when his mental and spiritual protective walls collapse and I can enter his brain in full force and at full volume. Imitating a siren or bellowing "Fire!" or similar utterances drives his pulse through the roof. Since I don't need to sleep, I can play that game all night long. Or two nights long. Or three.

"What should I wear?" The question already sounded like unconditional surrender, and I had a hard time suppressing my grin.

"Anything you like."

What did I care what he wore? It's not like anyone would be spotting me out with the awkwardologist here.

Martin didn't change his clothes, so I was fairly certain on this summer night that he was the only person in Cologne out on a pub crawl wearing creased wool pants; a ribbed undershirt made of unbleached, dye-free organic cotton; and a striped shirt, also made from organic cotton, which normal people might wear to attend the baptism of a niece or nephew. We made it to the Belgian Quarter around eleven, and of course the nightlife was still in full swing. The longest night of the year was coming up, it was pleasantly warm, and people were wearing jeans, chinos, or linen pants—but not wool and no creases. And they were living a life worthy of the word. Unlike Martin, who putzes around his slaughterhouse by day and at home by night before slurping some vegetable purée, organizing city maps, alphabetizing street names, and if possible going to bed early so he can get enough sleep. He isn't functional with less than eight hours a night.

"Which pub?" Martin asked.

"No idea. The owner is Greek and his name sounds something like 'Agatha.'"

Martin yawned.

"Well, let's get going to the first pub, and then we'll ask people if those details ring a bell."

Martin ordered a noncarbonated mineral water without ice or lemon, and learned that the Greek's pub wasn't on this street but maybe one over. We needed two more attempts until we found Die Werkstatt.

TWELVE

The pub was not only named "Die Werkstatt," which means "the workshop," but that's exactly how it looked too. All of the fixtures and furnishings were made from old machines, lathes, tools, and oil drums. They even had an old hydraulic lift, although it was just for decoration. Everything else had been metamorphosed with lots of love and elbow grease—but little money—into barstools, benches, tables, and chairs. It smelled of the usual pub must, with a hint of used motor oil. Heaven!

"P.U.," Martin gasped as he stepped to the bar. "These benzene vapors are toxic."

"Yeah, the medics haul a body out of here almost every night," I confirmed.

Martin froze.

"That was a *joke*," I said. "How many benzene-vapor bodies have you had on your table in the last few years?"

He didn't say anything.

"That's my point. So chill out, dude."

Martin walked up to the bar, which had formerly been a lathe, and ordered . . .

"A beer!" I bellowed before he could order another flat mineral water. I mean, how was the guy supposed to take Martin seriously if he only ordered water?

"So . . . a beer," Martin repeated.

The mountain of a man who pulled the beer and set it before Martin hadn't uttered a peep at this point. Not a hello, not a confirmation of Martin's order, not even a friendly *"Prost!"* The guy wasn't exactly accessible. Martin took a sip from his glass and managed the feat of sucking practically nothing through his defensively pursed lips and nonetheless swallowing.

"Go on," I pressed. "Ask him if he's Agatha."

"I-I'm looking for a friend of Susanne Hauschild's," Martin stammered as he looked across the bar at the belly of the bartender. He didn't dare look him in the eyes. That would have been hard in any case since the guy's eyebrows were fluffy enough to serve as a full head of hair on other guys.

"And why are you looking for him?" the guy growled. Although I was sure that the words had emanated from him, I hadn't actually detected any movement under all the old-growth forest of frizzy black hair between the nose and chest. Maybe he was a ventriloquist.

"A friend of mine is suspected of having murdered Susanne," Martin whispered.

In the end Martin managed to raise his eyes a bit, but it didn't help him much. The guy paused almost imperceptibly while drying off a beer glass, in which the reflection of his overgrown face showed no emotion. His imposing belly, squeezed into his black T-shirt and black leather vest, didn't respond either. The beer belly may have been able to talk, but it was no chatterbox.

"Are you the man I'm looking for?" Martin asked. He had shrunk so far down on his barstool that he could hardly see over the counter anymore.

"Martin, sit up straight," I ordered him. "Don't worry. The guy isn't going to thwack you off your stool here in front of all the patrons." Martin sat up straight.

"More," I ordered.

"I'm still waiting for him to answer."

I sighed. It wasn't like time actually meant anything to me anymore. But at this pace, Gregor would serve his full sentence and be released from jail before Martin got any information.

The guy set the clean glass aside, neatly folded and put down his drying cloth, rested both palms on the bar counter, and bent over toward Martin.

"My name is Ioánnis Anastásios Dimítrios Agathangelídis. And who are you?"

"Martin Gänsewein. Pleased to meet you."

Martin offered the wooly mammoth his hand, which Ioánnis stared at but did not shake.

"And what exactly do you want?" the Greek asked.

"A beer," someone called over from one of the oil-drum tables in the dark depths of Die Werkstatt.

"Shut it," Ioánnis roared back. "Can't you see I'm busy?" Then he returned to the trembling Martin.

"Concentrate," I scolded Martin. "Say everything in the proper order, with crossed t's and dotted i's."

"I'm looking for someone who knows why Susanne Hauschild was murdered," Martin whispered.

"Are you accusing me of something?" Ioánnis whispered back.

"No, not in the least," Martin frantically replied. He had sunken back down to counter level. "I'm just wondering whether you might have any idea. Maybe you know what Susanne

Hauschild was working on right before she died. Or perhaps she had mentioned having trouble with someone. . ."

With every centimeter Martin shrunk, the Greek bent a centimeter farther over the counter, so the distance between their heads had stayed the same. When Ioánnis pulled back, Martin straightened up accordingly. I had noticed the telescopic flexibility of Martin's spine many times before, so I wasn't surprised, but the Greek was obviously annoyed.

"The cops have already asked me about that," he finally growled.

"And? Were you able to answer them?"

"I only knew that she had been trying for days to get hold of that guy at the nightclub."

"Karpi," Martin said.

The hairy portion of the Greek moved slightly, which I interpreted as nodding.

"And then she was with him."

"And?"

The shiny black leather of the Greek's vest moved. A shrug?

"She didn't want to tell me whether she had learned anything from him."

Martin sagged, this time out of disappointment.

"And that's everything?"

The Greek scratched his beard, and a few crumbs fell onto the counter that he observed while lost in thought. Then he brushed them away with a single motion of his giant paw.

"Something occurred to me yesterday."

Martin stretched his backbone more and again looked like the nerd who sits in the front row eagerly anticipating who earned the only A on the final exam.

"She had been trying to find old blueprints or sketches of the layout of that bunker where Karpi's club is."

"Huh?" I said.

"Why?" Martin mumbled, a few centimeters smaller again.

"No idea."

"Did she find the plans?" Martin asked.

Ioánnis shrugged. "No idea, man."

"Did you provide this piece of information to Düsseldorf Criminal Investigations?"

The Greek made a sound that I interpreted, after some consideration, as laughter. "Do you think I'd call up the cops because Susanne was interested in an old Nazi bunker? Maybe the Amber Room is hidden somewhere in that fat Russian's nightclub?"

Martin shook his head.

"Besides, they've got their suspect already. Why should I butt in?"

Martin took a breath to profess Gregor's innocence, but I hissed, "Shut your mouth." There are just some situations where smart-assery can irreparably destroy a budding friendship like that between Martin and the Greek.

"This beer is on the house," Ioánnis said in a low growl as he turned around and stomped over to the table where the previous order had come from.

Martin, who had hardly taken a sip from his Kölsch, wanted to get up and go, but I explained to him that you just don't leave a beer on the house untouched, so he poured the liquid down his hatch with deathly disgust, burped, and then left Die Werkstatt. I stayed with him until he was safely back in his trash can; he's such an obvious target that anytime he's walking the streets alone in the dark I expect someone to give him a one-two. It hasn't happened yet, and it would probably be too embarrassing for bad guys to shake down a lame-o like Martin.

Why had Zuzubee been looking for blueprints for Karpi's bobblehead bunker? And why was she with him? Maybe getting a look behind the curtain would give me some clues.

So I zoomed over to the nightclub and took my time swaying back and forth between bobbing bazooms and bouncing belly buttons, surfing the wave of people to the door that separated the public area and the backrooms. There was some kind of commotion again in the storage room, where boxes and crates were being delivered while others were being hauled off. Some of them had those ridiculous-looking Russki letters on them and others were unmarked. The truck drivers all looked the same, like Putin had personally released them from prison to go and improve the trade imbalance between Germany and Russia. They didn't talk, they didn't smoke, and they didn't steal . . . as far as I could tell. They were functioning like a well-organized gang. I tried to see what was inside some of the cartons, but the darkness and all of the Styrofoam peanuts and wood wool made it impossible. I wondered what secret project Karpi had going, though I wasn't going to solve that puzzle tonight.

But I might be able to finish my actual mission.

I whooshed around, surveying the layout of the ground floor, but I didn't find anything out of the ordinary. Except for the ducts in this bunker, which were so wide even Birgit in her current condition could have still fit through them. On to the elevator.

I didn't need a door code, and I didn't need an elevator car to take me up and down, so I flew through the shaft, down the corridor, and into Karpi's office, where he was sitting at his desk talking on the phone. In Russian. Or one of those fur-hat languages; they all sound the same to me. This wasn't turning up anything useful, so I kept on looking.

The corridor that Martin and Birgit had waddled through a good twenty-four hours ago had three other doors along it. One was the back door that Karpi had sent them out through because the Düssel-doofuses were dropping in on him unannounced. That door opened into a damp stairwell that went up to street level, which is where Gregor's cousin's daughter had been found. I wasn't interested in that door.

Like the others, the last two doors were also made of iron. I presumed it was normal to have fire doors in a bunker; plus, a decorative wooden door with a white Swedish varnish would have probably looked a little swishy. I aimed for the first door and—bang. I can't describe it any other way. Naturally there isn't a real impact, like if some spindly dumbass rams his forehead into a steel bulkhead after forgetting to duck, but for me it felt like a big bang. I bounced off.

Not that I didn't recognize the sensation. I knew it all too well, since Martin's anti-electrosmog netting has the same effect. Except, the netting isn't made of steel. In this case, I had to sort out all of my electrons first to formulate a clear thought. The door was protected from electromagnetic waves, and as I quickly determined, it was absolutely impenetrable. There was no keyhole I could have whooshed through—only an electronic locking system, like up at the elevator door. And the slit between the door and frame, which should have been big enough for me to get through, was also secured with an electromagnetic field.

What the fuck was going on here? What was behind that door? Did Karpi live in there? Had anyone ever seen him outside his bunker? Not as far as I knew. This might be his Bat Cave. And the cave was as thoroughly shielded as the secret command center of a nation with nuclear weapons. Was Karpi worried about electrosmog? In a former Nazi bunker with one-meter-thick concrete walls? The guy wasn't just totally wacko; he was apparently paranoid to boot. But, please, if he was trying to get in his beauty rest without the prying eyes of extraterrestrial or supernatural powers spying on him, I was the *last* person who'd bitch about it. Still, I knew all too well that electromagnetic surveillance had more aspects to it than most earthly beings could ever imagine—because one of those aspects was me.

THIRTEEN

July 1, four days after Gregor's arrest

I hadn't been able to find anything new out via the bunker, so instead I had hung around the nightclub until last call. I just wandered aimlessly for the last few hours of the night. I rode along on a few ambulance deployments with the night-duty guys. I checked in on the four bonsais who had kept me company last November for a while. All four of them were spirited and healthy and, at this hour, sleeping like champs—logically. That was obviously part of being alive. Once the sun started to rise, I finally headed home, where I found Martin leaving for work and Birgit waving good-bye to him from their window. Then Birgit grabbed her phone, and I zoomed up to my cabinet.

WSUP, Birgit typed.

OK, I knew that one. What's up? She was feeling enterprising. Yeah!

Today, the Sonnenschein Home, I texted back.

Who are you? Birgit wrote in reply.

Did this woman never give up? I would have been tearing my hair out if I still had some.

Gregor's best friend, I texted.

Katrin? Birgit wrote back.

Katrin has bailed on us.

?????

Are you helping Gregor or not?

I had to wait quite a while for a response, but then it came: *OK. What should I do?*

What I would have liked her to do first is go check out Papa Hauschild, because he had been a cop and was living in the home. Maybe certain goings-on there had struck him as suspicious, and he had tipped his daughter off. Or maybe he knew what story his daughter had been working on. But since his current brain didn't much resemble that of a reasonable cop anymore, I decided to put Birgit on Paulina's trail instead. I knew that gossip was standard etiquette among the people you work with, even if you were already dead. So I tipped Birgit off to the ladies in white. That was the required component. She had the option of trying to elicit a clear thought from Hans Hauschild if she wanted.

I drove over with Birgit in her gray BMW convertible with red leather seats. Her ride was from the eighties, when cars still had boxy shapes and you could break into them without a degree in computer science. It wasn't some classic car right out of the glossy pages of an automotive magazine; it was an object of utility, an everyday car that showed its age properly. But that hoopty was still well maintained and in proper technical condition. I had played a not inconsiderable role in that, because whenever there was the slightest problem, I could quickly figure out what it was.

The auto shop I'd recommended to Martin for Birgit's ride was not strictly on the up and up. Obviously, right? By their nature, auto shops are the opposite of up and up. But if you drive up in a car like Birgit's 3 Series convertible and can correctly describe both the problem itself and its cause, even the dimmest nutrunner knows he better not screw with that customer. Even if that customer looks like Martin. The real feat was Martin articulating the correct words, because he knows absolutely zilch about cars. It knocks my socks off every time it comes up how clueless he is. I mean, he does get that wheels roll because they're round, but that pretty much exhausts his technical understanding.

So with my assistance, for instance, Birgit's car never had its fully functional windshield wiper blades swapped out, because I knew they would just end up on the mechanic's own car two minutes later. And her brakes also stayed untouched until they were really on their way out, and her service appointments didn't turn up a long list of parts that had "needed" replacing—which, again, the mechanic would just install on his car, his wife's car, his nephew's car, or his bed bunny's car. In short: I make sure that Birgit's ride is running well and that nobody leads her down the garden path. Sad that she'll never know about it.

Birgit parked her car with its top down in front of the entrance to the old fogy home and waddled into the lobby. She almost ran over the platinum blonde.

Once again she was here early in the morning. Had she somehow gotten infected with geriatric insomnia in this joint? I was going to have to check into that more closely. For now, however, I followed Birgit to the door of the break room for the White Coats. "I'm sorry to disturb, but I wanted to see about picking up Paulina's things."

The three achromatic attendants turned their heads and blinked at Birgit as though she'd asked how to get to the delivery room.

Birgit—you have to give it to her—doesn't take silence for an answer. She waited patiently for the women to respond, although it looked for a while like no response was coming. All three just kept staring this way and that, but ultimately two of them and Birgit settled their eyes on the beanstalk sitting stage right.

"The police took her things out of her locker," the beanstalk said.

"Oh!"

Birgit managed to convey surprise, disappointment, and bottomless grief all in one word.

"Who are you?" the beanstalk asked. She was at least sixty, had ugly eyeglasses and short hair, and looked like she had spent her whole life eating nothing but whole grains and carrots.

"A friend of hers. I'd offered . . ."

"Are you covering her debts as well?" the fat blonde in the middle butted in. Hers was a fake blonde, her eyelashes were even faker, only her teeth were the real McCoys. Which was too bad: if there was anything she should have invested in, it was false teeth. The aftermath of a Category 5 hurricane was nothing compared to the chaos in her pie hole.

"Or have we been taken for a ride yet again?" Her voice matched her foul mouth.

Birgit winced. "How much is it?"

"She owes two months' of money to the coffee fund, twenty euros for Dr. Wenger's birthday present, ten for the break room espresso machine . . ."—she pointed at an apparently new appliance in the corner—"and she still owes eight euros toward the barbecue."

"I lent her fifty euros as well," said the third woman, who reminded me of one of those tiny animals they just discovered a couple of years ago on Madagascar. Some kind of primate, super small, camouflage-colored coat, with huge black eyes. They had been baptized "mouse lemurs," and the creature before Birgit was confirmation enough that it was a good name.

"How awkward!" the blonde said corrosively.

"Well, shit happens!" said the whole-grain granny. "Unfortunately the stress just goes on for us, especially since Paulina's not here anymore. Break is over. *Auf Wiedersehen.*"

Birgit left the cat cage with the three white pines. The fat blonde and granny scurried away, and when they'd disappeared around a corner, the mouse lemur turned to Birgit.

"Have you spoken with Yuri?" she asked.

Birgit raised an eyebrow.

"If you see him, please give him my condolences, OK?"

Birgit raised her eyebrow even higher.

The mouse lemur was kneading her hands, her eyes frantically scanning the hallway for eavesdroppers. "I don't know why Paulina gave him his marching orders. Yuri's a good guy, despite his job."

Her giant monkey eyes starting filling with tears.

Birgit set her hand on the animal's shoulder.

"I'm worried he'll do something to himself," the animal said.

"Were you close to Paulina?" Birgit asked.

The mouse lemur shook her head. "She was—a little stuck up, honestly. But I talked with Yuri a few times, when he was waiting for Paulina." She blushed. "He really worshipped her."

"Can you tell me where I can find Yuri?" Birgit asked.

"I know only his first name, but he works at Karpi Diem."

I wished I could pat Birgit on the back for a job well done, but obviously that was impossible. And I couldn't congratulate her by text right away since I'd need to zoom up to my closet for that, plus she'd have surely asked how I knew what she'd just found out. So instead I followed her back out to the lobby, where she stopped for a second to think, and then turned toward the café. She sat down at one of the bistro tables, pulled a notebook out of her bag, jotted down her latest findings, and circled the name Yuri.

"Hello. Can I get you anything? Coffee, tea, cake?" The platinum blonde stepped up to Birgit's table.

Oh, shit. Now I couldn't quickly warn Birgit that this chick had been spying on Zuzubee when she was copying pages from the prescription log. Martin was a totally awkward investigator—and kind of a pain in the ass, too, with his constant backtalk—but at least I could spontaneously tip him off with new instructions. With Birgit I was as helpless as a model-car driver who realizes his ride is under someone else's remote control. And that's a crappy feeling.

"Yes, thank you. I'd love a latte and a giant piece of cake."

The platinum blonde smiled. "Which cake? We have apple strudel, cherry strudel, Black Forest cake, German cheesecake, whipped cream and quark cake, Frankfurt crown cake, and chocolate cake."

Birgit considered the options and then shrugged. "Which would you recommend?"

"Honestly?"

Birgit nodded.

"A slice of cheesecake and a slice of chocolate cake together. It's a brilliant combo."

"Good, I'll take that."

Should I text her now? *In case you run into a platinum-blonde chick, then ask her if she knows more about Zuzubee's strange behavior?* Maybe she talked to Susanne? Or she was on the same trail we were on. But what trail was it? I needed to talk to someone who understood all this medical stuff. What was so interesting on all those pages Susanne copied? Everything was boiling down to the fact that I needed Martin. Without him I couldn't make any more progress. An awful feeling.

Martin got in touch as though he'd somehow perceived my intense thoughts regarding him. Although, not in touch with me but with Birgit.

"Where are you?" he asked, panic in his voice. "Are you all right?"

"Of course I'm all right," Birgit whistled into her phone. "I was having a serious craving for cake. What's up with you?"

"You said you were going to go shopping," Martin said. "So I took the rest of the day off."

"Great!" Birgit said cheerfully. "I'll be home in half an hour."

And who was the fifth wheel yet again? That's right.

Birgit and Martin shopping for baby clothes for the ten-thousandth time, Katrin no longer trustworthy, and me all on my own to save Gregor. Wait—maybe Jenny was still on board? After all, she was still busy with the case that had put Gregor and his ex back in touch. Maybe I could find out something new from that angle. So I zoomed over to Jenny. Unfortunately, she was just explaining to her boss why she had closed the file on Paulina Pleve.

"No clear evidence of foul play or a third party. The issue of the traces of talcum powder is less strange than initially thought. If she hadn't been sweating, then the powder would have stayed intact for many hours. In that respect, the powder could just as well have come from work, where she routinely wore latex gloves. In addition, there is the fact that the attic was locked from the inside. So I think we should close the case." The boss nodded.

I was frustrated. Somehow I'd put a certain amount of hope in the Paulina Pleve case because Gregor investigated the case when he was being framed. If the Pleve case really was a straight-forward suicide, I still had no idea what possible reason there could be to blame Gregor for the murder of his ex-wife. I groaned out loud, which of course didn't impress anyone since no one can hear me.

Jenny-Bunny glanced at the clock, grabbed her bag, and hurried out to the parking lot. Offermannequin was out there, leaning on his ride—an Audi TT, which his envious colleagues said stood variously for twerking trophy, tranny tractor, or turbo Trabi.

"What's the boss say?" Offermann asked.

Jenny grinned at him. "A door locked from the inside is pretty clear evidence of suicide."

"So the case is closed?"

Jenny nodded.

"Good. We should go celebrate. Currywurst, or to the beer garden for Bavarian roast chicken?"

Jenny laughed. "Currywurst."

Offermann held the door open for her. "Do you need to come back to work afterward?"

Jenny shook her head. "I've got a hundred twenty hours of overtime I need to take time off for."

"Good. Then I'll drive you to the world's very best currywurst."

"Where is that?" Jenny asked, a sparkle in her eyes like a kid at Christmas.

"Buckle up," Offermann said, and then he took off.

Nauseating, all the hormone-saturated boot-licking while Gregor was wasting away in jail. I'd have expected a little more loyalty from someone on Gregor's team. But no: Jenny's blood was literally flooded with adrenalin and cortisol, and her nostrils were flaring as they snuffed up the pheromones Offermann was putting out. The two of them were a chemical spill.

I followed them on the autobahn all the way down to Aachen, but then I didn't feel like chit-chat anymore. It was obvious that Jenny was going to find herself laid flat at the next rest stop where there was some concession stand serving currywurst, but instead of stopping and screwing around, Offermann just jabbered her to death with anecdotes from his life. Please, these romantic types still existed? Wasting their lives making things unnecessarily complicated, buying buckets of bubbly and fressing currywurst for weeks on end before feeling the chick up. I'd hook up with them again later on . . . when things got that far.

FOURTEEN

Now that Team 2 was out of the running, I checked in briefly on Katrin, but she had been slicing up cadavers without a break because there had been a huge crash on the A3, which runs north-south on the east side of Cologne and has some of the worst traffic in the country. At least this way she couldn't fraternize with the Düssel-doofuses while Gregor slowly fossilized in the clink. As for Gregor, he was sitting back in his cell while almost all of the other cons were busy somewhere else in the facility. Lots of them worked in a wood shop, some in the kitchens or laundry, while others were sweating out their stress in the training room. Gregor was the only one sitting alone in his cell. I would have understood if he'd been locked up in Cologne; you wouldn't want to run into any former "clients," right? In other words, a Cologne cop doesn't have a lot of friends in a Cologne clink. But no one knew him here. So why was he sulking away instead of making some kind of sensible statement to the police and going home? I still did not get it, and I couldn't help anyway, so I bailed.

I wandered aimlessly through the streets. I could have watched the platinum blonde serving coffee, or Zuzubee's father drawing, but neither of them were in a good mood today. I wouldn't find Paulina the Pendulum's ex-boyfriend at Karpi Diem until ten thirty tonight, at the earliest, and without Martin, my sheriff's deputy, there was no point in showing up there. So I checked in on the Desperately Seeking Susanne crew up in Düsseldorf. They were in their afternoon briefing.

"The forensic analysis came up with a match on the fibers." Stein was lecturing. The projector cast an image on the wall of Gregor's jean jacket, which Katrin had given Stein. Traitor! Now CI had one more piece of evidence in hand against Gregor. The VIN plate, the witness statement from that liquored-up Mrs. Berger who had seen Gregor, and now some of Gregor's dandruff and fibers from the jacket he had on that Friday as well.

"All circumstantial evidence so far," the redheaded women's libber interjected with a grumble.

For the first time in my life, I found the ultrafeminist anti-man shtick pretty good. If only Agent Orange could just work in a comment between each of Stein's sentences as a reminder that Gregor had not made any confession . . .

"Well, I would sooner call it proof," Stein said.

"Let me summarize what we know," Agent Orange said nasally. "Kreidler's keychain fob was found at the crime scene, he was seen at the door to the building, and the deceased had flakes of his skin and fibers from his jacket on her."

"Pretty solid evidence," Keller mumbled. There was something stuck in the left corner of his mouth that could have been currywurst sauce. I would rather not consider other alternatives.

"Kreidler's fingerprints were found on the doorbell, but not on the body. There was a cup in the apartment that Kreidler had drunk coffee out of, confirmed by fingerprints and DNA."

Huh? Gregor had drunk some coffee inside Zuzubee's apartment? Had he in fact been in her apartment? He hadn't rung the bell in vain and taken off again without having achieved anything? I had assumed that the VIN plate had been planted at the crime scene by someone, but the more fingerprints and DNA of Gregor's they found in his ex-wife's apartment, the greater the likelihood he actually had been there. And that was fucked up.

Stein nodded.

"Forensic medicine couldn't provide a plausible explanation of how the skin flakes and fibers from the jacket could get under the victim's fingernails, because the strangulation had come from behind."

Aha, point to Gregor.

"And above all we're missing the most important thing so far," Orange said.

Stein, Keller, and the pretty boy sighed, grumbled, or mumbled in chorus with Agent Orange: "Motive!"

Stein pouted. Keller licked his fat lips, the tip of his tongue thereby discovering the saucy residue in the corner of his mouth. He focused on licking it away.

"I've got a few questions that urgently need to be addressed," Agent Orange said. "First, the most important question in the case of a journalist: what was she working on? Next: where is her computer or laptop? Only after we've figured that out can we can start conducting a proper investigation. All we've gotten so far, with all due respect, is shit."

I resolved never to drop any mean comments about women's libbers ever again.

Martin and Birgit didn't pop up again, not on my radar at least. I didn't zoom right over to the apartment because I didn't want to miss a second of the CI briefing, but they had pretty much said all the interesting stuff. Unfortunately I listened in for another few hours on random forensic analysis reports they had about unimportant details, realizing in hindsight I hadn't needed to take in all that drivel.

One by one the detectives started taking off for the day; the only one who stayed at work was Keller. He ordered a pizza and left greasy stains on the files while he thoroughly read all of the reports, page by page: autopsy report, forensics report, and witness interviews. He ate loudly and kept slurping off his greasy fingers to the point that I wanted to puke. I needed to get away from there.

Little Red Riding Hood was clearly right when she underscored the importance of Susanne's work, except that even the most ardent desire to locate Zuzubee's laptop didn't help much if no one knew how to come by it.

Where could that essential device to the work of any journalist be?

Was it even her main tool for doing her work?

Did Zuzubee dictate every word into her smartphone?

I didn't think so, because the detectives had found her phone. It had showed them the connection to Gregor and Karpi, and if there had been important data on it, the forensics guys would have found it.

So I guess the focus had to be on her laptop.

The detectives had searched Zuzubee's apartment top to bottom.

But I hadn't yet.

With a sigh I made my way over there.

I hate poking around in the apartments of murder victims. Usually what you find is just incredibly awkward. Titty magazines, dildos, ladies' panties in the head of household's toolbox, and all kinds of crap like that.

Zuzubee's apartment did not offer up any highlights along those lines, though. Furniture made of natural wood, a giant desk in the living room that a lot of cords and cables came up to but didn't connect to anything. This is where her laptop would have been.

The walls were hung with some of her father's drawings. Cars, people, flowers. A medium-size flat-screen TV hung on one wall, and the shelves beneath it held DVDs. Green peppers, lettuce, and onions were getting moldy in a bowl in the kitchen.

After the overview, I mentally divvied the place up into a grid, and checked each sector thoroughly. The hardwood floors had a few loose boards, but they weren't hiding any treasure underneath—only dust.

Refrigerators are dark inside when the door is closed, but I still whooshed in and carefully prowled around its contents. Bottles and Tetra Paks of juice in the door, marmalade, what I assumed was a mustard jar, a small unopened carton of kefir or whipping cream, a plastic container with something that smelled like cheese and had a moldy surface; the vegetable drawer held three sizes of organic dildos: carrot-skinny, Chiquita-medium, and cucumber-thick. Nothing to get excited about. I slid back out of the refrigerator and squeezed in behind the bathroom mirror and into the drains and traps under the sinks, which triggered a major gag reflex that, sadly, I had no way to resolve. Naturally I didn't think I'd be finding a laptop in those places, but a thumb drive could really have helped us along.

Teacups, sugar bowls, cereal boxes—I streamed my way through everything. I swooshed through every drawer in the kitchen, bathroom, and bedroom, and I was about to give up when I suddenly had a flash of inspiration.

Coffee cup. Stein had mentioned Gregor's fingerprints and DNA had been found on a coffee cup.

I had not found any coffee cup. I checked the kitchen again.

No coffee grounds. No instant coffee. No espresso machine. No equipment to make coffee at all.

Given those facts, even Desperately Seeking Susanne should have considered the possibility itself that the evidence against Gregor had been planted here.

I considered what I should do with this coffee information and finally came to the only sensible notion: I flew home and sent Keller an e-mail. It was time that the Düssel-doofuses digressed from their fixation on Gregor and set him free. Without him, everything was just going every which way. I was the only person who had anything like an overview of the situation, but my hands were tied and—even worse—my yap trap was stapled shut.

I just didn't see any connection between Gregor and his ex's murder, but *someone* had put the blame on him. Why him? I could think of only one reason, namely, that they wanted to put the kibosh on Gregor at the same time as Susanne. And why had they wanted to neutralize Gregor? The common denominator was the old folks' home where Gregor and his ex had run into each other. I had no idea what story Zuzubee had been researching in the old folks' home, but Gregor had investigated Paulina Pleve's death there.

Before I gave up this one—and, to be honest, only—line of inquiry, I wanted to check one more time that I hadn't overlooked anything. So I went back to the start—to the attic where Paulina had hanged herself.

This time all I found hanging up there was drying laundry. Even the wailing apron had calmed down and was carrying on with her life just two weeks after her neighbor had been fluttering in the warm summer breeze. Today the summer breeze wasn't warm, by the way. On the contrary. The sky had grown dark, gusts whipped through the attic windows, and a storm was brewing.

I tried to think back to the scene. The attic door had been open when I arrived, Paulina was hanging around, and both Katrin and the CSI team had supported the suicide hypothesis. Logical, if the attic had been locked from inside and the key was still in the keyhole. The old door had been pretty warped, as I recalled, but no so much so that someone could have pulled the locked door shut from the outside. Or? I whizzed into the gap between the door and jamb. Well, actually, I had plenty of room—but still I didn't think that trick would have worked.

Suddenly a wild clattering tore me out of my considerations. The door was rattling in its frame from the strong wind whistling through the two open windows in the attic and the open skylight in the stairwell. The attic windows were those old-style, single-glazed mullioned windows with rounded corners that you can open by using the sash lock as a handle. No one could get through those.

The door rattled some more. Something about that sound made me nervous. It wasn't just the wooden rattling of the panels of the door, but there was also this shrill jangling that resonated at an unpleasant frequency. I flew higher. The window pane in the top of the door with the etched frost-and-snowflake pattern in it was sitting so loose in its mullions that I could imagine the next dead person lying here on the floor with his carotid artery sliced open from a falling piece of broken glass. And then the detectives and CSI team would be standing in here again, and the slicers would be jabbering on about suicide— I stopped short.

Gregor and the CSI techs and I—we had all looked closely at the lockset on the door and determined that it was impossible to lock the door from the inside and then pull the door shut in its frame. But what if someone had taken the etched pane of glass out of the door? Could someone have then reached through the window and locked the door that way?

My form of existence had lots of advantages, but also disadvantages. One disadvantage is I've lost a bit of my sense of proportion over time. Duh, because in the end I'm floating around above everything.

So I tried to picture how high the window was, how long an arm needed to be to reach through to fiddle for the keyhole with your hand and actually insert the key and then turn around . . .

No way. It may or may not work, but there was no way I could determine that. So once again I needed help from an earthly being. Barf.

FIFTEEN

July 2, five days after Gregor's arrest

Jenny was late. I'd tried to check in on her in her office—nada. Cafeteria—nada. Her car was in the lot, so I did a lap through the whole department. The other detectives, the boss . . . but no Jenny. Then I got suspicious. I posted myself in the parking lot and waited with rising rage. And then it drove up: Offermannequin's turbo Trabi. And who was sitting in it?

Jenny!

The two of them were smooching like hormonal twelve-year-olds before Jenny finally got out. She walked to her car and—drove off!

Hello?

I followed Jenny home. She took a shower, which under normal circumstances I might have quite enjoyed, blow-dried her hair, got dressed, and dolled herself up. Her smeared mascara from last night was replaced with fresh, but she didn't stop there. No, today demanded the whole shebang: smoky eyes, blush powder pearls, and God only knows what all the other crap is called. At some point that felt like two hours later, Jenny-Bunny was finally ready. She drove to the office, passed Offermannequin's office without peeking in, poured herself a coffee in the break room, checked her box in the mail room, and went to her desk and turned on her computer.

I kept waiting. What else could I do?

Finally she checked her e-mail.

Mine was the seventeenth.

Jenny stared at it, blinked, shook her head, and stared at it again.

God, what would I have to do to get this detective frau to realize that she had closed the case prematurely?

Jenny printed my e-mail and ran to Offermannequin's office. It was empty. She hesitated, sighed, and moseyed to her boss's office.

"What should I do about this?" she asked him.

The boss read my message. *Subject: Paulina Pleve. The pane of glass in the attic door that was locked from inside is loose. If someone removes it, he can reach through and lock the door from inside. So, murder after all?*

The boss also blinked a couple of times, asked Jenny if she routinely got e-mail from Spirit of Truth, and then slowly shook his head.

"Have you released the apartment yet?" the boss asked.

Jenny nodded.

"Even so, drive over there and see if what this says is true. Then we'll open the case again."

I didn't trust the love-struck Jenny-Bunny one bit, so I texted Birgit. She hadn't had breakfast yet but said she was prepared to drive to the address I'd given her and meet Jenny there.

So you're a colleague of Gregor's? she replied.

I grinned. That woman was like a pit bull. Once she bit into something, she never let go. I needed someone with exactly that attitude to save Gregor's hide.

Something like that, I texted back.

I'm on the way, Birgit replied.

I watched how fast she downed her espresso and inhaled a bowl of müsli, stuffed her bag full of cookies, raisins, dried apricots and mangos, candied ginger, walnuts, two apples, and a whole roll of Spree candies so she could tide herself over in the convertible for about half an hour. Then she squeezed her bonsai belly behind the wheel and took off, convertible top up, in the drizzling rain.

Birgit and Jenny arrived almost simultaneously at Paulina's building. Jenny could hardly believe her eyes. "What are you doing here?" she asked.

The tone of her voice was ambiguous to me: surprised, pleased, or irritated? I couldn't tell.

"I was dispatched here," Birgit said.

"By Spirit of Truth?" Jenny asked.

Birgit smiled and nodded. "You too?"

They entered the building, Jenny climbing the stairs first and Birgit sweating her way more slowly up. She had to take at least five breaks and was still totally out of breath when she got upstairs.

"And now for the *moment* of truth," Jenny said. She put on a pair of thin latex gloves and told Birgit about the status of the case and the issue with the glass pane. Then she opened the attic door just enough to carefully touch the glass pane in the door from both sides. It rattled.

"It's loose, but not . . . whoops!"

Jenny was holding the glass pane in her hands. "Can you hold this for me?"

Birgit was clever enough to first conjure a handkerchief from the depths of her bag, then she used it to take hold of the glass, which she set in the corner of the landing, before turning back to the door. The pane had been adhered with putty, certainly first applied several decades ago. It was porous and had been completely and cleanly cut away on the long side with some kind of sharp blade. Birgit also noticed this and whistled softly. Then she pointed to that spot for Jenny, who in turn took a picture of it with her phone.

Jenny closed the door and reached her arm through the empty space left by the missing pane. She couldn't quite reach the lock.

"Are your arms longer?" she asked Birgit. They weren't.

"OK, that was a good theory, but it doesn't work," Jenny said, pulling off her gloves.

"Wait a second," Birgit mumbled.

I held my breath. The pit bull in Birgit had picked up a scent. She opened the door to the attic, took position under the roof beam that Jenny was pointing to. "That's where she was hanging."

Birgit didn't say anything for a couple of seconds, then she waddled back to the stair landing outside the door, fiddled around in her bag, and stuffed three huge cookies in her mouth at once.

"If I were going to hang a woman from the roof beam, I'd need a ladder," Birgit said.

"There was one lying below her," Jenny explained.

"My own ladder," Birgit mumbled through two dried apricots in her mouth. "Paulina stood on one ladder . . . she was standing on her own, right? Anything else would be very, very hard to pull off."

Jenny looked perplexed. "Yes. She had taken sleeping pills, so she would have been pretty woozy from that. But the autopsy showed she had still had enough muscle tension to stand."

Two walnut halves found their way in past Birgit's white teeth. "OK. So I've got a moderately drugged victim who can still stand under her own power. That means I need a ladder for Paulina to stand on, and one for me. I lean over to her, put the noose around her neck, and pull the rope up over the beam. And then I knock her ladder down."

Jenny nodded.

"Paulina's ladder stays here because it's necessary to stage a suicide scene, but I take my own ladder out."

Birgit walked to the door and measured the distance between the hole from the pane and the handle.

"Now, if I imagine I was standing higher up . . ."

She was absolutely right. If she were standing on a ladder or even some kind of chair or stool and her shoulders were at the height of the windowpane, she could reach through the hole with her entire arm. That way it was cake to turn the key in the lock.

Jenny called CSI.

Birgit got lost without being asked, because it wouldn't have been easily explained why the pregnant girlfriend of the friend of the murder suspect would be with Jenny at a crime scene investigation. Once in her car, she sent me a text message, which I could read off the screen on her phone, and she started her car. Instead of turning left at the nearest intersection and heading home, however, she took a right. She was heading to the old folks' home.

I needed to communicate directly with Martin. All the texting with Birgit was cumbersome and time-consuming; plus, at the moment there were way too many fronts on which we needed to make our presence shown if we wanted to be able to cover it all ourselves. My plan for Gregor to be free before the weekend wasn't realistic anymore, but I wasn't going to give up. So, I zoomed over to Martin at the Institute for Forensic Medicine. When I found him, I was flabbergasted, however. Keller and

Stein were standing at Katrin's desk, waiting for her to turn off her computer and activate call forwarding on her phone.

"That is ridiculous," Martin was saying in a trembling voice. "First you suspect Detective Kreidler, and now you suspect Dr. Zange as well. This is growing more and more absurd."

"I'm sure everything will be cleared up," Katrin told Martin. Her rage was seething like the brewing storm outside. I would not want to be anywhere near her when she exploded. Even though she couldn't be dangerous to me personally since I was dead, after all. But if Stein—the gussied-up fop—or Keller—who today was featuring a wide marmalade stain on his shirt—didn't watch out, they'd be the next corpses in this shadowy case.

Naturally I didn't stay close to Martin but instead followed Katrin, who was hauled off to Desperately Seeking Susanne in Düsseldorf, where she was interrogated.

"Dr. Zange, who can confirm that you were at the Dutch coast in Renesse last Friday night?"

"I've already given you the names," Katrin said with forced calm.

"We did indeed inquire with those ladies. However, an interesting piece of information came up at our second interview. Between Friday night at ten o'clock and Saturday morning at nine o'clock, no one can vouch that you were present."

"So?"

"Why didn't you join the group celebration on Friday night?"

Katrin rolled her eyes, took a deep breath, but still replied in a slightly bitchy tone. "I had a headache and wasn't looking for a guy for the night."

"And so you went blissfully to bed and slept for ten hours?"

"No, I watched TV for a couple hours, and then I fell asleep. But not until nine, only until seven. Then I went for a jog on the beach, took a shower, and then was at the breakfast table at eight."

"I'm not terribly interested whether you were in the breakfast room at eight or nine," Keller mumbled. "Either way, you would have had the whole night to drive to Cologne and back. Isn't that right?"

Katrin shrugged and said nothing.

"And since you wanted to get rid of not only your competitor but also your unfaithful lover in one fell swoop, you planted a few pieces of evidence in the victim's apartment."

Katrin turned pale.

"You pulled it off with great skill," Stein said. There was nothing left of the schmaltzy claptrap he had been priming Katrin with last Wednesday night. "First you plant all the evidence against Kreidler, then you play the loyal girlfriend routine and make a fuss when you're asked to hand over his jacket to us. But then you decide after all to help us find the truth, bringing us his jacket that you use to dig him deeper into his hole."

Katrin's carotid artery began to throb. I could feel it like the beats of a bass drum because I was sitting right next to it on her shoulder.

"Detective Keller noticed that the cups in your apartment were the same as the cups in Kreidler's apartment. However, the set of cups was complete on your wall shelf but not in his. One was missing from there. You placed that cup, with prints and DNA from Kreidler on it, in Hauschild's apartment."

Now Katrin's hands started trembling. I felt sick. Katrin was the sort of person who could fillet dead bodies that were diced, decomposed, mummified, or even coated in liquid polyurethane without her hand ever trembling, but this time she was at her limit. She was about to either ex- or implode.

"What do you have to say about that?" Stein asked.

Amazingly, neither -plosion occurred. Instead, Katrin suddenly relaxed. I watched the relaxation start right in the middle of her head, run down her temples and cheeks, loosening her neck, shoulders, and everything beneath. I'd never seen anything like it before. Even an Indian yogi could have learned something by watching it.

"No judge in the world is going to issue you a second arrest warrant for the same murder," Katrin said. Her voice was so cold that I could hear icicles clanking on her vocal cords. "So decide whether you suspect Detective Sergeant Kreidler or me."

Stein, who had apparently anticipated a different reaction, recoiled. Keller noisily licked his tongue over his fleshly lips like he was looking for something edible and then sighed. I couldn't tell if his disappointed sigh referred to Katrin's sudden aplomb or his futile search for fodder.

Katrin sat in her chair with her back straight and her chin raised. "If you don't have any other questions . . ." she reached for her bag and stood. "Good day, gentlemen."

SIXTEEN

I found Birgit with Susanne's father out in the garden. He was drawing faces again: the millenarian who had dozed off in her wheelchair, the two guys who were playing chess—or at least pretending to. *I* didn't see any motion at their table. They were just staring at the board and chess pieces.

And what was even splashing around still in old Hauschild's head? He wasn't really responding to Birgit's questions. Well, he was responding—not with straightforward answers but with drawings instead.

When Birgit asked whether Hauschild had seen Gregor recently, Hauschild drew Gregor when he was a teenager. Wow!

"How is he?" Hauschild suddenly asked. "Does he still have his kick-start moped?"

"No," Birgit said. "He's got a car now." Hauschild drew a Beetle.

Birgit laughed. "Not a Beetle. A new car. An Audi."

Hauschild drew an Audi TT. "Not as sporty," Birgit corrected him. His next attempt was a match: an A4.

In a remote part of my consciousness a little bell started ringing. The sound was bugging me, especially since I knew the ringing was trying to tell me something.

I'd overlooked something important. Zuzubee's car.

I zoomed back to Martin, who was still in his office doing the work of two, since Katrin hadn't come back to work after her interrogation.

"We need to go check out Susanne's car," I yelled.

Martin winced. "What does 'check out' mean?" he asked.

"Where is the car? I was just over at her apartment, and there's nothing there that can help. But what about her car? Did the detectives search it? Is it even still parked in front of her building?"

"How should I know?" Martin moaned.

True. How should he know? I needed to find that out. But before I could put my thoughts into action, Martin surprised me with an invitation. "I'm driving over to see Gregor. Are you coming along?" Who could say no?

Gregor seriously looked like shit. Years older, gray, wrinkly, and saggy. I'd not have expected him to decline that much in only five days in the clink. A good German cop should easily have a bit more staying power than this.

"Thanks for coming," Gregor said.

"My pleasure. I'm your friend. I'm standing by you," Martin said.

And he will. Sentimental crap like this is something Martin is great at.

"Stein was here and interrogated me again. He now suspects Katrin," Gregor muttered. "Do you know anything about that?"

Martin shook his head.

"I know something!" I bellowed, but Martin mentally waved me off.

"How do they get this shit in their heads?" Gregor asked.

"It's surely just a misunderstanding," Martin whispered.

"The evidence they found at the crime scene . . ." I began, but Martin apparently didn't want to get bogged down on the topic.

Gregor ran his fingers through his hair, and then he straightened his back and looked Martin in the face. His eyes were bloodshot, but now he had that killer look in them again.

"Martin, tell me the truth: How did they get Katrin in their sights? Did she get herself involved in the investigation?

"Not as far as I know."

This time I shut my trap voluntarily. I definitely didn't want to be the one to break it to Gregor that his beloved had schlepped his jacket over to Detective Stein so he could officially compare the skin flakes and fibers on it with what was found on the body.

"Katrin cannot get involved. Tell her . . ." Gregor swallowed. "Tell her to forget me."

Martin shook his head awkwardly, like a bobblehead at a soccer match.

"It's not a request; it's an order," Gregor said seriously. "Between friends. You guys need to stay out of it!"

"Bullshit!" I bellowed. The last thing I needed was for Gregor to quash Martin's already-feeble readiness to help with secret directives. How in the holy turbocharger was I supposed to find out the truth all by myself? I needed Martin!

"Why?" Martin asked.

Gregor ran his hands over his face, and then he sighed. "Do you remember how I got a phone call on Sunday, right before our colleagues from Düsseldorf hauled me in?"

Martin's did more of the bobbly wobbling. Well, whatever that meant, *I* remembered the call.

"Someone said, 'Keep your mouth shut, otherwise Katrin will be next.'" Martin went pale.

"Martin, that warning applies to you just as much."

"No!" I roared. "We can't just leave Gregor hanging."

"But if someone is manipulating evidence, you might really . . ." Martin's voice failed.

Gregor nodded. He had tears in his eyes. "I'd rather go to jail than have something happen to Katrin."

Martin said nothing for what seemed like an eternity, but then he shook his head. "We can't stand idly by."

Now Gregor turned angry. "I do not want anything to happen to either of you!"

Martin waved his hand. "You've misunderstood me." He looked out the corner of his eye at the guard who was standing near the door and then leaned as far forward as he could over the table. "Do you remember that case last year with the car thief?" he whispered.

He meant me!

"Yes."

"He's, uh . . ."

Gregor's eyes grew wide. "Is he still here?"

"Yes!" I screamed. "Of course I'm still here. Hello, Gregor!"

Martin moaned. Oy. In my excitement I guess I was being too loud.

"He can help you."

I hated always being at other people's beck and call back when I was alive. But for my favorite cop, I was prepared to make an exception. If Martin was going to pimp me out, it was fine by me as long as the john's name was Gregor and the trick was to save him. However, without Martin, it was practically impossible to pull off.

"We'll set a time when he'll come here, to you. You can talk to him."

161

"Have you been huffing paint?" I asked Martin.

"What do you mean?" Gregor asked.

"If you suspect something, then say it aloud. If you want Pascha to watch someone, then he'll do it. If you want him to look for something—"

Gregor seemed frustrated and anxious, but pensive. "Is he reliable?"

"No."

"Thanks, asshole," I said. "Why are you offering my services only to turn around and diss me?"

"Gregor needs to know what he's getting into," Martin scolded me.

"And what will happen with the information I tell him?" Gregor asked. "Suppose I had an idea who he should surveil. You're the only person he can tell about what he sees, right?"

Martin nodded. "Exactly. And I'll come to you and report—"

"No," Gregor said. "You all need to keep out of it. You and Katrin and Birgit and the Little Ghost too."

Now I was seriously disappointed. The Little Ghost! As though I was here to amuse children!

"I'm taking the threat very seriously," Gregor continued.

Martin nodded.

"If I find out that you are up to no good, then I'll confess to the murder!"

Martin turned as pale as his ribbed undershirt.

"Great," I said. "Now *der Kommissar* here has got you so scared, you're just going to put up your feet so no one steps on them. But then unfortunately Gregor is going to spend the rest of his—"

"Who says I'm putting my feet up?" Martin said, interrupting me. "You don't seriously think I'll allow my friend to settle into jail even though he's completely innocent?"

I drained my spirit of all mocking, snide, condescending, critical, or otherwise typical thoughts with respect to Martin so he couldn't sense any negative waves emanating from me. Of course I still thought he was a coward and he still needed to be shown what a serious situation the rescue operation was, but for the moment I felt like bursting out in song. Finally it seemed like Martin was back in the game.

I got a message from Birgit that she hadn't found out anything new from Hans Hauschild. Shit. But what did that matter now that Martin had promised his full cooperation?

"I've been thinking about Gregor's situation," Martin announced over dinner, which consisted of spinach soup, whole-grain veggie patties, and something that looked like green chitterlings but sounded something like "alpha sprouts." Birgit at least tossed back another half package of chocolate cookies afterward.

"I need to help him."

"Good," Birgit said. "What shall we do?"

"We don't do anything," Martin said emphatically. "You need to take care of yourself."

"I'm bored to death sitting around here all day," Birgit replied. "Plus, Gregor is my friend too."

"It's too dangerous for you."

I give Birgit some serious credit for not plopping onto the floor in laughter.

"What's so dangerous if I help out a little? I'm not sure if Jenny would have come up with the idea about the door on her own if—"

Martin turned white as chalk. "Birgit, have you been poking around in the murder case?" he asked with a trembling voice.

Birgit nodded cheerfully, stuffing one whole cookie into her mouth.

"You cannot do that! Do you hear? Y-you may not do that," Martin stammered. "Gregor is being blackmailed. They threatened him to keep his mouth shut so that nothing happens to Katrin. That's why he's sitting in jail now not defending himself. Because he's afraid for Katrin's life. And anyone who gets involved is also in danger."

Birgit turned pale. I did say she wasn't stupid. She's not afraid of her own shadow like Martin is, but she also doesn't run headlong into real danger.

She thought for a second.

"Who is threatening him?"

"Even he doesn't know! That's why the situation is so opaque. And the more opaque, the more dangerous because no one knows from what direction the danger looms."

Another cookie disappeared through Birgit's lips. She chewed pensively and swallowed. "But you're in danger as well, then."

"I owe it to my best friend."

Martin looks so totally lame whenever he plays the tough guy that I have to actively restrain myself from bursting out in laughter.

"Me too," Birgit said. "In addition, the danger is less for every individual if as many people as possible are aware of the situation. Making two people disappear is harder than just one."

Top-notch knowledge gleaned from watching *CSI* on TV—but Birgit was right. In this case, television had fulfilled its educational mission, even if the consulting TV crime shows got on forensic medicine was sooner something from the Brothers Grimm.

Before Birgit and Martin could reach an agreement, Martin's cell phone rang. He was on call, and they needed him on site somewhere. He commanded Birgit—there's really no other way to put it—not to get into any trouble, and then he left.

SEVENTEEN

Birgit arrived at Karpi's at around nine o'clock. It was much too early to make an appearance at a nightclub, but Karpi offered a Virgin Cocktail Hour every Friday between eight and ten. And, accordingly, there were people pushing and shoving to get in at the entrance. The bouncer was doing a good job, though, and had each of them show ID.

When it was finally Birgit's turn, he tried to wave her through, but Birgit gave him a friendly smile, put both hands on her belly, and cheerfully asked, "Do I look like I want to drink cocktails?"

"I can't say whether you want to or not. But whether you *should* is another question."

Even though the guy was pretty quick-witted with the chit-chat, he looked like a bouncer at any other club: tall and wide, with a polished bald head, black clothes, and a goatee. You couldn't make out his eyes through the mirrored sunglasses.

"Are you Yuri?" Birgit asked.

He pushed her to the side, waved the dolled-up chicks behind her through, and then pretended as though Birgit wasn't there anymore.

"I'm here about Paulina."

The mountain of meat continued with his cigar-store Indian routine.

"Paulina was murdered."

No reaction.

"The police aren't making any progress in their investigation because the investigator in charge was framed for the murder. I want to know by whom."

Still no reaction.

"The investigator is a friend of mine. If you're not Yuri, he's at least a colleague of yours. Paulina was his girlfriend. We all need your help."

"Beat it," I told Birgit, but of course she didn't hear me.

"All right, well, if you don't want to help me, I'm going to go talk to Karpi again."

Birgit walked past the bouncer into the nightclub and pressed her way through the twitching and bouncing figures on her way to the elevator. But the doors to the club stayed closed. I zoomed back to Mount Meat, who had his phone to his ear.

". . . about Paulina," he was saying.

"Cops?" squeaked a voice through the speaker.

"Uh-uh. A friend of the cop who's been framed."

"Excuse me?"

"Man, what do I know? The chick is pregnant and blonde. Does that mean anything to you?"

Silence on the other end.

"Come on, Yuri," the meat mountain finally said. "When are you coming around again? I'm sorry about your girlfriend, but I don't feel like standing the door here all weekend by myself. If you're not coming in, tell the boss so he can find a replacement."

"I'll think about it."

They hung up.

OK, we still hadn't found our desired outcome. I thought for a second how I could come up with Yuri's address when the meat mountain suddenly began to move beneath me. He stopped the influx of chorus girls by raising his hand, disappeared into the club, and closed the door behind him. The crowd outside the door protested vociferously, but the chrome dome waltzed a path to the dark cave, typed the entry code into the box next to the elevator, and went down to visit Karpi in his basement lair.

"Boss, Yuri has the cops by the balls."

Aha, loyalty to one's financial backer was greater than that to one's colleague.

Today Karpi was wearing a satin kiwi-green snakeskin-pattern suit. No wonder the foo dog didn't take off his sunglasses. The guy was afraid of going blind.

"Why?" Karpi mumbled around the straw in his mouth, which led to a bright-green drink that looked like the crap Iron Man has to drink to prevent palladium poisoning. The glass held at least a whole liter of liquid, and Karpi half emptied it with a single suck.

"Paulina."

"Idiot," Karpi mumbled. "That pussy fucked him over."

The meat mountain shrugged.

"Go back to your post."

I let the hamburger hill withdraw and waited to see what Karpi would do next. He didn't do anything for quite a while. Finally he grabbed one of his landlines. He had just dialed the area code for Cologne when the door to his office opened again. Birgit appeared at the threshold.

For as much as I love Birgit—right now her timing was shitty.

"How did you get in here?" Karpi asked with a sigh.

"I'm looking for Yuri."

"How did you get into the elevator?"

"One nine four three."

"Shit, girl. How do you know my code?"

"I watched the bouncer when he came downstairs."

Karpi shook his head and all of the bacon fat hanging off it shuddered.

"Yuri?" Birgit reminded him.

"I'm not hiding him."

Birgit thought for a moment. "Gregor Kreidler was framed. Someone is putting the blame on him for a murder he didn't commit. That and other issues have bogged down the investigation of Yuri's girlfriend's case. I have no idea whether this is all connected or not, but I'm sure Yuri knows something about this whole mess. So please. Help me."

"Why should I?" Karpi asked.

Birgit shrugged. "For justice's sake."

Karpi burst out in a chuckle that turned into an odd, spumy blubbering and then into a soft gurgling. He wiped the sweat from his brow.

"Do you know who I am?" he asked, still slightly out of breath.

"No," Birgit said. "I'm sorry, but may I sit down?"

Karpi nodded, and Birgit pulled a rickety wooden chair over in front of Karpi's desk.

"I'm one of the men your mamma warned you about."

"Investment adviser?" Birgit asked.

Karpi snorted with laughter and giggled for a moment, his chins wobbling away.

"Worse," he then said, suddenly dead serious. "You may be in danger here, little blonde lady."

Birgit blew a strand of hair out of her face. "Hmm, I hadn't thought about that until now. Should I be worried?"

"It's too late for that now anyway."

Birgit sighed. Her sigh transitioned into a little burp. "Pardon me. That happens to me constantly."

Karpi reached into his desk drawer and tossed her a bag of pistachios, from which Birgit took a handful. She started cracking them.

"So you don't want to help me? Me and Gregor Kreidler?"

"This is not CARE International here."

"And I'm not Mother Teresa. Still—"

Karpi waved his hand to silence her. "If I start doing good without something in return, it will ruin my reputation. Then I may as well shut my business."

"The nightclub?" Birgit asked.

Karpi snorted and waved his hand again to say no. "But if you're here to make me a business proposition, then that's something worthy of consideration," Karpi said.

"Whap biv ou have in mind?" Birgit asked with her mouth full.

"Make me an offer."

"Oh, I have no idea what you might be interested in." Birgit chewed faster. "Certainly not money. Maybe . . ."

"Maybe you'd like to name your child after me?"

Birgit turned pale. "Karpi?"

Karpi shook his head. "Karpi is a nickname. My real name is Anatol."

"And what if it's a girl?"

"Katharina."

Birgit took three deep breaths and tried to listen within her whether it was a girl or boy, and, fairly certain it was a girl, nodded. "OK."

"How will you explain this to the pajama suit who was here with you last time?"

"Let me worry about that," she explained coolly. "Deal?"

Karpi gently shook Birgit's outstretched hand, and then wrote some numbers down on a sheet of paper, which he handed her.

"Here you go."

"What's this?" Birgit asked in amazement.

"You're a smart cookie," Karpi said with a wide grin. "You'll figure it out."

Shit! I'd completely forgotten to tell Birgit to ask about the ray-shielded rooms, but it was probably actually better that we didn't try for too much information all at once. Once Birgit deciphered the number puzzle—and I assumed she was wholly able to do so—then she could bring up the strange fortress within the fortress and ask why it was hermetically sealed.

I accompanied Birgit home and watched her set the paper from Karpi on the dining table, sit down, and stare at it. It listed ten digits, each occurring only once. The first two were 0 and 2, but it didn't continue with 4 and 8 or some recognizable pattern. It was just a muddled-up mess. If it were on a math test in school, it'd say "Complete the pattern" or something—but I couldn't see any rhyme or reason. Apparently Birgit was having trouble, too, because she rested her forehead in her hands, and nothing happened for a long time. Until her head fell onto the table and she started to snore. Oh, great!

I whooshed back to Karpi, hoping I could find out a bit of info about Yuri, but Karpi wasn't in his office. He wasn't at the nightclub either.

I hung out for a good while in the bobblehead bunker, relaxing my brain for the first time since Sunday night. There was plenty to see here, and I was just enjoying the tricked-out chicks gyrating their bodies in ecstatic convulsions to try to catch the eye of one of the testosterone bombs. I had rarely played this age-old game back when I was alive, because my assets during my earthly existence were less of a physical nature. I tended to win chicks over with the ride under my ass and the horsepower under its hood. I wallowed a little while in the memories of the rides I used to drive during my short life, but at some point I needed to admit to myself that being a ghost among earthly beings was even lonelier than being alone, so I bailed.

July 3, six days after Gregor's arrest

Even before I could reach Martin the next morning under his anti-electrosmog netting, a cell phone rang in his and Birgit's apartment.

Birgit's cell phone.

Martin jumped up, alarmed. He determined it wasn't his and answered it anyway.

"Hello? Hello? Who is this?" he asked.

"Who are you?" a voice squeaked back.

"Gänsewein," Martin said, introducing himself. "Speaking on Ms. Arend's phone."

"That's exactly who I want to speak with. The apartment has been released."

"Which apartment?" Martin asked.

"Ms. Hauschild's, of course."

When Martin gets angry, his cheeks turn red, and the tip of his nose turns white. It's pretty funny to see, especially when he's trembling on top of it all. Which he was doing now.

He was seriously at his limit.

"You're behind this!" he hissed at me.

"Well . . . what can I say . . ." I began. I'd have grinned if I could have, Martin was being such a ridiculous little snit pixie.

"You have the audacity to involve Birgit in this life-threatening matter?"

"Chill out," I advised him. "Birgit was dying from boredom. Plus, she wants to help Gregor. And I needed someone who could ask—"

"How did you communicate with her?"

"Guess."

Martin was holding her cell phone in his hand, but even so it took him several seconds until he stared at it as though he'd never seen such a thing before.

"You can make phone calls?" he whispered.

"Cold," I replied, although there were devices I could use to make phone calls, as long as a certain kind of wireless headset was connected. Unfortunately those things had almost disappeared from the market.

"Text messaging?" Martin asked.

"Hot!"

"But where did you get a cell phone?"

"Ice cold."

Birgit staggered into the kitchen. She was white as the wall and had drops of sweat on her forehead, holding her belly as though it would splash down onto her feet otherwise.

"I think it's time."

And with that, me and my little difference of opinion with Martin were instantly forgotten. And for once I could even understand, because suddenly even I was—well, yeah—even I was *excited*. While Martin frantically called the midwife, I started circling Birgit and watching her suspiciously. She really

173

didn't look good. Tensely, I followed Martin—now apparently somewhat reassured after the telephone-based care provided by the fret nurse—as he maneuvered the whimpering Birgit and her long-since-packed suitcase downstairs, into the trash can 2CV, and to the hospital.

Once in the maternity ward, Birgit was hurried into Delivery Room 3 by the midwife, who was already there and ready for the kid to pop out. "This is the nicest one," she whispered to Birgit, who at the moment seemed uninterested, even though these special delivery rooms are the reason Birgit wanted to give birth in this hospital. "Having a baby isn't a disease," she always said, which is why it was important to her to deliver her baby in a friendly, colorful environment and not in a shitty white-tiled maternity ward.

I tried to get Martin's attention. "Martin, could we please—"

"No! Not now!" he thought with intense energy toward me. "Right now I'm interested only in Birgit." Then he closed all bulkheads.

Great! Despite this, I stayed at the hospital for a long time, feeling sorry for Birgit and trying to block out Martin the Drama Queen, which wasn't going that well because he was constantly wiping off Birgit's forehead with a cloth, like she was driving a vintage car in bumper-to-bumper traffic, or bringing her water, or squeezing her hand flat. Birgit was enjoying it; she smiled at Martin and whispered reassuring words into his ear. The midwife was also taking more care of Martin than of Birgit, but nothing they did helped. Martin's nerves were fluttering like the eagle-emblazoned presidential standard on the State Car, which by the way is an armored Mercedes-Benz S600. I couldn't take the suffering anymore, so I cleared out of there.

I did a tour through the empty offices of the Cologne PD and then headed to Düsseldorf for visiting hour at the jail. But there wasn't anything new going on here, either. In the conference room for Desperately Seeking Susanne, however, I did find Keller and Agent Orange. The two of them were embroiled in feminist disputes that had nothing to do with Zuzubee's murder. I listened for a bit as the women's libber chattered on and on while Keller seemed to be enjoying chewing some kind of open-face sandwich whose rémoulade was dripping down onto his shirt. But I didn't glean any new information about the murder or the hunt for the perpetrator.

I found the platinum blonde at the old folks' home café busy bringing millenarians and their visitors coffee, tea, and cake. She scuttled back and forth, wiping tables, sitting down occasionally at tables with old folks who were by themselves and not having visitors today. I resolved to stop by again later to see what happened when she left the raisin ranch and whether she at least had any fun at night. Maybe she went to the movies or something or other that normal people at her age do: smoke weed, screw, steal cars.

EIGHTEEN

Around seven o'clock Birgit was feeling better, but the kid apparently didn't want to make an appearance yet.

"We'll keep your wife overnight for observation. Go home and come back tomorrow morning," the doctor advised Martin. "If nothing has happened by then, you can take her home."

So things were chill here for now. Fine by me, but now I *really* didn't need to be here. So I checked in at the home again. The platinum blonde was still schlepping dishes back and forth. Odd bird. I noticed again that she did everything with a smile, but she smiled only with her mouth—not with her eyes. Whatever her reason for being here, it was definitely not out of some major love of old farts.

I hung out under the ceiling light, watching as the visitors took off and the café employees cleaned up until the final table had been wiped off. Then the last two back-combed cookie monsters said bye and disappeared, leaving the platinum blonde all on her own.

She stood for a while at a column in the corridor, looking in all directions like she was waiting for someone. Suddenly she left the column and walked to the stairwell. She went down the stairs, cautiously looked down the long corridor toward the break room where Birgit had chatted with Paulina's colleagues, and then she quickly scurried past it. Her objective was the last door on the right. She rummaged through her pocket and pulled out a key, unlocked the door, and slipped inside.

I flashed through the door—and could not believe my eyes. Apparently this was the junk room. Bed frames, IV stands, tables, chairs, room dividers, a defective trolley cart, and all manner of knickknacks and junk were lying around everywhere. In the backmost corner, behind a room divider and two bookcases, was an air mattress on the floor with a sleeping bag and a gym bag on top of it. The platinum blonde swept the gym bag aside and plopped down onto the air mattress. And just a few minutes later, she was sound asleep.

What was I supposed to think from all this? I ruled out child slavery in a German old folks' home. As well as work for room and board. In principle there could be only one explanation: the platinum blonde was a runaway hiding out here.

But how would someone come up with the idea to do this?

She was a chick, true, but she wasn't dumb.

So. What does someone in Cologne do on a Saturday night all by themselves? Someone goes to a pub. I was in the mood for a pub crawl even though I rarely do that since I can't get tanked anymore. It's also pretty lame for me, watching people get lit all around me while I stay dead sober. Actually, that's pretty much the lamest thing about being a ghost: not being able to get fucked up anymore. I couldn't even get the tiniest bit buzzed to make it through the long, tedious periods or send all my problems down the Rhine for a while, as they say.

So if I was going to go barhopping without getting dead-drunk, then at least I was going to do something beneficial and stick close to Zuzubee's hairy boyfriend. So, off to Die Werkstatt.

Halfway there I put on the brakes, though. I had an even better idea. Before I spent a lonely evening among well-oiled motorcycle aficionados, a little screwing couldn't hurt. Of course I couldn't do that myself anymore either, and watching nookie is way less exciting than most people think. But there was a couple that appealed to me. Sort of scientifically speaking, actually. See, I just could not for the life of me imagine Jenny and Offermann getting it on. Did Jenny just giggle the whole time? Was Offermann a teddy bear or a tiger? I had no idea. By this point I was pretty adept at sizing people up, figuratively. Which makes sense if you can spend every night watching hormone junkies go stalking, tearing up their prey, and then getting to the point—it hones your eye like you wouldn't believe. But . . . Jenny and Offermann? No idea.

Those two were on the verge, as people say, so I popped in on Offermann early, like at eight thirty. Their duds were strewn between the front door and the bedroom. They led off with Jenny's blouse, followed by Offermann's T-shirt, quickly moving to a shoe, a bra, a second shoe, Jenny's panties, then there wasn't anything for a few steps until Offermann's bed, next to which lay his jeans and aloha-print boxers. It's a sign of male dominance when the chick is naked before the guy even takes off his jeans. At least, that's what some old psycho broad was saying over breakfast TV the other day. So my survey of what had gone on didn't really surprise me. Anyway, Offermann was on top, which also didn't surprise me. And he kept asking how he was doing . . . OK, to tell the truth, he was asking how it was for Jenny. She was cross-eyed with pleasure and was apparently having difficulties formulating complete sentences, but I doubt Andy would really have wanted to know that much detail. There are limits, after all. A guy just wants to confirm and finish.

Offermann fell asleep for a moment but came to again when Jenny got up. He followed her into the shower and kept her company. Which didn't present a problem at all since his shower was not one of those rickety stalls you can get on the cheap at the hardware superstore but instead took up a full third of the bathroom, separated from the sink and toilet by a long glass wall and with one of those awesome tropical rainforest shower head setups that douse you in twenty or thirty liters of water a minute.

The shower corresponded to the level of finishing in the rest of the apartment, which I was free to notice now that the action was over. At least a hundred twenty square meters of floors covered variously in authentic granite, slate, and Brazilian hardwood. Few walls, little furniture, lots of space. Jenny noticed this as well when she came out of the bathroom freshly blow-dried and dressed in the clothes Offermannequin had so kindly brought her.

"Wow, this is amazing!" she breathed when faced with the spacious dance floor between the freestanding kitchen island and flatscreen TV. "I've only ever seen something like this on television before."

"Exactly. I'm actually just the house sitter here. I look after this joint for West German Broadcasting."

Jenny's eyes opened wide.

Offermann tousled her still slightly damp hair. "Joking. Actually I inherited it."

"The apartment?" Jenny asked.

Sure, my fairy godmother's place looked like this too.

"A building. Ancient and ugly as sin, but in one of the best locations in Bonn."

I wasn't interested in real-estate transactions in Bonn, which is merely a glorified suburb of Cologne, and since these two were about to take in a romantic comedy at the movies, I bailed. I can stand a lot, but joining in with a hundred fifty hand-holding couples to watch a flat-chested Hollywood honey seek her Mr. Right is far beyond my limit.

At eleven o'clock all hell was breaking loose in Die Werkstatt. Every stool, every chair, and every bench was full, and people were standing packed between them all. A minority of patrons were female. Had I found myself in a gay bar? I looked around. None of the guys were making out, and I didn't see any of the traditional tarted-up queens. No, it was mainly men's men here, and the conversations in Die Werkstatt were mainly about men's topics. Motors, tuning, dynamic suspension adjustment, engine capacity, horsepower; some were even jabbering about kilowatts. But, on a serious note, anyone who was tinkering around on mopeds, gopeds, or light motorcycles before manufacturers started wrapping their crotch rockets in streamlined fiberglass bra cups would definitely consider performance expressed in kilowatts to be bureau-crap.

I listened in on a couple of conversations and did not regret that I'd never set foot in this joint when I was alive. That I had never been here was due to the fact that the Belgian Quarter was so not my thing with its hip pubs and silly bistros filled with cockalorums. Given that Die Werkstatt wasn't all plasticky design but *actually* reeked of motor oil, it didn't really fit in in this neighborhood. If it had been located somewhere else in town, tonight's patronage would likely have included more people like me. Genuine motorheads who had dedicated their lives to speed. But the men meeting up here were unmistakably middle-aged, trying to recall how they used to speed home five kilometers over the speed limit when they were sixteen. And then only to make it home in time for their dinner with sweetened rosehip tea sitting at mommy's kitchen table. Most of them were wearing designer jeans instead of work pants, with wide gold bands on their ring fingers right where the priest had had their wives place them.

Ioánnis was standing behind the bar with two sufficiently attractive girls wearing pit-chick outfits, who were serving not just beer but also colorful, modern mixed drinks throughout the shop. This was *definitely* not an authentic biker bar. Still, it had a nice enough atmosphere and the music was all right, so I stayed a while, swirling through the room and listening in when people sounded like they were qualified to talk tech. Although I'd never been a fan of vintage vehicles, I'd spent many hours tinkering on those old things. There's no better education than taking apart a couple of mopeds and putting them back together. People don't learn that in automotive school anymore nowadays. A real shame.

My interest was aroused for a moment when I was hovering over a table where the guys looked like they were setting up some kind of flea market. Among the beer glasses were various metal logos, badges, and plates that had previously been applied to the gas tanks or gearboxes of motorcycles, from the days before beautiful embossed lettering was replaced with cheapo stickers. And between a BMW badge and a Kawasaki GPZ900 logo was a Kreidler motorcycle VIN plate. Exactly like Gregor's, which was now rusting away in the evidence room at Düsseldorf PD.

"For twenty yoyos you can even pick your own chassis number," one guy was saying, whose jeans were clearly *not* from a designer connection but a discount department store line.

"Any number?" a guy *with* designer jeans asked.

"Totally any chassis number," cheap jeans said. "If you want, he'll even put your birthday on it. Nice and neat."

"And they look genuine?"

"Absolutely. On genuine ones from the original Kreidler factory in Kornwestheim. They couldn't use them anymore after Kreidler was taken over by Prophete GmbH because the manufacturer name was already engraved on them. See, here's a blank one; it says 'Kreidler Fahrzeuge GmbH & Co KG.'"

"And where exactly did you get these?" the designer jeans asked.

"Well, here. From Ioánnis's parts sale. Every Sunday morning, out back."

July 4, seven days after Gregor's arrest

"You need to go to that pub again. Out back they do a parts flea market where you can buy VIN plates," I excitedly explained to Martin on Sunday morning as soon as he lifted the anti-electrosmog netting over the bed.

"Is there any hope for you?" Martin asked. "Our child may be born at any moment, and you want me to attend a flea market? The only thing I am doing now is taking care of Birgit," Martin said dismissively.

"Good idea. Bring her along. A very pregnant blonde—"

"You can forget it. Birgit needs to rest," he yelled indignantly.

I had already checked in on Birgit at the hospital and found out she was doing splendidly. She had had coffee at five thirty with the ward nurse; after that, she took an extended tour through the maternity ward, bringing various pregnant women on bed rest all manner of things they requested, from vending-machine coffee to the Sunday paper.

"Birgit's fine, the kid's fine, and the only thing bothering Birgit is you babying her."

"It's not babying. It's concern. Taking care of each other isn't something you understand in the least."

"Birgit can take perfectly good care of herself and you at the same time," I replied. "And because she's a woman and good at multitasking, she can even take care of Gregor too—and that's exactly what you two need to do right now."

"Birgit needs to rest; that's what the doctor—" Martin repeated, almost desperately.

"He only prattles off bullshit like that so he doesn't lose his liability insurance."

"Most doctors think first and foremost of their patients."

"Income, liability, screwing during office hours, weekend plans, golf course handicaps . . . and THEN they think about patients," I enlightened him.

"As though you had any idea . . ."

"Under no circumstances am I lying in bed at home," Birgit explained. She was already dressed and ready to go when Martin arrived at her hospital room. "I need exercise, and I need distraction. Otherwise I'm going to go completely crazy from all this waiting."

"But the doctor said—" Martin began.

"He has no idea, Martin. He's never been pregnant."

I love that woman. I do all the time, but especially so sometimes. Like right now.

Once Birgit was home preparing her second breakfast, I zoomed up to my closet and sent her a text message: *Zuzubee's apartment has been released by the police. What are you waiting for?*

Birgit read the message while Martin was in the bathroom. Her eyes lit up. She flipped on her espresso machine and poured a big bowl of müsli. She sliced banana on top, poured whole milk over that, and grabbed a soup spoon from the drawer. She had downed half the bowl when Martin sat beside her. "Martin, I need to tell you something." Martin turned ghost-pale.

"She wants to look for the laptop or a thumb drive in Zuzubee's apartment," I yelled in explanation so that he didn't have a coronary from the sheer anxiety of the revelation about to come. "And you should *not* talk her out of it!"

"I got a text message from a friend of Gregor's," Birgit began cautiously, watching Martin very closely.

Martin nodded hesitantly.

"I, well, it's like this . . ." And then Birgit burst out in tears.

What was up with that? Why was she crying? Well, OK. With pregnant women you're not allowed to ask. They just cry. With or without müsli.

Martin leaped up and served Birgit the espresso she had totally forgotten. Normally Martin considers the drinking of espresso during pregnancy to be at least nearly as hazardous as jumping from the Deutz Bridge over the Rhine, but whenever Birgit deploys the water cannons, he'll do anything to dry up the tears.

"I kept it a secret from you because you're always so worried about me."

Martin knelt beside Birgit's chair and took her into his arms.

"Otherwise I'm going to go completely crazy if I just sit around here waiting for the baby to finally arrive. And, secondly, I need to do something to help Gregor."

"I know," Martin whispered. "I am very protective. Sometimes perhaps even too much so."

Birgit laughed.

"Stop with the schmaltzy chit-chat and get going!" I roared at the sap fest before me on the kitchen floor.

It took Martin a second to regain his senses. "Come on. We're going to save the world."

NINETEEN

Birgit absolutely wanted to walk, so Martin and she waddled their way through the summer streets of Cologne. Birgit's waddling in particular pained me because she actually has incredibly beautiful, long legs and a very graceful gait. At least there was some hope she would grow back out of her waddling in the near future. But Martin was a dead loss, doomed to galumph his way through life.

They made it to the parts flea market behind Die Werkstatt by around ten thirty. The showroom was the garage, with the door open and accessible to anyone. The walls were lined with shelves and cabinets of drawers in various sizes that held anything that could be mounted on a motorcycle, legal or otherwise. Orderly labels on each drawer revealed the contents: brake levers, brake cables, clutch levers, pedals, footrests, flashers, chains, pinions, shock absorber springs, and of course most other technical parts for engines and transmissions. The larger parts were along the back wall: moped, scooter, and light motorcycle frames; a motorcycle frame in a screaming green that could only be from a Kawasaki; some front forks; and a sidecar, including a dog harness. The serial numbers had been filed off most of the frames or the VIN plates removed. I was careful not to point that out to Martin, because he would certainly have wanted to make an immediate exit from such a criminal place.

There were only three customers there, one of whom was the guy wearing the designer jeans. He was buying a Kreidler VIN plate as a gift for his beloved's birthday. Ioánnis muttered something through the wild thicket of fur on his face as he embossed the date into the metal. Ioánnis's next sales were an original headlight from an '85 Manxy Racer and a BMW tailpipe.

"Manxy Racer?" Martin asked, who had apparently been following my train of thought.

"An affectionate nickname for the Yamaha SR500."

Martin shook his head in disbelief. You just cannot have a man's conversation with him.

Finally, Martin and Birgit got their turn.

"What do you need?" Ioánnis asked, standing akimbo in front of them. Again, there was no discernible movement in the oral region.

"We're looking for Kreidler VIN plates," Birgit said.

During their walk here, Martin had told Birgit about his visit to Die Werkstatt last Wednesday. Birgit was surprised that Martin hadn't told her earlier, to say nothing of how he focused in on this Ioánnis specifically, but ultimately they dropped the topic. I had advised Martin to let Birgit do the talking this time, and so far he was taking the suggestion.

Without looking, the Greek grabbed a drawer under the counter, reached in, and set out a VIN plate.

"How many of these can I get?" Birgit asked.

A second reach under the counter, and whole handful of the things came jingling down onto its surface.

"I'll take all of them," Birgit said. "With this ID number embossed on them."

She set a piece of paper onto the counter with the serial number from Gregor's VIN plate written on it. Overnight I had zoomed up to Desperately Seeking Susanne's conference room to get the VIN number from Gregor's file. Although the only illumination was from the streetlights in front of HQ, I could still make out the numbers.

"They run thirty each," Ioánnis said.

Martin counted seventeen plates and was calculating the total, which drove the blood from his face, but Birgit beamed a grin at Ioánnis and started haggling.

"A hundred for all of them?"

"For a hundred you get three and a lollipop," Ioánnis countered.

"A hundred twenty and a piece of information."

From somewhere between the leather vest and the facial thicket, a hissing sound emerged that reminded me of an overheated radiator.

"Who's bought a plate like this recently?"

"That is currently the most popular souvenir on the scene."

"With *this* number?"

"I don't log my customers or their birthdays."

"It's not a date of birth. It's the number borne by the most important piece of evidence in the murder of your girlfriend."

Ioánnis bent so far forward that his eyebrows grazed Birgit's forehead. "Are you threatening me?"

"No," Birgit said, whose smile was still beaming brightly. "I want all of the plates with this number for a hundred twenty. And I want to know who bought one with that number last."

"I can't give you that information."

"Because you're protecting someone?"

"Because I've sold about two hundred fifty of those plates in the past six weeks. How am I supposed to remember the numbers all those people had me emboss?"

Birgit thought for a moment. "Then all the plates for a hundred. That's a lot, given that Criminal Investigations would certainly be interested in you if they know that you are manufacturing these pieces of evidence by the hundreds, right?"

Martin had shrunk more and more during the course of this interaction, pulling on Birgit's blouse from behind like a toddler who wants his mommy to get moving.

"Martin, let go of Birgit's apron strings. Nothing's going to happen to you," I reprimanded him.

He told me off mentally for twisting the facts, saying he was standing so close to Birgit to protect her, blah blah blah. Birgit had an ATM-fresh hundred-euro bill, which she waved in front of Ioánnis.

He took the plates and the paper with the serial number and walked over to the embossing machine, where he embossed all seventeen plates in a few minutes. Birgit stowed the plates in her bag while Ioánnis pocketed his hundred, shooed Martin and Birgit out of the garage, and pulled down the garage door behind them.

Birgit plopped down in a chair at the nearest street café and ordered a tall latte and croissant.

"Can you let me in on what you're planning to do with all of those plates? We don't know who purchased the one in evidence that incriminates Gregor," Martin said.

"We're not even sure that the evidence they have is the wrong plate," Birgit said. She rested her head in her hands and rubbed her eyes. "But if they ever bring it to trial, that piece of evidence will be worth precious little if we can produce seventeen others that are exactly the same, right?"

I wanted to puke at the notion of someone bringing Gregor to trial, but Birgit was right. Nonetheless, I hoped we would never have to put it to the test.

Mrs. Berger met Martin and Birgit at the door to Zuzubee's apartment.

"The landlord was notified by the police that they've released the apartment. Ms. Hauschild has only her senile father, who can't look after anything. That's what everyone at that home told the landlord as well." Mrs. Berger said. "But he knows that I've got the key, and so he naturally asked me if I knew of any other relatives, and I said that a girlfriend of Ms. Hauschild's had been by saying she could take care of her things. He asked me to have you get in touch with him."

The neighbor lady was totally high, at least on caffeine, probably with some kind of dessert liqueur on top—and that was before noon on a Sunday. She couldn't really stand up properly, she was slurring her speech, and her face was covered in red patches.

Martin looked at the floor. He was naturally displeased with the white lie Birgit had told Mrs. Berger about being a long-lost friend.

But Birgit was fully at ease. She took the key, which was on a felt-piggy fob, out of Mrs. Berger's hand, thanked her warmly, and unlocked the door to Zuzubee's apartment. Martin performed a sort of Dance of the Vampires with the curious neighbor, because the undead rum cake was determined to come inside as well, which Martin tried to prevent with equal determination. I would not have wanted to bet on how this would play out, but amazingly Martin won. He pressed his back against Birgit to push her into the apartment, and Mrs. Berger stayed outside. She wore her failure with very little composure, stomped her foot, and walked off—presumably to indulge in a small glass of liqueur.

Martin and Birgit were now standing hand in hand inside Zuzubee's apartment, kind of like Hänsel and Gretel, staring at the painted outline on the wood floor where the body had been found. Martin cleared his throat.

"What are we looking for?" he whispered.

"The story she was working on," Birgit whispered.

If you're now wondering why the two of them are whispering, well, you try sneaking into a stranger's apartment. It's a weird feeling. I've gotten used to it because I am constantly passing through other people's apartments to hang out with folks watching the boob tube or to spy on their banking data. But for earthly beings it's weirder because they can actually get caught. Fine, these two can't get caught—at least, not by the neighbor lady who just handed them the key—but the apartment of a murder victim is an order of magnitude spookier than a normal apartment.

"OK, get busy."

They split up. They searched every drawer, every cabinet, every cupboard. Martin looked in every tea, sugar, salt, and other canister in the kitchen. He even looked inside the pepper mill, but he found only peppercorns there. Birgit was rummaging through the living-room cabinets. I was already familiar with the apartment and had checked all of the obvious hiding spots, but naturally I couldn't have touched, emptied, or otherwise handled anything. There needed to be a hiding spot in the apartment that divulged its secret only on second glance.

I used to keep my money in socks. So I suggested that Martin check Zuzubee's socks. Nada. Stuffed between pillowy layers of a push-up bra? Nada. Inside the heel of a shoe? Nada.

USB sticks could fit practically anywhere; that was the problem.

The millimeter-by-millimeter search was boring me to death, so I considered asking Martin to turn on a movie for me. Most of the DVDs in Zuzubee's collection were out of the question. Romantic comedies, family dramas, and Hobbit movies. There are few things that I hate more than Hobbit movies. But maybe the short, fat Zuzubee felt some kind of connection with the short, fat Hobbits.

Even so, she did have a few TV classics that were acceptable. The first season of *Alf. Magnum, P.I.*, *MacGyver*, *Miami Vice*, and—yes!— rarely does one Duke come by himself. How is it that that series was in a collection owned by a chick? Who otherwise preferred schlocky chick flicks? I whooshed over to Martin to ask him to put the DVD in. He was hugging Birgit tightly in the kitchen. "Tightly" being a relative concept due to the bowling-ball belly.

"Hey, Martin! Could you put a DVD in for me? This woman has perfect taste in old TV series. Lots of crap, of course, but there's one winner!"

Martin tried to drive me out of his brain, but he was unsuccessful. In a potentially dangerous environment he always leaves a gap open so I can warn him, if needed. Yeah, I guess I'm good for *something*. By the way, before you ask: no idea what would be so dangerous here.

Martin punished me with a brainwave of contempt.

"Martin! I haven't seen *The Dukes of Hazzard* in ages! It's totally cool. It's got rockin' cars, a totally hot brunette, and—"

"Are you able to think of anything other than cars and sex?" Martin asked, irritated.

"Hey, I'm the one who's been fighting practically nonstop this whole time to get Gregor out of jail!"

Martin sighed but walked into the living room with me like a good boy. He traced along the DVD collection on the shelf with his finger to find the box set I meant.

"Keep going, keep go—" I started to direct but cut myself off.

"What is it?" Martin asked.

"Wait. Go back!" I yelled. Martin's pudgy finger slid backward obediently. And there it was again, the DVD that reminded me of this ancient and—even then—superlame joke that my buddies told each and every time the slimy guys in pastel suits started a nighttime race through the drug-ridden metropolis of Miami. "What do you call a pink strap-on in the morning?" one would ask, and another would say, "A dawn johnson."

Like I said, har-dee-har-har. We used to watch that show just because of the cars. Admittedly, we also watched it for the hot women, but definitely not for the cool dudes. Men in pastel suits aren't cool, but at least they could still draw their guns just as well. The reason why I stopped short now in front of the DVD had nothing to do with the quality of the old joke but with the element of surprise in it: hearing "pink strap-on" you expect something totally different than what you get.

"*Miami Vice*, Martin! See what's in it!" Martin grabbed the DVD case and opened it. A DVD was inside, but—surprise!— it was an unmarked rewritable data DVD, and I was pretty sure that we wouldn't be seeing any cops in toddler-blue polo shirts and beach sandals when we slid it into Martin's laptop.

TWENTY

The three of us were sitting in front of Martin's computer back at their apartment. The air was thick between Martin and Birgit because Martin wouldn't explain why he had suddenly released Birgit from his hug in Zuzubee's kitchen to march single-mindedly into the living room and then pick up the *Miami Vice* DVD, specifically, from the shelf. Plus, Birgit now understood that Martin seemed to know the sender of the secret text messages she had been getting, but he wasn't giving her any clear answers on that topic either. At this point, Birgit's almost endless patience had finally been stretched to its limit.

Martin sat unhappily in front of the computer because he couldn't decide how much he wanted to tell Birgit about me. She knew only that he was some kind of medium or something and was occasionally sought out by the ghosts of the dead. She didn't know anything about me. Martin wanted things to stay that way; I wanted the opposite. But Birgit just wanted to know what Martin was keeping secret from her.

So this created a bad vibe in the apartment, which was pissing me off because Martin was focusing his lugholes, his peepers, and ninety-five percent of his goose brain on this interpersonal relationship problem. Birgit, by contrast, had glued her eyes to the screen.

Zuzubee's records were comprehensive. There was a file labeled "DEATHS," a file labeled "PHARM," and a file named "NOTES." Martin opened the deaths file. Twelve names were listed, each with birth date and death date. It wasn't explicitly stated, but I assumed these were deaths that occurred at the Sonnenschein senior sanctuary. All of the dates of death were between early April and late May. True, I had no idea what a normal attrition rate looked like at a zombie depot like that, but if you annualized that two-month rate, you could project sixty deaths a year. In other words, almost a third of the residents went out feet first. To me that seemed way too many. Martin and Birgit had also come to that conclusion, because they kept glancing at each other with furrowed brows.

Martin opened the next file. Aha, pharmaceuticals—and the information Zuzubee had pinched from the pharmacy. This list had about forty or fifty names on it, including the names that were on the death list, and the prescription drugs for each patient.

The third file of notes confirmed my interpretation of the first two lists. Zuzubee wildly speculated about everything from Paulina Pleve as an "angel of death" who released the most care-dependent residents from their suffering to turnover planned by the home's management as a way to accommodate a waiting list. Even Till Krämpel, the pharmacist, had fallen under her scrutiny. She theorized he was embezzling expensive pharmaceuticals to sell the pills on the black market. The price of some of the drugs would have been a thoroughly attractive motive.

But unfortunately Martin and Birgit couldn't agree on what angle she was going for with her illegally acquired flow of data.

"We'll inform Jenny," Martin said. "She's investigating Paulina Pleve's murder, so she should have this data."

"Not a good idea," Birgit replied in an unusually snippy tone. "Jenny will have to explain to her boss where she got the data. Then her boss will inform the police in Düsseldorf, and they will come breathing down Jenny's neck. And all of that would happen even though we have no idea whether there really was anything to Susanne's suspicions."

Birgit was unappeasable, which is quite unlike her, and Martin didn't want to antagonize her any more by acting against her expressly stated opinion, so the debate ended without a resolution. Terrific. So now we had first-class stolen data and couldn't do anything sensible with it because the thieves were arguing like two snotty-nosed brats over a lollipop. I could have puked.

"Martin, why don't you drive over to the home and talk with Mr. Hauschild," I suggested. "Maybe he'll remember some name or other from the list."

Birgit switched to stubborn mode, so Martin left without her. I did a quick check in on her five minutes after Martin drove off and found her sitting at the table, mulling over the piece of paper that Karpi had given her. Yuri's name, address, or phone number—or whatever Karpi's sequence of numbers had encrypted—was waiting for its solution. I had to admit Birgit had fooled us all. She hadn't been nearly as angry as she pretended, but her campy performance had induced Martin to let her out of his paranoid surveillance for a few hours. Now she had her head free to solve her puzzle. With a big grin I wished Birgit good luck and flew off.

Hans Hauschild was in the café eating chocolate cake. His coffee cup contained the deepest-black muddy mush I could imagine, presumably a mixture of coffee and cake. Most of the other tables were occupied as well, but today it was primarily residents and their personal visitors—no schoolkids.

"May I join you?" Martin asked.

"Are you a witness?" Hauschild replied.

"I'm a friend of Gregor's," Martin said.

"Gregor! Yes, he's a good boy. And clever. He'll make detective sergeant someday."

Martin gulped.

"Would you like some coffee? Tea? Cake?" The platinum blonde appeared tableside.

"A chamomile tea, please."

She didn't even flinch and went into the kitchen to get him some. Presumably chamomile is prescribed by the bucketful here.

"Did you know Paulina well?" Martin asked.

"The doctor," Hauschild said.

"No, she was a nurse here."

"Good doctor," Hauschild said. "I could see it in her eyes."

The platinum blonde brought the tea. "You've gotten your cake in your coffee, Mr. Hauschild. Wait and I'll bring you a new cup."

"It wasn't sweet enough," Hauschild said.

"I'll bring you a coffee with sugar."

"Did you know Gregor was here about Paulina?" Martin asked.

"Good boy, that Gregor."

"Did your daughter like Paulina?"

Hauschild suddenly stared at Martin with narrowed eyes. "You knew my daughter?"

Martin shook his head. "Unfortunately, no."

"She's dead, isn't she?"

The platinum blonde set a cup in front of Hauschild and stayed next to the table.

"Yes, unfortunately. And your daughter's death may have something to do with Paulina's death," Martin said.

"Yes," Hauschild said. "I think so too. Paulina was a good doctor, but a bad person."

Then he dumped another piece of cake into his coffee cup.

"His lucid moments are usually brief," the platinum blonde whispered. "He used to be a cop, right?"

Martin nodded.

"Pity. I had so hoped he might be able to help you."

I accompanied Martin home, but Birgit was asleep already when he got in. Unfortunately she hadn't left the solution to her puzzle paper out on the nightstand. Maybe she hadn't cracked the code yet. I softly wished her a good night, although I could have yelled for as much as she could hear me.

July 5, eight days after Gregor's arrest

Martin had headed into work early, and Birgit turned on her cell phone. Martin kept asking her not to use the thing to avoid unnecessarily toasting the unborn child, and Birgit mostly ignored him. But she no longer wore it in a pocket, and she didn't play around with it unnecessarily. Right now, in any case, she sent me a text message.

Who are you?

Pascha, friend, strictly secret.

Bullshit. I want to see you.

You can't.

Then call me.

Can't either.

Why?

I stared at my screen. Why was I showing so much consideration to Martin all the time, actually? I could spill the whole truth right here and now to Birgit.

But the fact was: I was scared. What if Martin was right and Birgit would feel freaked out by my continual presence? What if Birgit sent me away and made sure I wasn't welcome? What if Birgit hated me? Maybe it was better to stay on the down-low. Martin wanted to keep me under wraps, and lately I was tending to think he was right.

Complicated, I replied.

Why does everyone think I'm stupid??? she wrote.

Shit. This was going in totally the wrong direction now. I should be letting Martin lead this conversation. Or at least I would have preferred not to be the instigator of it.

I flashed downstairs to Birgit and saw her flip off her phone and set it down. Then she took the puzzle from the nightstand drawer, made herself a latte, and sat down at the computer. She typed the numbers into the search engine but didn't come up with any relevant results. She typed various area codes in front of it and looked in online phonebooks, but those didn't turn up anything either. Then she converted the numbers into letters following a pattern that wasn't clear to me. Again, nada. She didn't give up, but I couldn't stand watching this process for an extended period of time, so I said bye. I'd catch wind of it soon enough once Birgit landed a hit. I wasn't so sure if she'd send her text buddy Pascha a message about it, though.

I looked in on Jenny to see about the status of the Paulina Pleve investigation. Honestly, I had lost a bit of perspective. The case had been closed but then reopened after Jenny and Birgit uncovered the possible deception of the door locked from the inside. And now?

Jenny was sitting at her desk with the Pleve case file open in front of her. She had spread out all of the documentation, notes, and phones and was staring at them when her boss came in.

"Detective Gerstenmüller, what are you working on right now?"

"Paulina Pleve. The suicide that may not have been a suicide."

"Oh, right. You activated that file again. News?"

Jenny shook her head. "CSI confirms that it would have been possible to lock the door from the outside so that the key was in the lock on the inside, but that's far from proof that that's what happened."

"Good. Because I have another case—"

"Maybe you could assign Detective Offermann to the case with me, and then we take it from the top and—"

"I just put Offermann and Becker on a gang killing," the boss interrupted. "And for you I've got an urgent case. We have a traffic accident with a dead teenager." He handed Jenny a piece of paper. "The girl had her school ID on her, but we need the identification—"

Jenny turned pale but nodded.

"Do you want to bring someone from the counseling unit?"

"No."

Duh. Because otherwise the whole force would find out that Detective Gerstenmüller was bawling with the parents when she informed them their teenage daughter died. So far, only Gregor and I knew about her secret, and he wasn't telling.

"Good."

I zoomed back to Birgit, but she hadn't found the solution yet. She was still nursing her coffee and playing brain games. She had done cross totals and digit sums, changed the order of the numbers, and looked pretty spent. I decided to give her a break and sent her a text message: *The platinum blonde girl at the home may know more than it seems.*

Maybe Birgit could find out who that young thing really was and what she knew about the strange happenings that had drawn Zuzubee in. After all, the platinum blonde had been spying on her.

Birgit read my message, tossed the phone onto the sofa, kept puzzling a bit, picked the phone back up, gave the phone the finger, finally sighed with irritation, and put away the secret sequence of digits. Then she stocked up supplies for the drive over and got on her way.

I don't know how I could tell, because everything *looked* the same as always. The lobby and the café were full of people, the platinum blonde was serving coffee and tea throughout the area, and even out in the park there were wheelchair acrobats and benchwarmers out and about. But everywhere there was a sort of tension that I couldn't explain.

Birgit arrived and sat down in the café, ordering a coffee and two slices of cake and asking the platinum blonde to sit with her. She hesitated.

"I'm not going to do anything to you," Birgit said. "I'd just like to chat with you a little."

The platinum blonde sat down.

"You notice a lot of things here in the building, don't you?" Birgit asked with her mouth full.

Cautious nodding.

"The police suspect my friend Gregor of killing Mr. Hauschild's daughter."

The platinum blonde's eyes and mouth opened wide.

"But he didn't. He had been married to Susanne Hauschild years ago. They ran into each other here at the home because Gregor was investigating Paulina Pleve's death. Did you know her?"

"By sight."

Birgit nodded. "At first the investigators thought Ms. Pleve had killed herself, but now there's evidence it may have been a murder."

The platinum blonde pursed her lips.

"In any case, Gregor and Susanne coincidentally ran into each other here, but Susanne seemed to be really happy about running into him because she had discovered something she wanted to talk over with Gregor. Do you have any idea what that was?"

The platinum blonde looked at the floor, down the hallway, at the table, studied her tightly closed hands with great interest, and gulped a few times. Then she looked up and asked, "Do you think that what Ms. Hauschild discovered had to do with the home?"

A classic question to stall for time and land some information before giving up some information yourself. The platinum blonde was a skillful tactician.

Birgit took a sip of coffee. "No idea. Maybe, but not necessarily. We know that Ms. Hauschild was working on some leads in another case."

"Leads in another case?"

"She was a reporter."

"Oh."

The platinum blonde chewed the nail on her right thumb until Birgit set her hand on her arm to stop her. "So, you do have an idea, right?"

She shook her head. "I have no idea what Ms. Hauschild wanted from your friend. I also don't know if the case has to do with—"

"What case?" Birgit asked.

The platinum blonde looked around like she was afraid someone was eavesdropping. "Well, when Paulina died, it upset everything around here, and then Ms. Hauschild was murdered, and now Dr. Krämpel has disappeared without a trace."

TWENTY-ONE

Birgit called Jenny as soon as she was back in her car.

"Have you already heard that the in-house pharmacist at the home has disappeared?"

"So what? I don't work for missing persons."

Birgit rolled her eyes but continued in a friendly tone. "Of course, Jenny. But isn't it strange that, at the same retirement home, first a nurse is murdered . . ."

"Which hasn't been proved. After seventy years, the glazier's putty on an old attic door can just get brittle."

"And then after the nurse, a resident's daughter—who was a reporter apparently on a hot story—is murdered, and then the man who was responsible for distributing pharmaceuticals disappears. It's all a coincidence?"

Jenny sighed. "I'll look into it as soon as I can."

I didn't trust Jenny, so I zoomed over to police HQ to see if she kept her promise. The wording "as soon as I can" was pretty vague; it might mean in two or three weeks, actually, because Jenny-Bunny had a lot going on.

My suspicion wasn't wrong, and when I got there Jenny was just picking her bag up from her chair and walking out of the office.

I followed her and was amazed when she drove her car to the visitor lot outside Weiz Pharma AG. She checked in at reception and asked to talk to Mr. Bastian Weiz personally. After repeatedly making mention of her official position as a detective with Criminal Investigations at the Cologne Police Department, she was directed to the desk upstairs and outside the CEO's office. The dragon whose job it was to protect her boss from the evil outside world could also have done well as a model. She had Jenny show her badge and ID and offered her something to drink. Jenny declined.

"The only thing I'd like is to see Mr. Weiz and nothing else, thank you."

Jenny had to wait another five minutes until the door finally opened and the bore in the blue suit asked her into his office. Jenny sat down in front of his desk and took a deep breath.

"Mr. Weiz, I'm terribly sorry to have to tell you this, but we think your daughter was killed today in a traffic accident. We will need a DNA sample to make the official identification."

Weiz turned white in a flash, faster than I thought it possible for a living person to do.

"Dead? But . . ."

"Have a drink of water," Jenny said, pointing at the glass on his desk.

Weiz drank like he was on autopilot.

"A-a t-traffic accident you say?" he stammered. "B-but how . . . wh-where?"

"Please, Mr. Weiz. I need a sample of your daughter's DNA—perhaps from her hairbrush—to identify her. Could we drive you home now together to get it?"

"No."

Jenny froze. "No?"

"I'll identify my daughter myself."

"That's not how it's normally done," Jenny nervously said, blinking away a few tears. She was presumably afraid of breaking down bawling together with Daddy here once they were down in the basement at Forensic Medicine. "Today we always identify someone using DNA—"

"I want to see her."

Jenny took another breath, but Weiz was already standing.

"What are you waiting for?"

Jenny had no reply for the pharmaceutical CEO. No natural authority, no official authority, and no other such weapon. She was apparently already focusing all her power on not turning into a blubbering mess. So she let Weiz lead her out of the office and to the elevator, softly mumbling, "Mr. Weiz, this approach is . . ."

Whatever this approach was, Weiz wasn't one damn bit interested, and Jenny apparently wasn't either because she didn't provide any active resistance after that. On the contrary. Jenny drove ahead, and Weiz followed her in his car to the Institute for Forensic Medicine. Katrin was on duty, and Jenny had warned her by phone first, which is why she was already waiting for them at the front door.

"Hello, Mr. Weiz. This way, please."

Katrin conducted herself professionally but not cold-bloodedly, leading Weiz to the room where family members can see the deceased one more time. Jenny tailed him like a sad dog.

At the door, Katrin turned to Weiz again. "You still have time to think about doing this, Mr. Weiz. Normally we make identifications with DNA samples. It provides just as certain a result, and it's easier for family members."

Weiz shook his head absentmindedly.

Katrin shrugged and opened the door.

The body-viewing room was in the basement of the Institute for Forensic Medicine. It's actually uncommon now for German family members to come in person, what with DNA identification and all that; Germans prefer to see their dead loved ones only *after* the mortician has cleaned, clad, and made them up. But whenever the toe tags had names on them like Vladimir, Yıldıray, or Kemal, the remains had to be sealed up inside special human-remains cargo containers and shipped out by train or plane so they could be buried in their respective homelands. And the thing is, after a few thousand kilometers as freight, no mortician can work enough wonders to make an open-casket funeral a good idea. *Those* are the families who rush in to see their dead in the body-viewing room. So it was odd that Weiz wanted to be here.

The girl was laid out in the dimly lit room. Weiz stepped next to the body and stared. Then he put a hand over his mouth and made a gurgling noise. Katrin watched him closely, but he didn't puke. He just stood there like a plaster figure, staring at the girl. Her dark-dyed hair mercifully covered the slice across the head that Katrin had made to saw into the skull and take the brain out of its case.

The girl's white skin was almost translucent, as much because of the unnatural hair color as anything. I recalled an old book of fairy tales where Snow White had looked this way lying in her coffin—obviously though without the diamond pimple a.k.a. nose ring, or the roughly sewn seam under her chin.

"Mr. Weiz?" Jenny whispered, pale and trembling, about to burst out in tears.

Weiz didn't stir.

"Mr. Weiz, is this your daughter Lila?" Katrin asked, although that wasn't her job.

It took a few more seconds for Weiz to move. He took his hand from his mouth, straightened up, turned around, and looked past Katrin and Jenny. "Yes," he whispered. "That is my daughter."

Martin had worked through his lunch break so he could leave work early that night. And since there were no late or urgent cases, his plan actually worked. And now he was sitting in his trash-can car, going through Zuzubee's records one more time. He knew one of the family doctors who turned up in the documents. He called the office of Dr. Andreas Steinhauer and made it clear to the secretary that he urgently needed to speak with the doctor. The chick promised the doctor would call him back—and he actually did within just a few minutes. Martin reminded him that they had gone to college together, and they agreed to meet at a quarter to six. Since the doctor's office was on the other end of town and Martin could barely match walking speed in his trash can on wheels, he got going right away.

"Still with the chamomile tea?" the red-haired roly-poly doctor asked as he plopped down next to Martin on a bench in the café. Each bench was made of butt-contoured wood with clothes and hat racks overhead, like in an old train compartment. Black-and-white photos of steam locomotives decorated the walls. Nice, if you were a fan of vintage trains. I've never considered myself a ferrosexual, and I'd prefer a high-end RECARO bucket seat over a wooden bench, but it's not like I needed to torture my ass on any kind of seat anymore.

Martin gave an embarrassed smile.

"To what do I owe the honor?" the doctor asked. "I apologize for coming right to the point, but I've got another appointment right after this."

"Thank you for meeting me on such short notice," Martin began.

"Your gentleman's courtesy blather isn't getting us any-where," I impatiently interjected.

"I've got a technical question that sooner falls under your area of expertise than mine," Martin continued.

"What is your area now?" the doctor asked.

"Forensic medicine."

The roly-poly flashed Martin a smirk. "You were always an odd fellow, Martin."

Martin smiled as though that were a compliment.

"Here in town there's a retirement home that has recently seen a fair number of deaths."

Martin recited the information that we knew from Zuzubee's file but in a medical specialist's jargon. The roly-poly listened with so much focus that he didn't even look up when his cappuccino was served. He moved again only once Martin slid a stack of pages from a computer printer in front of him. Martin had sorted the available information by medical criteria on the first few pages, but those were followed by copies from the home.

"You've got the prescription lists?" Steinhauer asked with eyebrows raised. "Is this an official investigation?"

Martin shook his head.

Steinhauer dropped the papers back onto the table as though they had burned him. Obviously I couldn't read his thoughts, but I was pretty sure that the terms "doctor-patient confidentiality" and "criminal prosecution" were flashing through them promi-nently. He crossed his arms in front of him and closed his eyes.

"O ... K ..." he finally said slowly. "I'm going to assume that these are templates. Example documentation. A sort of continuing education. A hypothetical situation that you are studying for educational purposes."

Martin took a breath and was about to correct his friend until I roared "YES!" into his ear.

Martin winced and reflexively gasped for breath but then, like a good boy, finally said, "Yes." Whew. That was close.

"OK, then. Let's have a look."

Steinhauer studied the pages for a long while, and then he took a few sips from his cappuccino, and closed his eyes again. Evidently this guy could think only with his headlights off.

"Now, if I were to comment on this interdisciplinary educational exercise, then I would say that something here in fact does not look kosher. These patients were, judging from these sample documents, not so sick that their sudden death would be expected. And in the case of these two"—he tapped his finger on two names—"I would state that with some certainty since they were my patients." He paused deliberately. "Purely hypothetically, of course."

Martin drank the rest of his chamomile tea lost in thought.

"What do you suspect? An angel of death?"

"Is it that obvious?" Martin asked.

"It's entirely plausible," the roly-poly replied, glancing at the clock. "Another scenario might occur to me after I've had some time to mull it over. Can I take these papers with me?"

Martin nodded. "Please do. However ..."

"Confidential." He smiled awkwardly. "Got it."

July 6, nine days after Gregor's arrest

On Tuesday morning, Martin had to testify in court, and Birgit slept in until almost ten thirty. I was worried about her, but when she finally got up, she sang loudly in the shower and looked all in the pink, despite her ghastly warbling—because if there's one thing that even the awesome Birgit can't do, it's sing. I exhaled with relief. Soon after she was sitting in front of a huge bowl of fruit salad, still staring at the piece of paper with the numbers Karpi had given her. She'd turned on the radio and was tapping to the beat with her foot. Inane, droning blah la la crap. But at least she wasn't listening to schlocky German hit mix or magic violin.

Despite the noise from the radio, Birgit was brooding over the number puzzle. Like a good Doberman pinscher, she refused to give up—but she stuck to her guns with style, not all doggedly. I was damned proud of my Birgit. She was going to solve the puzzle. The only question was when.

Much as I wished it was my own electromagnetic vibrations that had turbocharged her brain, it was actually the radio waves that led to her breakthrough. In the form of an ad whose stupidity was beyond my ability to exaggerate.

The company in the ad sounded like the name of a robot in a space opera: O2, which is apparently a cell phone company or something. But the sound of "oh-two" got Birgit to thinking, because the first two digits in her number puzzle were 0 and 2. At her moment of realization, Birgit froze—her foot stopped tapping, her jaws stopped crushing fruit salad, and her hand holding the spoon stopped halfway between the bowl and her mouth. She stared at the paper, dropped her spoon in the bowl, heaved herself over to the computer, looked up the area codes assigned to that company, and then dialed the numbers off of Karpi's sheet of paper preceded by one of those area codes. Wrong number. Birgit apologized and tried the next area code.

"Have you finally solved my puzzle?" Karpi asked after the second ring.

"How did you know it was me?" Birgit asked.

"Do you want your prize now or not?"

He said he'd give her the information she wanted in person only, and then he hung up. Birgit glanced with yearning at her fruit salad but grabbed two bananas and her car keys and headed out.

TWENTY-TWO

While I was following Birgit, Martin radioed me. Since Birgit had to drive across town to Karpi, I had at least a half hour free, so I followed the call of my lord and master. OK, that bit about lord and master was a joke. But I was curious what he wanted from me, because usually Martin prefers to have me as far away as possible. When he actually calls me, it has to be something important.

I was surprised the summons was coming from the Belgian Quarter, and I was even more surprised that Martin was at Die Werkstatt. Ioánnis and Martin were sitting next to each other at the bar staring at the bottles filling the shelves up the back wall. In front of Martin was a cup of tea, whose color suggested chamomile. The Greek was drinking red wine.

"Susanne Hauschild's car is here. Ioánnis was supposed to change the tailpipe. We can take a look at the vehicle," Martin shared with me mentally.

I was speechless for a long while. Martin, my little goose, had found a potentially important piece in the puzzle that was our case—independently and at his own initiative.

"A reporter without a car is hard to imagine, right?" Martin explained to me. "And if she has a Saturday mechanic for a boy-friend, then he would likely know where her car is."

"How did you and he get to be such good friends that he's serving up the car to you instead of to the cops?" I asked.

"Ioánnis isn't merely a motorcycle aficionado; he's also a Citroën 2CV enthusiast," Martin said. He could not contain a certain malice in his voice.

"At least the trash-can jalopy has finally been good for something," I growled graciously.

The three of us went out to the garage where the parts flea market had been held. That garage was closed up tight, but Ioánnis walked mindfully toward another garage next to it. He flung it open, and there it was—the 1973 Volkswagen Beetle, Type 15, belonging to Susanne Hauschild. The Greek unlocked the Bug, came back out of the garage, and waved Martin inside. "Haven't you looked inside it yet?" Martin asked.

Ioánnis shook his head. "What for? She's dead."

Martin put his hand on the shoulder of the giant with the hair-growth problem. Ioánnis turned around and hugged Martin tight. Then he began to sob.

I was torn between laughing hysterically and bawling with him, because I felt sorry for the Wild Man. Maybe he really had loved Zuzubee. On the other hand, it just looked super embarrassing, a giant bawling on Martin's shoulder, which he had to bend way, way down to even reach. I quickly turned away and took a quick fly-through of the Beetle. Kleenex with wiped-off lipstick in the driver's footwell, a hairbrush and scrunchie on the passenger seat. As far as I could tell in the half-light of the glove compartment, there were a couple of street maps, an ice scraper, and an eyeglass case whose contents I didn't check. It's cramped and hauntingly dark inside a closed eyeglass case inside a closed glove compartment.

Martin finally liberated himself from the Greek's grip and helped me by raising floor mats and by opening the glove compartment, taking the sunglasses out of the case, and unfolding the maps. Unfortunately, no conspiratorial messages or references to the murder fell out. Hope briefly flared up in us when Martin discovered an envelope between the backseat and side panel, but it had just been some junk mail Zuzubee had used to write a shopping list on. Butter, sugar, flour, and baking powder. From the look of the envelope, the list might be several months old.

Martin wanted to go to the back of the vehicle and open the trunk, but I warned him he was heading in the wrong direction. A guy who didn't know the trunk of a Beetle is in the front of the car actually doesn't have any reason to exist, does he? I've been saying that the whole time.

The trunk was empty except for a blanket, some granola bars, and a first-aid kit. Martin was about to drop the hood when I remembered where we had found the data from the old folks' home in Zuzubee's apartment.

"Look in the first-aid kit."

Martin hesitated, understood my mental reference to the *Miami Vice* DVD, and opened the box. It contained the usual stuff like bandages and iodine, but there was also a prehistoric disposable camera and some sheets of printer paper stapled together and folded in half.

Martin took the papers out and held the box under his arm as he unfolded them. On the cover sheet, there was a drawing of a man in "recovery position," lying on his side with his arms and legs locked for stability and his mouth down. The usual drivel about first aid at the scene of an accident.

"No dice," I said, turning to Ioánnis. He had rediscovered self-composure. Good.

Birgit must have arrived at Karpi's by now, and I wanted to play fly on the wall over there.

"Martin," I called. "I'm—"

The rest of what I was going to stay got stuck in my throat. Martin was staring spellbound at the pages in his hands.

"What's so interesting?" I asked. "Given that you're a doctor, I'd think you'd be familiar with first aid."

Martin didn't react.

"Even though your patients don't usually need any first aid."

No laugh, but also no scolding that my jokes at the expense of his deceased clients aren't funny. No reaction at all is always a sign of total mental captivity.

I zoomed in and looked over his shoulder. It took me a while to figure out this was the floor plan of the bunker that was Karpi Diem. GF stood for ground floor, where the bouncy house was. BT stood for basement, where Martin, Birgit and I got to know the elevator, hallway, and Karpi's office.

There were three connections between GF and BT. One was the elevator, the other two were stairwells that I hadn't noticed before. They led to a large underground area that we hadn't seen. It was gigantic—at least five hundred square meters, about the size of a professional basketball court.

Karpi was living pretty damned large.

Provided that was really where he lived.

Martin flipped the page, and there were individual photographs of people coming out of Karpi Diem's back door. Lots of the pictures had names, but not all did.

I recognized one guy, although I didn't know his name and it wasn't with his picture. His photograph had been on the shelf at

Mrs. Berger's; he was the one paying his grandma five euros not to tattle on him to his mother about his secret job. Apparently, that job involved working for Karpi, in the basement. What in the hell did that guy do there? Was Karpi's basement a meth lab?

In any case, Martin couldn't make any more sense of the papers than I could, but unlike me he began to tremble.

"I-I knew it—this man is dangerous," he stammered.

Uh-oh . . . good thing he didn't know Birgit was on her way to Karpi's basement right now.

"Birgit?" Martin screamed and instantly went to DEFCON 2.

Shit, I wasn't shielding my thoughts well enough. Martin raced to his trash can. Well, what he might call racing. A one-legged rabbit with a five-kilogram weight on its tail would have been faster, but he was doing his best. The Greek watched him, mouth agape.

TWENTY-THREE

"What exactly do you want from Yuri?"

Karpi was wearing pink today. A pink silk suit, a white shirt, and a red tie with polka dots on it. I was sure he was color blind—or that he had only black lights in the ceiling cans in his dressing room.

"Yuri was a friend of Paulina Pleve's. She was murdered, and I—"

"I thought she killed herself," Karpi mumbled. He spoke unclearly because he was nibbling on a fruit kebab of grapes, halved kiwis, strawberries, and slices of banana. The thing was about as long as a samurai sword.

"Give me Yuri's full name." Birgit's voice was firm and determined. "I don't need to remind you about our deal . . ."

Karpi nodded and said, "Gernot."

"Yuri Gernot?"

Karpi spit out a grape seed, along with a noise that sounded like "gilgh."

From Birgit's face, she must have found the sound as repulsive as I did.

"Gesundheit!" she said.

Karpi gurgled and then turned serious. "Jürgen."

"Jürgen Gernot?"

"Exactly."

"Do you know where he lives?"

Karpi uttered a street name with an oozing sound to it. The word was having trouble getting out around the piece of banana clogging up Karpi's throat.

"Thank you." Birgit hesitated. "Is there anything else I should know?"

Karpi stared at her with his mouth open, as though she had just told him she wanted to tie a string around his leg and fly him in the sky over Cologne like a hot-air balloon. It was not a pleasing sight due to the half-chewed banana in his yap trap.

"You're good, Blondie," he whispered. "Maybe you should be asking yourself why Yuri dumped his old flame even though he worshipped her."

"Asking myself?" Birgit replied. "I'd rather ask you."

Karpi giggled. "I don't know. I've only wondered about it."

One of the phones on Karpi's desk rang. He picked it up, grunted, and hung up again.

"Your pajama suit is standing outside the door and wants to save you."

Birgit turned red.

"Do you want to take the back exit?" Karpi asked.

Birgit at first looked grim but then she smiled. "No, thanks."

Karpi puckered his greasy face into something that might resemble a grin, shrugged, and raised his index finger as a gesture of good-bye as Birgit laboriously got to her feet. She left by the front door to pacify Martin until his pulse was normal again.

I didn't follow them because I was more interested in what Karpi was up to in his secret basement lair. Finding that out was a problem, of course, because the magnetic screen was gapless. I was going to have to wait for a door to open. That had to happen eventually, because otherwise people like Mrs. Berger's grandson couldn't come and go. So I paced slowly, pausing in front of the two steel doors until I remembered there were other access points that led directly from the ground floor to the basement. I looked for the stairwells I had seen in Zuzubee's diagram, which were both in recessed areas that also provided bathroom access.

What were the people up to down there? I had no idea, but I couldn't stomach hanging out anymore to find out, now that we finally knew Yuri's name and address.

I was about to bail when one of the steel doors opened. A pubescent pimpleface appeared in the doorway. He looked horrible. Greasy hair, glazed-over eyes with huge rings under them. I zoomed to the door but braked before slamming into his schmaltz head; I didn't want to accidentally skid inside that shielded room. Because if the door closed behind me, I'd be trapped.

Maybe I could risk a quick peek? The pimplehead shuffled on rubber soles over the threshold. I zoomed halfway down the stairs. A soft blue light shined up at me. A steady hum filled the air. I cautiously floated deeper. The light grew more and more intense, the humming louder and louder. Only a meter or so separated me from a clear view into the room.

But then a stream of air suddenly flowed over me, forcibly pulling me into the basement. *Help!* I had been discovered, sucked in, and presumably would be toasted with microwaves until I couldn't pose any danger . . . I panicked and paddled upstream, no longer worried about what I might have discovered below. Instead I focused solely on escape. Up the stairs, against the stream of air flowing through the narrow stairwell like a jet stream. The door came into sight, slowly closing behind the shuffler. I doubled effort in the air channel, because even if the jet stream was a simple physical effect and not a sneaky ghost trap, the situation was still dangerous for me.

At the last moment I made it back into the unshielded area of the nightclub. The pimplehead took the back exit from the ground floor, which led out behind a row of dumpsters into the alley. I still hadn't discovered Karpi's secret, but I didn't feel like waiting around for the door to open again. Yuri was more urgent now, anyway.

Martin and Birgit were struggling through the clogged streets, but I got to the address in less than two seconds. The building had almost a hundred units, and the buzzers at the street entrance didn't reveal which floor each apartment was on, so it took me a while to find Yuri. To be precise, for me to find the apartment that I *assumed* was Yuri's. I deduced this from the fact that Till Krämpel, the pill apportioner from the old folks' home, was lying tied up and gagged on the bed. No one else was there.

It was a studio apartment, with a kitchen the size of a closet and a tiny bathroom. Apart from the bed itself, the main room had a giant desk, an armchair, and a wardrobe. A flatscreen TV was hanging on the wall. No expensive furniture, and only the one boob tube, but everything was new. The bookshelves next to the desk were full of medical textbooks and reference books. One wall had a framed diploma on it, proving that Gernot had successfully completed his medical degree. The other walls were full of photos, just pinned to the wall. They were all of Paulina. Only one photo showed Paulina together with Yuri. It was a selfie with distorted perspective—Yuri's long arm stretched to the corner of the image, their noses too big, and their ears too far back. Typical smartphone picture, but it was annoying to me because

I wasn't sure if I would recognize the guy again on the street just from that shot.

I couldn't find any clues to where Yuri could be hiding.

Krämpel was gasping away; apparently his nose was stuffed up. So he was still alive. The only question was, for how much longer.

I decided to wait for Yuri, passing the time studying the titles of the books on the shelves. *Internal Medicine, Angiology, Cardiology, Naturopathic Medicine, The Pharmaceutical Lie, Emergency Medicine* . . . If this guy knew everything in these books, his next job could be professor. But if he did know it all, then he wouldn't have the books lined up on these shelves anymore. If I had to bet, I'd say Yuri had finished his medical degree and was now a resident somewhere.

I met Martin and Birgit at the front door of the building where Yuri lived. They were standing, also clueless, in front of the buzzer board. Some of the buzzers were labeled with the apartment number, some only with first names, and some weren't labeled at all.

"Yuri isn't here," I announced to Martin.

Martin's finger had been hovering along the buzzer board names, and then he dropped his hand to his side.

"But Dr. Krämpel is tied up and gagged in his apartment."

"Krämpel?" Martin asked in shock with a wince, as though he had misheard me. But I don't mumble when I communicate mentally.

"Yes, Krämpel. The pharmacist from the Sonnenschein Home."

Martin froze and stared at the buzzer board as though it were giving him the lotto numbers for next week. Birgit tugged on his sleeve.

"Hello? Earth to Martin!" Birgit said.

Martin's thoughts were swirling around the irksome issue: *What do I tell her?*

"Just tell her like it is," I suggested for the two hundred thousandth time.

"No."

Aha. His majesty doesn't know what he wants, but he *does* know what he doesn't want.

Martin cleared his throat and then turned to Birgit. "You told Jenny that Dr. Krämpel disappeared, isn't that right?"

Birgit furrowed her brow. "Why? What does that have to do with Yuri?"

"Ahem, well . . ."

"Coward," I moaned, but then I took off. Martin was going to have to come up with his own explanation as to how he knew that instead of Yuri, the tied-up Dr. Krämpel was currently in apartment No. 63.

Jenny wasn't at police HQ, so I looked for her at the Sonnenschein Home. If she were keeping her word, she would be looking into Krämpel's disappearance, and so it would be logical for her to stop by the home. And I had not been mistaken.

"Did he frequently miss work without calling in?"

Jenny was sitting in Dr. Wenger's office with her notepad on her right knee, which she had crossed over her left. As always, she reminded me of more of a university student than a police detective.

"No, never. Dr. Krämpel is exceedingly reliable."

"You'll recall that we asked you some questions in connection with Ms. Pleve's death about the management of medications." It didn't sound like a question or a statement, and Dr. Wenger just nodded, evidently unsure how the comment was meant.

"Do you think it's plausible that Dr. Krämpel, who of course had access to the drugs, was not, uh, dealing with them entirely properly?" Jenny asked.

Dr. Wenger at first looked annoyed and then the big light went on. "Do you mean to claim that he was stealing medications?" she asked in a tone that had dropped below room temperature by a few degrees.

"It would be a, uh . . ." Jenny mumbled. Then she cleared her throat and straightened her back. "It would be one plausible explanation. Dr. Krämpel embezzles medications, especially painkillers that cost a lot on the black market. Ms. Pleve noticed this deception and—"

"I can't possibly imagine that being the case," Wenger said piercingly. "Our residents would naturally have reported it if they weren't getting their medications."

"You have incapacitated residents here who receive continuous care, if I'm not mistaken," Jenny said. "Perhaps not everyone is able to articulate him- or herself accordingly."

"Ridiculous. Our staff would have noticed it, in any case."

Jenny gave a conciliatory nod. "It's just a scenario for the moment, one that conjectures a connection between the death of Ms. Pleve and the disappearance of Dr. Krämpel."

"Maybe there's no connection at all," Wenger said.

"Perhaps," Jenny replied. "We'll see."

I trundled along after Jenny, who crossed the lobby without checking in on the platinum blonde. But I looked in on her and found her standing frozen in the middle of the café. In her left hand she was holding a plate full of cake, in the right a cup of tea. She was staring at the TV, which was on a local Cologne station.

". . . could not be reached for comment."

Floating beside the curly-blonde Lorelei type, who was squinting slightly as she read her copy off the teleprompter, was a photo of the pharmaceutical company CEO and philanthropist, Bastian Weiz.

"After the previous death of his wife and murder of his brother-in-law, fate has struck a third time with the death of his daughter."

How were the news vultures breaking that story already? Weiz had been at the institute that morning to identify his daughter. Was someone there observing him? Or had the funeral home leaked it to the press? Or maybe Weiz himself . . .

And why did the platinum blonde drop the cup of tea, set the plate with cake down on the nearest table, and run out of the café and to the park?

Everywhere I turned, there lurked questions I didn't know the answers to.

I observed the platinum blonde for a little while longer, but I still couldn't figure out why the news about Weiz's daughter had thrown her. After talking with Dr. Wenger, Jenny had driven home. And no one was up in Yuri's apartment anymore. Neither Yuri, nor Krämpel. *Great!* Martin had screwed it up. If he'd just blurted out what he knew from me, Krämpel would be free by now and probably could have said a few words to help solve the case. But no. Martin's secretiveness about me was apparently way more important than saving the pharmacist.

I could sense trouble brewing between Martin and Birgit. Probably because of me as well.

"Of course," Martin said, scolding me when he noticed me and my suspicion. "I should never have accepted you moving in here with us."

Well, I *had* offered to stay out of his life forever back when that thing about the leased-out morgue drawers got out of hand. But after I'd saved several of the parties involved, Martin had gone soft.

"That was a mistake," he chided me.

"So, bye," I replied.

I left him in the uncertainty of whether my farewell applied just to tonight or to forever, but, really, we both knew perfectly well that I'd come back.

Tonight I was focused on finding out what Karpi was hiding in his basement. A workshop where he was mixing knockout drops? A meth lab? I could imagine tons of things a greasy-haired pubescent zit head could help out with. Or was he the lab rat? That was a possibility, of course. If you're synthesizing new drugs, you need test subjects. And then after the rats you need to test it on real people. Well, *I* was going to find out.

I found Karpi in his usual spot. Snoozing. While sitting in his chair. Maybe a fat slob like him can't sleep lying down anymore. Maybe he can't get up again by himself if he lies down. Or maybe he suffocates under his own weight. Or . . . no idea. I wondered if I should stay with him or post myself at one of the two bathrooms next to the secret doors. I decided on the latter.

It took two hours for someone to show up who wanted to go downstairs. It was the grandson of Mrs. Berger, Zuzubee's neighbor lady. He approached the secret door and waited maybe two seconds, the door cracked open, and he stepped through. He hadn't pressed any button, entered any code, or said anything. I didn't have time to check the Open-Sesame trick because I flew right behind him through the door. We climbed down the stairs into the basement toward the blue light and hum. This time I decided to go all the way in. And what I saw, I had not expected.

TWENTY-FOUR

At first glance the room looked like a mixture of youth center, a punk band's practice studio, and the laboratory of Professor Hubert J. Farnsworth. Half-baked guys were sitting, hanging, and lounging around on beanbags, at regular work desks, or in hammocks, all with computers. Lots of them had earbuds in; others were wearing the latest trend in giant cans over the ears. But almost all of them had beats pounding through their lugholes into their brains.

Surprisingly, laptops and tablets were in the minority; giant computers with or without cases were in the majority. Mrs. Berger's grandson tossed his cell phone into a bin, and walked through a full-body scanner like the type at the airport. He had to step back because it detected a flash drive in his pocket. He threw the drive in the bin, and then the scanner stopped beeping, and the guy was finally in. He plunked down in a beanbag in front of a giant monitor about the size of a twin bed hanging on the wall, then he grabbed a wireless keyboard and logged onto the computer, a half-meter-tall box on the floor below the monitor. The bastard started hacking away at the keyboard without looking right or left.

The surfaces of the desks were covered not with computers and monitors but packages of food high in calories and low in vitamins. Chips, hamburgers, pizzas, and similar crap. My mouth started watering.

This was not a cybergambling den. And there wasn't a single screen with someone taking a pop at something. No first-person shooters, no racing, no conquests of alien worlds. The screens were all filled with what looked like lists and lists of insurance company information or banking data or . . . Hey. Suddenly, I saw a little birdie pop up on the grandson's monitor. I recognized it from the news. An eagle. Not the whimsical logo of the day for an online search engine. No. A heraldic eagle displayed sable, armed, and beaked on a gold field—the coat of arms of Germany, in fact. The grandson had landed on the site of the German federal government. That wasn't unusual, because obviously our government has its own spots online where it verbosely and inaccurately conveys to the electorate how awesome it is. But that's not what was going on here. On the contrary. The system these guys were logged onto required one password, then another, and then a third. The grandson didn't enter the passwords, however, but instead at each level activated a search algorithm to circumvent electronic data protection. I could come up with only one possible interpretation for this digital den: I had found myself in a hacker club.

A grand moff was sitting at one table separate from the others, clicking through the screens the boys were working on. One key press and he would see what Number 7 was up to; the next click showed Number 8's monitor; and so on. Clearly, the guy was controlling what was going on in this joint. Everything down here was set up wirelessly, and that was undoubtedly the explanation for the electromagnetic shielding. Any normal user just secures his Wi-Fi with a password. But a hacker club like this knew that wasn't sufficient to keep uninvited guests out. So here they shielded what the equipment all contained. No one could get into their network.

I ambled back and forth a little. Number 3, if I wasn't mistaken, was logged into a banking system to check account balances and cash flow. Number 6 was retrieving data from a computer at the German Federal Office for the Protection of the Constitution, which is Germany's domestic security agency. And Number 8 was checking the registration information for various vehicles. Another hacker had infiltrated the computer systems at Germany's most important weapons manufacturer, and yet another had accessed the internal servers at several major corporations.

As I hovered over the hackers' heads, Number 2 logged off.

The grand moff checked how his work had gone, nodded with satisfaction, and counted out a couple of fifties from a fat wad of euro notes.

"See you tomorrow?" he asked.

Number 2 shook his head. "My little sister's birthday is tomorrow. But the day after."

They fist-bumped each other, and then Number 2 disappeared up the secret stairs I had come in through. I disappeared with him.

July 7, ten days after Gregor's arrest

When I got to the office, Jenny was already there. She had a cup of coffee in front of her and was staring—yet again—at the Paulina Pleve file open on her desk. She didn't even notice Offermann, who suddenly filled the doorway.

"Even when she's up so early, she looks good," Offermann soft-soaped.

Jenny looked up and blushed. "Hi. How'd you make out last night?"

Offermann walked in, sat down, and shrugged. "Some good luck, some bad. Guns and drugs in the house they were operating out of, but still no trace of the perp. In gang wars like this, everyone covers for each other. It's hell."

"Sorry."

"And how are things going with you?"

Jenny let out a soft sigh. "The in-house pharmacist at the retirement home where Paulina Pleve worked has disappeared."

Offermann frowned. "I thought the Pleve case was closed."

"Oh, right," Jenny said shaking her head. "You hadn't heard yet. We reopened it because there was evidence it could have been a murder after all. And now this Krämpel guy is gone. That naturally casts a fresh light on the matter."

Offermann listened intently, studying Jenny and demonstrating his mental engagement with little reactions. According to early-morning talk shows, active listening is important to a relationship. And Offermann was all about it. It straight-out looked like Jenny was important to him, even out of bed. "What's the latest trail?"

Jenny-Bunny shrugged. "Honestly, I don't have one. I was thinking . . ."

Her phone rang.

"It's rather unfair that the boss is putting you on the case all by yourself," Offermann said as he stood. "But I'd be glad to help you." He blew Jenny a kiss and vanished.

Jenny had a sizeable information deficit. She didn't know anything about Yuri yet, she didn't know that Krämpel had been bound and gagged in Yuri's apartment, or that now he *and* Yuri were missing, and she still didn't have access to Zuzubee's data. Martin was going to have to either put her on the right track or get his feet out of the quark, as we say in German. Otherwise at this rate Gregor was going spend Christmas in the clink. So I made my way to my wonderful team partner to exchange a few serious words with him.

The way he looked, I wasn't the only one who needed to have a serious word with Martin. Birgit was standing in front of him screaming at him, her face totally red.

"If you don't tell me where you get this information from, then I can't live with you anymore!"

Martin was pale as the kitchen wall he was leaning back on; evidently he no longer had the power to stand upright.

"How is it possible you know what was going on in Yuri's apartment when we hadn't even found the right buzzer yet?"

"I . . ."

"Who is speaking to you?"

The constant repetition of this same topic was getting on my nerves, but at least I could bail whenever things got too lame. Martin had to withstand the discussion again and again and again. Well, he's got only himself to blame.

"Martin, we need to start getting serious and get Gregor out of jail," I cheerfully piped in, just to increase his stress level another couple notches.

Martin moaned. Loudly.

"Oh? You don't have anything you want to say?" Birgit asked.

"I wasn't groaning at you," Martin whined.

"THEN. WHO. ELSE?" Birgit roared.

"Tell her!" I shouted.

"His name is Pascha!" Martin screamed.

Birgit and I were so shocked we instantly fell silent.

"Sorry?" Birgit asked softly.

Martin sank to the floor along the wall, put his head between his knees, and sobbed.

Birgit stared down at him, evidently not knowing whether to laugh or sob along. I was excited to see if he told her the truth, the whole truth, and nothing but the truth—and I held my breath.

"Please. Let's go into the details later," Martin whispered. "At the moment I'm out of strength. But I promise I'll tell you the whole story from the beginning, exhaustively. Just not now."

Birgit sat in front of Martin and took him into her arms.

"It's OK. I'm sorry I yelled at you like that," Birgit said.

Martin sniffled.

"When will you tell me?" Birgit asked.

"As soon as Gregor is out of jail," Martin said.

Birgit stroked him with her hand, and Martin cuddled into her. One more reason to get my favorite cop out of the clink as soon as possible.

I zoomed to Düsseldorf to check on the status of things and found myself yet again in the middle of a meeting. I wasn't surprised that these detectives hadn't found any sensible suspect given that they spent so much time blathering on about lame crap while sitting in a poorly ventilated room.

". . . is how I imagine it," Stein was just saying. "Katrin Zange had an argument with Kreidler before her vacation and suspected he would be meeting another woman during her trip. So on the day of the murder, she heads to Cologne, sees him with his ex, follows them, and kills Susanne Hauschild. Then she retrieves a coffee cup from Kreidler's apartment and leaves it in the victim's apartment."

Agent Orange shook her head. "What was the VIN plate fob doing in Hauschild's apartment? Where did the traces of DNA come from on Kreidler's jean jacket and under the victim's fingernails? And why did Zange bring a coffee cup into the apartment, but leave the jean jacket on her own coat stand?"

"The skin and fabric traces from Kreidler himself and his jacket got under the victim's skin when he body-checked her, obviously," Keller mumbled. "And he lost his VIN plate in her apartment on this or a previous occasion."

"Dr. Zange's odometer more than allows for a trip to Cologne, as we've known since yesterday," Stein added. "That is, if she correctly logs her business trips."

"And if the log she uses to keep track of kilometers driven for her job isn't correct?" Agent Orange interjected.

"Like yours?" Keller mumbled with a suggestive grin.

"The kilometers she's logged are plausible, especially when compared with her colleagues," the pretty-boy snot replied.

"So if everything is now pointing at Dr. Zange, why is Detective Kreidler still in jail?" Orange asked.

Stein grinned. "Because he confessed."

TWENTY-FIVE

Gregor confessed? Apparently it took only ten days in the joint for him to completely lose it. With Gregor's confession in the bag, there was little hope Criminal Investigations would get on the right trail. Either they believed Gregor's confession, or they believed Gregor was trying to protect Katrin. Apparently no one was giving any thought to Susanne and her laptop anymore. And on that point we had two leads to follow: the hacker den at Karpi's club that Zuzubee was tracking down right before she died and the strange cluster of deaths at the old folks' home. Because—and this idea occurred to me suddenly and unexpectedly—maybe the two deaths weren't even connected. Maybe Paulina had surprised Krämpel during one of his drug deals, and he killed her, and maybe Susanne had gotten wise to Karpi and fallen victim to that fat rabbit-food junkie. Pure coincidence that both deaths happened right around the same time and that Gregor had a connection to both.

I zoomed off to the institute to see Martin and Katrin. Normally there were positive vibrations in Katrin's office, but today—as in the past ten days—the air was thick enough to cut. Katrin the Volcano was spewing toxic clouds of sulfur, and Martin was fluctuating between a hysterical seizure and catatonic depression.

"Gregor confessed," I explained to him.

Martin froze, totally motionless. That meant he stopped dictating midsentence and stared at his screen with his mouth agape. It took a while for Katrin to notice something was wrong.

"Gregor confessed," Martin whispered, answering her question about what was up.

Katrin shrugged. "Good. Then those stupid cops will finally stop butting their noses into my affairs."

Martin and I don't really have much in common, but we were both shocked.

"Katrin, you don't really believe—" Martin began, but Katrin shook her head.

"The subject of Gregor Kreidler is dead to me. Please never mention his name again in my presence."

What were we supposed to think of that? The vacuum of our minds was interrupted by the ringing from Martin's phone. He mechanically picked up.

"Hey, I've got news about your list of prescriptions."

Aha, Dr. Steinhauer.

"Shall we meet in about half an hour?"

Martin suggested a small Vietnamese restaurant where he enjoyed the fodder—I wouldn't even torture a pet rabbit with it—and got going. The roly-poly good doctor was already there, drinking a beer.

"I do know some of the patients, as I already told you. I looked at their medical records and compared those with other cases from my practice."

"I see."

A tiny Asian woman came to the table, took Martin's order of jasmine tea and some dish that other people would use as organic fertilizer, and scurried through the bead curtain into the kitchen.

"Naturally I can't say what happened with the patients or with the medication at the home. However, I did notice something that doesn't have much to do with the home."

Don't torture us anymore, Jabba, I thought, for which I earned a rebuke from Martin. He can listen to professional prattle until it puts him in a coma, regardless of whether the storyteller ever gets to the point.

"Any detail could be important," Martin admonished me.

"Yes, then, get him to hand over some details!" I suggested.

"You're familiar with the situation in the German health-care system?" Doc Andy asked.

Martin stopped short. "Uh, not as an insider," he said. "I work more on the law enforcement side than with the health-care system."

"Of course," the doc said, sipping his beer. "So, with a universal health-care system like ours that has both public and employer-provided insurance, what people have really focused on for years is limiting costs. It hasn't been about the health of our patients for a long time—I'm sure employers would love to abolish pesky services like treating the sick or curing them if only they could just to save some money."

He finished his beer and nodded at the bartender in back to order his next one.

"The government keeps cutting doctors' fees, but it's not like a doctor can switch to a better-paying job after ten or twelve years of medical school, residency fellowships. You see what I mean?"

Martin nodded unhappily. He hated tirades of this kind, but he couldn't exactly interrupt Bones here, since he needed something from him. So he kept listening, sipping on his jasmine tea the whole while. Caffeine-free, cholesterol-free, sugar-free, gluten-free, alcohol-free, allergen-free.

"The insurance companies would love it if they could save money the same way on pharmaceuticals, but the drug lobby is damned powerful in Berlin. So, instead of explicitly peeing on the legs of the large brand-name manufacturers, some insurance companies have come up with a new strategy to save money. Doctors are allowed to prescribe only the specific active ingredient itself and not a brand-name medication, and pharmacists are required to dispense the cheapest formulation of that active ingredient available, often a generic."

Martin nodded.

"Most of the patients whose prescription orders you showed me were suffering from the usual ailments of old age. High blood pressure, cardiovascular disease, diabetes. Many of them had other conditions, but the lowest common denominator is that set of three common ailments."

Martin sipped his tea but looked up with interest over the edge of his cup. He nodded like an excited dachshund.

"All of the patients on your list were given prescriptions for the active ingredients to treat those three ailments, and they must have taken the inexpensive versions of those medications that are typically dispensed for those ailments. But again, the prescriptions specify only the active ingredient itself and not the brand name. I wrote this all out for you."

The doc reached into his jacket pocket, pulled out a sheet of paper, and set it in front of Martin on the table. Then he downed his second beer.

Martin picked up the sheet of paper and read the three names.

"Thank you very much," he said softly.

The information he had just heard just kept swirling around in his brain, unable to find a proper hook to hang itself on.

"What could this mean?" Martin asked after his friend ordered a third beer. Apparently the doctor's existence was so brutal that he needed to get lit.

"To this point, my explanations don't constitute much more than an analysis of the information you gave me," Steinhauer said, all smarty-pants-like. "Some possible interpretations, and I remind you that everything I'm about to say is pure speculation."

Martin nodded again.

"If these people did not receive one or more of the three medications for the medical conditions they each had—I'll call these their 'baseline medication'—it would have fatal consequences, specifically in patients who were not taking any additional pills. But it would be extremely dangerous for those who are taking other medications as well. Example: an asthma patient takes a bronchodilating medication, which, aside from its intended benefit, can also cause a side effect such as cardiac arrhythmia."

That means irregular heartbeat, in case you haven't been hanging out with doctor types lately.

"I am obviously familiar with that group of substances," Martin explained. "It has a strong anabolic effect, it's banned as a doping substance, and that status has earned it extremely dubious attention in the media. We all too often have top athletes show up on an autopsy table, and that's the sort of substance we would look for."

Steinhauer grinned. "Exactly. Doping at the retirement home. Something new for once."

Martin considered for a moment with a wrinkled brow. "So you mean if these patients with concomitant conditions don't receive their baseline medication, sooner or later the side effects of the other medications will kill them."

"That's true as well for people who take only one of the three baseline medications, but it's more dangerous for the ones with other ailments."

"But why would they not be receiving their baseline medication?" Martin mumbled. "These are not substances that you steal and move on the black market."

Steinhauer ordered his next beer and leaned forward toward Martin, conspiratorially. "I'm an avid mystery reader, so I'm sure I have a special talent for this kind of speculation."

Another shit-eating grin that I'd have loved to clock off his face. Martin remained outwardly calm, but inwardly he rolled his eyes at the mention of mysteries.

"So I came up with the following scenarios."

Martin's vitamin mush and the doctor's next beer were served. Whereas the beer was empty within seconds, Martin nibbled with devotion at his greenery.

"First: an angel of death. I think that's unlikely in this case, however. Those people weren't sick enough. Angel-of-death types usually 'release' only very serious cases. But you never know. Maybe the patients were fussy, and that's why . . . well, you know." Steinhauer ran his finger across his throat.

Martin looked tormented.

"Second possibility: drug counterfeiting."

"Drug counterfeiting?" Martin asked with surprise. "Of medications like these?" He pointed to the sheet of paper listing the three baseline medications.

Steinhauer nodded.

"I thought that happened more with impotency drugs online . . ."

"Don't you remember that heparin scandal?" The doc let out a laboriously suppressed belch. Martin shuddered. "It must have been back in 2008. The manufacturer bought cheap raw materials from China that hadn't been properly monitored. The whole thing blew up, if I recall correctly, at dialysis centers, where patients are under continuous monitoring. But the drugs we're talking about here are ones that any doctor prescribes fifty times a day. Maybe a patient comes in at some point reporting that he isn't tolerating the cheap drug very well, so the doctor is *then* allowed to prescribe a specific brand name—and not just the active ingredient this time." He suddenly sounded more depressed than smug. "But how many patients stop complaining about their deteriorating health and never get put on a more effective drug?"

"I can't imagine," Martin replied thoughtfully. "But how likely is it that these cheap medications are actually being counterfeited?"

"You're still thinking about counterfeiting all wrong," Steinhauer said. "Expensive drugs are counterfeited by a fraudster who sells them online for a lot of money. But *inexpensive* drugs are mixed together from the cheapest possible raw materials or sold past their expiration dates. The more pressure put on the health-care system to save money, the more fatalities like yours there will be."

"B-but such things must be subject to oversight . . ." Martin stammered.

"Germany's drug agency is completely overwhelmed when it comes to large quantities of raw materials from low-wage countries or the opaque trade channels among manufacturers, pharmacies, wholesalers, middlemen, EU importers, and e-commerce. Who is supposed to oversee and pay for it all?"

After a glance at his watch, Steinhauer stood up, swaying slightly.

"Could you write down the names of the companies that manufacture these medications here?" Martin asked.

Next to the first medication on the list, Steinhauer wrote the name Weiz Pharma AG—which made me wince. Next to the second and third, he wrote "MelinaMed," which didn't mean anything to me. One Weiz, two Melinas. I was anxious to see how Martin would proceed because there was no way he would actually go visit Weiz.

My brain was spinning, so I went and holed up in my cabinet and worked through the night. I wrote out everything that I knew for sure, and then I came up with a whole slew of questions, which I then narrowed down to the most important questions:

Did Zuzubee know about Karpi's hacker den?

Did Zuzubee's murder have anything to do with the Paulina/Krämpel case?

Did the raisins at the home die not from someone intending to kill them but from adulterated or counterfeited pharmaceuticals?

If that was the case, why was Paulina Pleve murdered? Or was it a suicide after all? But then what did Yuri want from Krämpel?

By the time dawn broke, I was more confused than ever before.

TWENTY-SIX

July 8, eleven days after Gregor's arrest

It was high time we got some answers. Naturally Martin would need to help me with several of the various questions, but in one case Birgit was my assistant of choice. She was connected to the hacking grandson via his grandmother, so I texted her right after breakfast. Twenty minutes later Birgit was underway.

I whooshed off to Martin and found him by himself in his office.

"Martin, we urgently need to clear up a couple of things."

Martin nodded.

Huh? No objections?

"We need to know whether the Paulina and Zuzubee cases are connected; otherwise we'll be looking in the wrong direction."

Martin nodded again.

"We need to find Yuri and Krämpel. Or better yet, have someone else find them. By which I mean put Jenny on it."

Martin nodded yet again. Was he catatonic?

"The drug counterfeiting that your buddy suggested is something we need to check out. Do you think you could have some of the toxi—"

"Not here," Martin said. "But I know of a laboratory that can test the items. I only need a prescription to obtain to the pills."

"Shit, you could have gotten that from your buddy," I grumbled. "How long will it take to do that now?"

Martin shrugged. It's not like he was normally bubbling over with joie de vivre, but at the moment he was seriously giving me the creeps. No idea what happened to take him to empty. Yes, that's all I felt around him: emptiness. No thoughts, no power, nada. Empty bottle.

"Katrin's gone," Martin mumbled. "She had so many untaken vacation days and so much overtime that the boss had to dismiss her."

"Wait a minute," I said when the word "dismiss" seeped into my braincase. "What do mean by 'gone'?"

"She quit. She's not coming back. She wants to move away."

Now that seriously threw me off track. Katrin, my hot little Katrin. Gone. That was inconceivable!

"Gregor suspected of murder, Katrin gone . . . everything is falling apart," Martin whined.

"You still have Birgit and me," I said trying to console him, and on mentioning Birgit a tiny light flickered through his soul that disappeared the instant I referred to myself. Dumbass.

I left him wallowing in the clouds of his dark mood. While he was thinking how to get his hands on the drugs, I had something else planned.

Birgit had since arrived at Zuzubee's neighbor's house and was again sitting amid all the doilies on the couch.

"I urgently need to speak with him," Birgit was saying, and I got the impression it wasn't the first time she'd said it. It seemed clear enough to me that she meant the grandson.

"And I'd like to know why." Mrs. Berger's voice sounded shrill, and her posture indicated she was ready to do battle.

Birgit took a deep breath and raised her chin. "The job your grandson has . . ."

"Yes? What about it?"

"I think the work he's doing is illegal."

"I don't have to stand for this," Mrs. Berger said indignantly. She reached for the glass of juice on the table in front of her, downed about half its pulpy contents, and shuddered at the death-defying taste.

"That's true," Birgit said. "But Criminal Investigations needs to hear this, which is why I'm going to the police next."

"Why are you butting into the affairs of my grandson in the first place?" the aggressive grandmother screeched. Without her schnapps, she was seriously spoiling for a fight.

She held up her juice glass, yelled "To my blood pressure!" and downed the rest in one gulp. Then she let out a massive burp. The smell of sauerkraut spread throughout the living room. "Disgusting stuff," she mumbled. "But insanely healthy, my daughter says."

Birgit gasped for fresh air and struggled to her feet.

"Sit down!" the old bag commanded, reaching for her phone.

While Birgit waited for her witness to arrive, the grandma restlessly shuffled through her apartment, presumably hunting for alcohol. She went into the bathroom, opened the medicine cabinet, found some Spirit of Melissa in a bottle with three nuns on it, and took a major swig. It relaxed her immediately. The question of whether the calming effect was from the lemon balm or from the 158 proof alcohol was answered once the grandson arrived.

He turned immediately to Birgit and asked, "Did you give my grandmother anything with alcohol in it? That stuff is toxic to her liver."

Birgit stopped short, shook her head, and then did something few chicks can do: she focused on the important stuff.

"I know that you're working for Karpi in the basement. Can you tell me what exactly you're doing down there?" No warm-up, no foreplay. Which was a good thing.

Jonas—he had introduced himself by name despite his grandmother's warning not to—nodded. "Sure, lady. We hack into databases and stuff like that."

Grandma frowned, although I couldn't tell if her response was from lack of understanding or worry.

"Is that legal?" Birgit asked.

"No idea," the bastard said, with pointed disinterest. "I just do what the guys tell me."

"And what exactly do you do?"

"I open the door. If there's content in there, one of the bosses takes over."

"What door?" his grandma asked, annoyed.

Jonas rolled his eyes. "Not a real door, Grandma. We're talking about computer systems here."

"So you've never actually changed or deleted data in a third-party database yourself?" Birgit asked, keeping the conversation on track.

Jonas shook his head. "They totally pay attention to that. No changes, no copies, nothing. Door open, and gone."

"Why?"

"I think they're selling the stuff they draw off those systems, to the Russians or Chinese or whoever." Jonas tried to provoke Birgit with a dirty grin. But he was barking up the wrong tree.

"How do your, uh, employers make sure that you don't take anything out?" Birgit asked.

"They've got body scanners and security equipment that would put airport security to shame. And the joint is shielded so you can't send out data by cell phone. No guy with any sense would even try to smuggle something out of there."

"What do you get per hour?"

For the first time, the high-rolling Jonas turned bratty, preferring not to answer the question. He glanced quickly at his grandma.

"Fifty," he whispered toward Birgit.

"Sorry?" screeched the grandma. "Fifty euros? And you're paying me a measly five euros for an alibi?"

"What are you doing with all the money?" Birgit asked in surprise.

Jonas rolled his eyes again. He was really good at eye-rolling.

"Savings account, lady. A computer like the one I need is at least three thousand."

"Your hush money has just been increased to ten euros," Grandma intervened. This family really understood business.

Meanwhile and as planned, Martin had arrived at police HQ and was sitting with Jenny in her office.

"Paulina Pleve was dating Jürgen Gernot, but they broke up shortly before Paulina d-died," Martin said. "This Jürgen Gernot was seen dragging Till Krämpel, the pharmacist at the retirement home, into his apartment bound and g-gagged."

Well, fine. A little of that was a lie, which is why Martin stuttered a little, but Jenny ignored his speech impediments and pounced on the information.

"By whom?" she asked.

"By me." And now he developed hiccups.

"When?"

Martin blushed. "The day before yesterday."

"The day before yesterday? And you came strolling in here with all the time in the world only today . . . ?"

"I-I didn't fully understand what I was seeing. I didn't know Dr. Krämpel or this Yuri fellow by sight . . ."

My God, what gibberish was the man jabbering? If Jenny were paying attention, she might have wondered how Martin was able to recognize the two in front of Yuri's door when he didn't know them at all. Or why the whole thing didn't occur to him until two measly days after the fact! And what was Martin even supposedly doing in front of Yuri's building? Oh, Martin. We were definitely going to have to practice the lying thing some more.

"OK, once more from the top." Jenny whipped out a pen and took notes as Martin served her up with an extremely simplified version of the facts we knew to that point and what our suspicions included, except he left out the whole part about drug counterfeiting. That wasn't proved yet and it didn't fit into the story, which focused on Krämpel and Paulina, one of which was up to something crooked with the pills, while the other had clued in on that fact.

"And Jürgen Gernot suspects that Krämpel killed Paulina Pleve," Jenny summarized, the look on her face vacillating between concentrated and annoyed. "That's why he kidnapped him—to force him to confess?"

"Or to kill him," I suggested.

Martin turned pale. "Or worse," he told Jenny.

Jenny sighed. "The Paulina Pleve case is a hot mess. There's not a single piece of evidence that she was killed, and now you're telling me I should not only continue my investigation in the case, which I'm doing anyway, but I should also put out an APB on two men, neither of whom has previously been under any suspicion in this case whatsoever." Martin nodded.

"I'm going to discuss this with my boss," Jenny said. "Thank you for your help."

Martin and Birgit met up in the parking lot outside the Sonnenschein Home. Today, the boxy building looked gray and flinty because the sky was dark and promised more rainfall. There was a somber mood in the lobby as well. The café was deserted. It was dinnertime. At five thirty in the afternoon.

I directed Martin and Birgit to the pharmacy, but the door was locked. Shit!

Unfortunately opening a locked door isn't as easy as they make it seem in movies. Ramming a door open with your shoulder is practically impossible. Your shoulder suffers way more than the door. The credit card trick might work in America, but German doors aren't usually crackable that way. And certainly not if they're locked. My assistants pressed the button for the down elevator without achieving anything, but this time fate smiled on us. When the elevator doors opened, Mr. Hauschild was standing there.

"I know you, don't I?" he asked Birgit and taking her hand. He was beaming. "I've painted you. It's a girl, yes?"

Birgit shook his hand and her head. "I don't know if it's a boy or girl, but you did paint me. That's right."

The elevator doors started to close, but Hauschild had stepped forward when he took Birgit's hand, so he was in the way of the doors. The elevator beeped, and the doors opened again.

"And you're investigating my daughter's murder." Hauschild still hadn't let go of Birgit's hand but was now staring at Martin. "What did you want up here on the second floor?"

I'd never seen the guy so lucid. Who knows what dinner had been doped with.

"We were going to the pharmacy, but . . ."

"No problem," Hauschild said. "I'll let you in."

He walked straight to the pharmacy's door and fumbled around in his pants pocket for something. He pulled out a used handkerchief, then a button, a piece of chewing gum, a pencil, an eraser, another button, a candy wrapper . . . and a key.

"A master," Hauschild said absentmindedly as he unlocked the door. "It's always good to have a key."

None of us knew what to say to that. And none of us cared how the crazy old man had gotten a master key to the home, either. Martin went to steal pills while Birgit kept Mr. Hauschild happy.

"And the doctor who hanged herself?" he asked out of the blue.

"Paulina was a nurse," Birgit said.

"In Germany."

"And where was she a doctor?" Birgit asked.

"It's a girl, I'm sure of it," Hauschild said, locking the door behind Martin, who emerged from the pharmacy with his face red and his hands atremble.

Martin dropped the pills off at an analysis lab and spent the rest of the night with Birgit at home. They discussed all possible links, but they found it particularly interesting how Paulina had apparently studied medicine to become a doctor, and they wondered if she could have noticed the same things that Dr. Steinhauer had—or if she really was an angel of death. They wrote up lists similar to the ones I had drawn up, and without seeing any concrete solutions, went to bed at ten.

I checked in on Jenny and Offermann, following them from their pizzeria to a pub and from there into Offermannequin's freestanding bathtub. They got the water seriously splashing, took turns showering off afterward, and then guzzled champagne on the couch by candlelight. Personally, I thought the twenty white candles were kind of kitschy, but overall Offermann's pad had style, which anyone could objectively see. But Jenny wasn't sighing sweet nothings at him. She was piling on good old Andy about Paulina, Yuri, Krämpel, and the question of whether and how all of these things fit together. She was assuming that Zuzubee's murder was completely unrelated, because there was no evidence of a link between the two cases.

Offermannequin patiently listened to every detail again, nodding at the right spots and encouraging Jenny in her view that Paulina had hanged herself, which had made Yuri flip out and then take his frustration out on Krämpel because of some kind of misunderstanding and then kidnap him. The fact that Zuzubee didn't fit into this scenario proved her murder was totally independent from the events at the old folks' home.

This glaring misjudgment made me see once again that neither Jenny nor the Düsseldorf detectives knew anything about the information we had gotten out of Zuzubee's apartment. True, the information wasn't complete, and Martin was waiting on the analysis on the pills he had pinched from the home. But how much longer was he going to need to get a teensy tiny piece of evidence to Düsseldorf Criminal Investigations showing that Zuzubee had been on the trail of a series of strange deaths at the home—which could constitute a genuine motive for murder? In other words: how long would Gregor have to stay in jail while Martin played amateur gumshoe at a snail's pace? Although I didn't think much of Keller and Stein, I was sure Agent Orange would enthusiastically pounce on the new lead from Zuzubee's files. I was going to have to light a fire under Martin's ass.

TWENTY-SEVEN

July 9, twelve days after Gregor's arrest

I was tailing Jenny early Friday morning. She had met with her boss first thing and laid out the latest developments in the Paulina Pleve case for him.

"Good," the boss said after she mentioned Yuri, Krämpel, and the suspected kidnapping. "Rustle up this Jürgen Gernot. He's a former boyfriend of Paulina Pleve and thus an important witness on the question whether this is suicide or murder. Once you find him, we'll also know what to make of this kidnapping accusation."

Jenny managed to figure out Jürgen Gernot's address and phone number lickety-split. She got his mommy on the line.

"The police? But why are you looking for Jürgen?"

Jenny blathered the usual wish-wash in which the word "routine" featured prominently with the word "questions." Naturally I can't see into the heads of people who use stupid expressions like that, but I don't think any of them had ever once thought they were asking "routine questions." Or do you think phone calls from Criminal Investigations are routine? That's what I'm saying.

"My son is a doctor. He will probably be at the hospital. If he's not there, he might be at our weekend house. Or at my husband's apartment, which he uses when he's in Bonn on business.

Normally he's in Berlin, so the Bonn apartment is empty most of the time. Or, Jürgen could be at my husband's hunting lodge. Or, really, anywhere."

Wow, lady, thanks. That last bit of information would help our case exactly zero-point-nada percent.

Jenny got the addresses for the family's real estate as well as Yuri's cell phone and work numbers and hung up.

At the hospital, Jenny found out that Jürgen Gernot had not shown up at work since Monday.

"Did he call in sick?" Jenny asked.

"We haven't heard a word from him. Very unusual. He's actually incredibly reliable, Dr. Gernot."

Now, I'm not exactly a GPS system, but I did have access to the Internet and could figure out where all the addresses his mom had given us pretty fast. It took me less than half an hour to check the weekend house in the hills of Berg County northeast of Cologne as well as the apartment in Bonn, which is southeast of Cologne. Both empty. I couldn't find the hunting lodge out in the Sauerland, which is the mountainous region due east of Cologne. Once you get more than ten trees all together, it overwhelms my sense of direction. So maybe Yuri was holed up there, but maybe the first two places I had superficially checked out might have some clues where Yuri was if someone looked closer. The pros that Jenny would mobilize for this purpose would find the answers. The question was only when.

The boss called Jenny into his office right after lunch. She held the Paulina Pleve case file under her arm as she sat.

"How exactly did you identify Lila Weiz?" he asked.

Jenny's face derailed. "Sorry . . . ?"

"Lila Weiz. How did you identify her?" He emphasized each word individually, and it was obvious that the pressure in his veins was enough to fill up any fire hose.

Jenny pulled herself together. "I'm sorry, but that's not relevant now. In the Jürgen Gernot case—"

"You have just been pulled from the Paulina Pleve case, including Jürgen Gernot and anything connected to them, Detective Gerstenmüller."

Jenny's eyes opened wide.

"Offermann is taking over the case. So, again: Lila Weiz."

Jenny shook her head and pushed a few strands of hair behind her ear. "The girl had a wallet with a school ID, student bus pass . . ."

"I know that. Continue."

"I found the father and asked him for a DNA sample of his daughter, but he refused. He wanted to see his daughter and identify her himself."

"And you accepted that."

No response was necessary. The boss slammed a file on the table. It was open to the first page, which was a missing person's report. The girl in the photo was clearly the one who Bastian Weiz had identified as his daughter Lila. However, there was another name below it: Maureen Micaela Kerkenbosch, who had been missing since May 27.

Jenny was in shock when she tossed the file onto the desk in her office and sank into her chair.

"Hey, the boss just tasked me with finding Jürgen Gernot."

She hadn't noticed Offermann at her door, and she winced. Tears glistened in her eyelashes. She wiped her eyes with her hand.

"Can you quickly bring me up to date?"

After a sleepless night, Offermann looked unkempt and wrinkly, but more or less alert. He stepped into Jenny's office, leaned over her desk, and kissed her on the lips.

Jenny blushed and gave a rough summary of the phone call with Gernot's mother and the call to the clinic.

"That's not a lot," Offermann said.

"That's all we have so far."

"OK, don't worry about this. Starting now, the case in good hands with me."

No idea if he meant to sound as condescending as he did to me. But Jenny-Bunny seemed unbothered by his wording, in any case. Offermann stroked some hair out of her eyes and took a breath to say something but was interrupted by the boss, who appeared in the door.

"When you're done whispering sweet nothings, do you think you could get back to work?"

Jenny looked like she wanted to dematerialize. I could have told her that, after a while, that would feel crappy too.

"Offermann, into my office. This case needs to get closed once and for all."

I felt torn. It was going to get pretty interesting over the next few hours with Jenny and with Offermann. But Jenny made the decision for me about who to shadow. Really, she was just faster—she grabbed her bag and practically fled the office. And I followed her.

It was almost lunchtime when Jenny arrived at Weiz Pharma AG. The chief dragon welcomed her like an old frenemy and declared the CEO wasn't in.

"Where is he?"

"He's at a private engagement."

"You're mistaken," Jenny replied coldly.

"Wh-what . . ." the dragon stammered, authentically scandalized. "I beg your pardon?"

"Beg all you want, but if your boss is lying through his teeth to the police, then that's not private. That's a crime."

I'd never seen Jenny like this. She sounded like a real cop—just an octave higher.

The chief dragon first flushed red, then went white, and mumbled, "He's at his daughter's funeral."

"Oh, it gets better and better!" Jenny said with a curt, sarcastic laugh. She listened impatiently while the dragon lady gave her the funeral details and then she drove to Melaten Cemetery.

"Ashes to ashes, dust to dust," said the coat hanger with an afghan over his dark cloak, and he cast a small shovelful of dirt onto the casket. The white paint on it shone up from the bottom of the pit that Papa Weiz had had dug up for his little girl. Or whoever she was.

It occurred to me that he might really have mixed up the girls, but somehow I couldn't quite believe that. Even if he were a bad father and spent too little time with his offspring, he should be able to recognize his own child. So Weiz was staging the funeral of his own daughter, even though she wasn't the person inside the shiny box. I was looking forward to finding out the reason for this.

Standing around the pit were incredibly abundant flower arrangements, most of them red and white, some in pink, and all with tons of bows and ribbons and frills. A whole clutch of chicks Lila's age were standing together at one corner, their arms holding teddy bears as they wept in unison.

"You can raise the casket back up and spare yourselves all further ceremony," Jenny-Bunny said loudly and with undeniable anger in her voice. "The girl in that casket is not Lila Weiz. Mr. Weiz has been lying to all of you."

The ones who were crying stopped briefly and then started crying even louder, the silent types stayed silent, and only a small group in the back of the crowd started whispering among themselves.

"How dare you!" a woman standing next to Weiz hissed. Her expression made me think I'd landed in the wrong movie. I looked into the grouse's giant, round eyes. For those who don't know what grouse are: they've got eyes like cue balls with a little black dot in the middle. This human-size model wore thick horn-rimmed glasses, which only magnified her scary, icy, staring pupils. Her beak-like nose, the drooping corners of her mouth, and the smoothly combed, fluffed-up perm gave her look that final spooky touch. I literally needed to pull myself away from the sight of this apparition.

"Mr. Weiz," Jenny said through the now-hushed assembly.

"Please do not address Mr. Weiz," the grouse explained. Her wattles wiggled in time with her jaw opening and closing. "You're standing at the grave of his—"

"I'm not doing any such thing!" Jenny retorted. "Mr. Weiz is burying Maureen Micaela Kerkenbosch here under a false name, and dammit, I want to know why!"

Jenny had now adopted a fighting-hen stance.

"Stop it, Mother," the father faking his grief over a different girl quietly said.

The grouse's head jerked around, the wattles waggled, but the expected cackling failed to sound as Weiz removed himself from the group and greeted Jenny with a curt nod.

"Let's walk over here."

He didn't wait for her to reply and didn't make sure she was following him. He just started walking off.

Weiz headed toward the cemetery chapel, his head lowered. The Holy Joe pounced on Jenny, catching her asking what, pretty please, was going on here, he'd never before had someone interrupt him in the middle of a funeral . . . Jenny held up her badge in front of his eyeglasses, which were fogged up from excitement, and she ordered him to calm down the mourners but to leave the grave and everything around it exactly as it was. Then she followed Weiz.

"What did you say the girl's name was?" Weiz asked when Jenny caught up to him.

"Maureen Micaela Kerkenbosch. Do you know her?"

Weiz shook his head.

"Where did the girl get your daughter's wallet and student ID?"

"No idea."

"Why did you lie?"

Weiz ran his hand through his hair, sighed softly, and shook his head.

"Mr. Weiz?"

"I can't explain it to you now."

"You would have actually laid that girl to rest in that grave and leave her parents in the dark forever about what happened to her?" Jenny's tone made it unmistakable how inconceivable she found this notion.

"Will you file charges?" Weiz asked matter-of-factly.

"I want answers," Jenny said sharply.

"I can't give you any."

"Do you know where your daughter is?"

Silence.

Jenny was still enraged, but she had managed to regain full control over her voice so she didn't sound like a hysterical twelve-year-old anymore. "Are you being threatened? Are you afraid for your daughter? Is that the reason you want her to disappear officially?"

Silence.

"Or did you have an argument? Did you try pointing out to your daughter that she was 'dying' for you?"

"I can't answer you," Weiz said.

Jenny slumped.

Well, what now, sweet Jenny-Bunny?

She didn't seem to know either. She walked behind Weiz and shook her head.

"Mr. Weiz, please don't be childish," she said after a while. "Whatever sort of problem you're having, tell me. The police can help you."

Weiz forced a laugh.

They had nearly made it to the chapel. Weiz stopped and looked Jenny in the eyes.

"I need to ask you a favor," he said.

Jenny raised her eyebrow.

"Please treat this case as confidentially as possible."

Jenny straightened up. "You're afraid," she said, more or less certainly. "I'm guessing you're being blackmailed. Maybe your daughter has been kidnapped, or you're afraid of a kidnapping. Either way, the best thing would be to tell the police the truth. Otherwise we can't help you."

Weiz shook his head. "The police? The guys in white hats?" he mocked. "No, thanks."

Jenny looked like she wanted to stomp her foot in frustration, but she maintained her self-control and instead handed Weiz her business card.

"It wouldn't be good for my reputation as an entrepreneur if this story were to be spread widely in public."

"I'll be waiting for your call, Mr. Weiz. And to know what's going on here," Jenny said, spinning around and walking back to the grave to stop the cemetery workers from filling in the grave.

"I'm counting on your discretion," Weiz called after her.

I followed Weiz into the chapel, which some hired pussyfooters had cleared out. A woman was gathering up the song sheets, some kind of mole schlepped the huge portrait of Weiz's daughter out of the chapel and loaded it into a truck labeled on the side with the name of a large local funeral home. I caught a glimpse of the picture and felt like I'd raced head-on into an ICE 3 high-speed locomotive. The platinum blonde was grinning back at me.

TWENTY-EIGHT

I was so shocked I didn't even notice Martin radioing me.

"I have the pill analysis results in front of me," he broadcasted while I was still making my approach. "You will be surprised."

Nothing surprises me anymore, I thought. My mind was on the platinum blonde who was alive and well and staying in the old folks' home while her father faked her funeral. What could top all this bullshit?

"Of the three pills we had tested, two didn't show any active ingredients at all," Martin interpreted as he went through the highbrow blah-blah of the lab report. Dr. Steinhauer was next to him, nodding in agreement. Martin had asked him to join us and provide expert confirmation of our conclusions. "In addition," Martin continued, "the medications without an active ingredient contained some impurities that can presumably be traced back to bulking agents or excipients."

"What in the hell are excipients and bulking agents?" I asked, wondering if that was what was in breast implants.

He unleashed a hard-to-follow explanation with tons of technical jargon, out of which I shall now isolate the facts and translate into generally understandable parlance. If you want to manufacture a pill with an active ingredient that weighs only a few milligrams, either you can make the pill so small that it'll get lost in the crud under your fingernails, or you can take ten grams of flour and compress it into a tablet shape, adding the one or two milligrams of active ingredient, and—boom—you've got a Smartie.

"So then, MelinaMed is some kind of bungling operation that presses flour dummy pills but, unfortunately, forgets the actual medication," I said, summarizing Martin's blathering.

"Or the company is the victim of counterfeiting that is being committed at some point during the manufacturing process by a supplier," Martin said.

"Or a victim of counterfeiting pills that are being slipped in somewhere in commercial channels," Steinhauer added.

"Slipped in, in commercial channels?" Martin asked. "But these are drugs that can be issued only by a pharmacy."

"So?" Steinhauer said with a dark laugh. "Do you think that manufacturers deliver their products directly to pharmacies? Nope. In Germany, there are fifteen hundred pharmaceutical manufacturers, over twenty thousand pharmacies, and just shy of fifteen major pharmaceutical wholesalers with myriad logistics centers, warehouses, and suppliers. Those are just the major ones that are part of the national pharmaceutical manufacturers' association. On top of that, there are middlemen, importers, exporters, and reimporters. In Austria and Switzerland, for instance, there are hundreds of wholesale operations, some with a full range of offerings. Some medications are intended for export, unpackaged during stopovers, and then slipped back into the German market. In other cases it's exactly the opposite. Theoretically it's all subject to incredibly clear regulations, but it's so complex that efficient oversight is impossible."

The whole legally regulated pill parade sounded way less respectable than a cocaine or opium supply chain controlled by some hierarchical cartel, but maybe that was just my impression.

"What do we do with this new information?" Martin asked. He seemed disoriented. I couldn't blame him. My bright idea about an angel of death serial-killing the home's residents had unraveled, and the theory about Krämpel dealing legal drugs without a prescription was down the tubes. What else was there? A drug manufacturer whose pills had been counterfeited. How unspectacular was that? And, much more importantly: did that counterfeiting even have anything to do with our murder cases?

I left Martin, who was already glued to his computer researching drug counterfeiting and whooshed over to police HQ, where I hoped to find Offermann. After all, he was the one tasked with finding Yuri and Krämpel now, and maybe he'd have more luck than Jenny. Not that I had zero confidence in Jenny . . . but I didn't have very much confidence in her. Fine, call me macho, but Jenny is a mouse. And a mouse can't catch a tiger.

Offermann wasn't at his desk or anywhere else at HQ. Too bad. Where should I look next?

Naturally I could try to find Yuri and Krämpel again myself. I hadn't put much effort into locating the hunting lodge, for instance, but since the two other addresses drew blanks, I could try again. So I headed out to the Sauerland.

The Sauerland is a disturbingly large and disturbingly forested area of hills and mountains east of Cologne popular with bikers, hikers, campers, and the like. I knew that the hunting lodge had to be somewhere in the Arnsberg Forest Nature Park, which is a protected natural reserve in the Sauerland. So I zoomed out along Autobahn A46 toward Arnsberg, sure I was on the right track. I never was a Boy Scout, and when I was alive

I rejected any route that wasn't asphalted and that most vehicles couldn't drive on, so I had no ability to orient myself using natural phenomena such as the position of the sun or the growth of moss on trees, or other New Agey practices.

Which is exactly why I was too late. But I hadn't needed to look very hard the last few kilometers. Hordes of SWAT SUVs tore up the dirt roads at full speed, which could have been because international terrorism had struck once again from among the pines. Or because it was the violent end of a hostage situation. I picked up their trail and flew right past them, but the action was over by the time I made it. Offermann was standing right inside the door to the lodge with a smoking Colt in his hand. The part about a smoking Colt is meant figuratively, naturally. He actually had his service weapon in his hand. Those things don't smoke. In the middle of the lodge on Offermann's side of a tipped-over table, I saw Yuri lying on the floor. His eyelids were fluttering. At the other end of the lodge there was only one thing fluttering—namely, Krämpel's little soul already on its way past me.

"Asshole," the little soul was whining. "That scumbag of an asshole."

"Hey, calm down," I replied.

The little soul stopped short.

"Life isn't that bad on this plane. Stay here, then I'll show you—"

But, no. Krämpel's little soul just whooshed off, whining all the way.

Krämpel's body stayed behind. An entry wound graced his chest, and another his right shoulder.

I turned to Yuri. In his case, the entry wound was in his left pec. From my rich experience in matters pertaining to autopsies,

including my own, and to emergency medicine, which, personally, I had never had the chance to enjoy, I knew that he should be
dead. But he wasn't. His eyelids were still fluttering. Offermann
saw that too. He tried to work his way over the tossed-over chair
to Yuri when the order came to stop. Offermann stopped mid-
motion. Then the dark-clad Clone Troopers swarmed the lodge.

"Shit, man, what did you do?" the head honcho in black
bleated once Offermann handed over his weapon and ID badge.
"Were you playing Rambo?"

"I heard a shot. Then I went in."

"And?"

Offermann shook his head. "The second shot was fired while
I was going in," he pointed at Krämpel. "So I stopped the shooter."
He nodded at Yuri.

"Both dead?"

Offermann shrugged.

The head honcho put a finger on Yuri's carotid, raised his
eyebrows, whistled two of his helmet heads in, and assigned them
the task of keeping the guy alive. Then he led Offermann outside
and put him in one of the SWAT team's SUVs. They waited in
silence for the medics and CSI team to arrive.

I was pretty rattled. It was just three o'clock, and even though
Offermann had only been assigned the case a few hours ago, he
had at least one if not two bodies under his belt. Plus, they were
exactly the two guys Jenny-Bunny had been looking for and not
found. At first I didn't get how he had tracked them down so
fast. But then I was pretty pissed he had found them but also
snuffed them out. OK, Yuri apparently wasn't totally dead yet,
but that was just an issue of time. Who else were we going to ask
all of our clever questions? For instance, why had Yuri cast his

beloved out into the desert even though he still worshipped her? And had Paulina hanged herself because she couldn't take the separation? Or was there something going on between Paulina and Krämpel that no one was supposed to find out about? Had Krämpel revealed the truth to his kidnapper because he was afraid for his life? Or had Krämpel known something about Yuri that left Yuri no choice but to take Krämpel out of circulation? God, Offermann. You're a stud and all, but I'd have preferred you left at least one of the two guys able to talk.

Two hours later, Offermann was sitting in an office at Criminal Investigations with the Arnsberg police, patiently answering the questions that a Brigitte Nielsen double was asking him military-style.

"How did you find the hunting lodge?"

"Jürgen Gernot's mother had given the address to my colleague, Detective Jenny Gerstenmüller. It was the third possibility after the first two possible sites had been inspected and excluded."

"You are outside the jurisdiction of the Cologne police department."

"I put in a call to the Arnsberg police to let them know."

"After you fired your weapon?"

"No, before. If you'll please just let me explain . . . I was convinced that Jürgen Gernot was holed up in the lodge and—"

"How?"

"I could see in through a gap in the shutters."

"Continue."

"Then I called Arnsberg SWAT and waited."

"And why did you enter without SWAT?"

"I heard gunfire from inside the lodge."

"How many shots?"

"One."

"Then you ran in?"

"Yes."

"How exactly did you do that?"

"The lodge has functioning wooden shutters over the windows and door. These shutters were open. The actual door wasn't locked so I needed only press the handle. The kidnapper, Jürgen Gernot, had fired the shot; the other man had been hit but was still standing upright. I identified myself as the police and ordered the kidnapper to drop his weapon, but he fired again. Then I fired my weapon."

"Where on the man did you aim?"

"I wanted to hit the arm he was holding his weapon with, but he turned toward me just as I fired."

"You're lucky he's still alive."

"He's alive?"

"We hope he'll survive surgery."

I found Yuri being rolled out of the operating room—still alive. From what I could discern from the nurses' gossip, he owed his survival to an anatomical abnormality: he had some benign bone tissue growth from fused ribs where his heart should have been, so his heart was located slightly farther to the left than normal. In fact, the bullet itself wasn't the problem but the spray of bone fragments in the surrounding tissue from the fused ribs. One fragment had gotten stuck a half-millimeter into his actual heart muscle, and he had two more in his lung.

The shorter nurse studied the patient with a very unprofessional twinkling in her eyes, which started to waver when she noticed the cop take up his post outside the door to the intensive-care unit. Yuri was being treated as a dangerous criminal and was thus the beneficiary of extremely personal attention from the big boys in blue. There was nothing for me to do here other than damage, so I made my way home to Cologne.

I looked for Martin and Birgit, but I couldn't find either of them. Martin wasn't responding to my hails; his mental shielding was perfect. I had no idea where they might be, but I wasn't worried. They were likely at the OB for the thousandth time looking at shaky black-and-white movies of their progeny sucking its thumb. Disgusting. So I gave up looking for them. I hung out for a while until I decided to fly over to Karpi Diem. It was a warm night, the music there was OK, and I could float around in the fug of wriggling bodies, slip inside a T-shirt or two, and let the pounding beat blast my braincase clear for a while. I thought. Until I noticed someone in the throng I hadn't expected here.

The chick looked good, but she wasn't a model or anything. She was striking not for her heavenly beauty but for combining her good looks with incredible radiance. Her radiance was sending out multiple pieces of information on a continuous loop. "I know how good I look" and "Fuck off, jerk-off" being the two most important. No one even semipartially in his right mind would try small talk with that chick. Not without drawing up a will first. And not even a stone fuckwit would dare to grope, rob, or kidnap her. Which is exactly why Katrin stood out to me in the midst of all the bouncing disco bunnies, although her long dark hair was now short and blonde. Thanks also to her radiance, none of the big, broad, bald gorillas in Karpi Diem stopped her from making her way toward the elevator.

Maybe the bouncers knew her too.

Presumably she had been announced, because she didn't hesitate when she stepped into the elevator and took it to the basement.

And then I was sure I must have taken a deep draw from a mind-altering drug, because I watched as Katrin was hugged in the basement corridor by an upright Karpi. I swear!

They went through one of the doors into the hacker den. Obviously I flew in behind them, but I didn't want to get locked inside, so I stayed out in the hallway. Alone, completely confused, and frustratingly unable to get loaded. A miserable way to exist.

TWENTY-NINE

July 10, thirteen days after Gregor's arrest

Jenny spent Saturday finishing the paperwork and other odds and ends she'd botched in the case of the mixed-up dead girls. Offermann, who was put on desk duty after his shoot-out and thus didn't have any weekend work to do, whiled away his afternoon in his apartment, went jogging, rented a couple of DVDs— none of which indicated if he was troubled because Krämpel was dead or glad that Yuri was still alive. Martin was putting in some overtime at turbo speed because the slicers had way too much work on their plates without Katrin.

Katrin hadn't surfaced again, although I looked for her several times at Karpi Diem and her apartment overnight. No luck. And Birgit was spending her day using a template she'd bought to spray-paint humorous creatures onto the wall in the nursery. "Spray-paint" is the wrong term. Technically, she was using a toothbrush to scrub paint through an upside-down tea strainer. The paint was kid friendly, ecologically sound, and VOC-free—so natural that Birgit might as well have been drinking it. Instead, she was sitting on the floor with a can of freshly stirred paint by her side, the tea strainer in her left hand, and the toothbrush in her right hand, applying seahorses, fish, and cross-eyed octopuses to the orangey pastel-pink wall. I watched the performance for a long while, but then I couldn't take it any-more. I tried to text Birgit, but her cell phone was off.

So I was sidelined. For a whole day, while the world kept turning, Gregor kept rotting in jail, and someone out there kept laughing morning to night because he'd framed Gregor so beau-tifully. I felt shitty, I can tell you that.

July 11, fourteen days after Gregor's arrest

Saturday night among the clubs in Cologne's Old Town had ended with a mass shooting and two dead, so Martin was at work again on Sunday and he was consistently blocking me from his mind.

I was frustrated, so I decided to at least make some headway on something I didn't need Martin for: the platinum blonde. I checked Birgit's cell phone and was relieved to find that it was turned on, so I zoomed to my cabinet and texted her.

The coffee fairy at the home is a runaway. Living in the junk room in the basement. Can you help her?

Birgit texted back: *Who are you?*

Get Gregor out of jail, then you'll find out.

Birgit set her phone down and turned back to her toes. I had interrupted her nail polish routine. Which is hard work for an extremely pregnant woman with the baby balloon blocking her view and impeding her reach. Twice her little paintbrush slid off and she painted her whole toe instead of just the nail. She franti-cally rubbed her toe, but then she needed to paint the nail again. Distractedly, she kept squinting at her phone. Finally she picked it up again.

Who is she?

Lila.

"Lila *who*? God, you are really into guessing games, aren't you," she yelled in irritation, but then she typed: *OK.* Attagirl.

About an hour later, Lila and Birgit were sitting at a table in the park outside the home sipping lattes. Birgit also had a plate with three slices of cake, which she slowly and systematically shoveled into her mouth.

"How do you know that?" the platinum blonde asked for what seemed like the seventieth time.

Birgit just kept munching.

"Are you from Child Protective Services?"

Birgit shook her head.

"From the police?"

"Uh-uh." That was the only utterance, more of a noise really, that she could get out around the chocolate torte.

"My father sent you."

Birgit swallowed a few times. "I have no idea who you are, but your reaction shows me that my runaway theory is correct. You're hiding out in the home. Clever of you. But not a permanent solution. I'd like to help you."

"Why?"

Birgit pointed at her belly with a smile. "I like kids."

For the first time since I'd known her, the platinum blonde showed the tiniest hint of a smile. Pretty cute, honestly.

"But you won't send me back, right?"

Birgit shook her head and raised her hand. "Scout's honor."

"My name's Lila. Lila Weiz. My father is the guy who started the student program here at the home."

Birgit's cake-laden fork stopped midway toward her mouth. "Lila Weiz? But . . . I heard in the news that you . . ." Birgit blushed.

Lila nodded. "That I'm dead. Surprised me too."

Birgit stared at the cake on her fork like she couldn't explain how it got there, but then stuffed it resolutely into her mouth and leisurely chewed. Birgit is one of the few women who knows you can find out more if you keep your mouth shut.

"I gave my wallet and cell phone to a girl who looks like me. She's always with some of the burnouts who hang out at a totally rundown playground near my school."

The chick looked similar to her? If I recalled correctly, the dead girl was a goth. Everything black—hair, eyes, lips, nails. Plus tons of metal piercing various parts of her face. I studied the platinum blonde closely and, in actual fact, discovered tiny holes in her eyebrows and nose. OK. Add longer hair, dye it black, and that might be enough. Plus, both girls had strikingly narrow noses and pointy chins.

"If my father looked for me, he would have found her. Money withdrawn from the bank, cell phone locator, stuff like that."

She might not have been more than thirteen years old, but she was damned clever. And with her hair cut short and bleached platinum blonde, face freed of scrap metal, fake-out electronic trails laid . . . she was going to have a brilliant career. The only question was on which side of the law.

"But he apparently didn't look for me." Her voice was so quiet that I had to strain to hear her say it.

Birgit started her assault on the third slice of cake. "Why did you run away in the first place?" she asked softly.

The platinum blonde was quiet for a while. She seemed to be wrestling with how much to tell Birgit, but then she shrugged and sighed. "The usual."

Great. She apparently took after her daddy when it came to chattiness.

273

"You need to have those snuffed-off seniors exhumed," I roared the second I was with Martin. He dropped the brain that he had just sawed out of one of the banditos. Suspiciously small, by the way. The brain. Not the bandito.

"Average," Martin corrected me. "Yours wasn't bigger."

Asshole.

"I heard that."

Martin weighed the brain, sliced off a sliver that would end up as a sample in a pickle jar, and the rest was stuffed back into the cranial cavity.

"So, back up a little," he ordered me.

"You'll need to serve up some kind of credible theory why you're suggesting it," I explained. "Krämpel offed the old folks, and Paulina clued in on it. She blackmailed him, and Zuzubee got wind of it."

Martin considered for a moment as his scalpel hovered over the bandito's body. The colleague standing on the opposite side of the table to document the autopsy was looking at Martin with one eyebrow raised.

"But it doesn't look as though Krämpel had his hand in this. It's much more likely that the patients died from deficient medic—" Martin began.

"The facts are irrelevant for the time being," I said.

"That's exactly your style," Martin retorted spitefully.

"Crap trap shut, lugholes open," I said. "The crucial point is this is the only theory that will let us work together with all the different detectives."

Martin realized with some shock that the idea was brilliant, even though he took pains to hide this recognition from me. But he had to admit that we currently had the problem of three detectives all muddling along at cross-purposes. The Düssel-dweebs were responsible for Zuzubee's murder and had already locked up their suspect; the Cologne PD was responsible for Paulina's case; and now the Sauerland police were on the Hunting Lodge Case, as they were calling it.

"I'll see about using Susanne's data to justify more or less plausible suspicion," Martin said.

No idea why he had to express it in such a complicated way, but the main thing was he was getting the case going again.

That night Martin wrote up a report in which he characterized Zuzubee's data as his own research, referring to the fact that the mortality rate at the Sonnenschein Home had noticeably increased. He noted that other fatalities had some connection to Sonnenschein, such as Susanne Hauschild as the daughter of a resident of the home and Krämpel as one of its employees, and he indicated that all of these facts justified a more thorough investigation of the circumstances of all deaths within the past year. Finally, he e-mailed his report to his boss, to Desperately Seeking Susanne, to Jenny, to the Sauerland cops, and to the Cologne city attorney's office. Then he explained to me that he didn't want to be bothered for the rest of the evening, and he lowered his brain blinds.

I was thrilled. But once again I was totally left up in the air. Martin and Birgit sat on the couch in front of the boob tube taking in some kind of instructional video for new parents, Katrin had disappeared, and Gregor was still in jail. Yuri was still in the ICU hooked up to devices that beeped their ghost alarm when I checked in on him. Embarrassing, but not surprising. I had always interfered with the monitoring functions of equipment in the ICU. It was a nice piece of proof every time that I was still alive in some way.

275

When I left Yuri, Offermann was just coming around the corner. He inquired about how the victim he had shot was doing, but the nurse clammed up, mentioning patient confidentiality. Not even the desperation on Offermann's face as he explained he hadn't done anything wrong but was still troubled could change her mind. So he chatted with the uniform guarding Yuri's door for a while, then eventually bailed and went home to spend the night alone.

July 12, fifteen days after Gregor's arrest

On Monday morning I had expected some kind of birthday serenade or an annual subscription to a movie streaming service . . . or some other acknowledgment from Martin, but he had completely forgotten me. Me and my twenty-sixth birthday. Provided I was allowed to keep counting birthdays although I was dead. But I wasn't quite dead.

"I think it's very, very sad," I said in greeting to Martin over breakfast. "You two have been talking about your son's birthday now for months, but when other people also have birthdays and might enjoy receiving some kind of acknowledgment of it, I guess they're shit out of luck."

"Moderate your mode of self-expression," Martin reprimanded me.

"I'd like to celebrate my birthday with you," I demanded.

"Under no circumstances," Martin said dismissively. He still had sufficiently unpleasant memories from last year's celebration. Some really bad things happened right after that . . .

"Well, at least a present!"

"I'll think about it," he said, lowering his brain blinds again because Birgit had joined him at the table.

"I'm going to explode," she whined. "And a week to go still."

"At least," Martin said with prophetic doom, and Birgit moaned some more.

"The first child usually comes a few days after the due date."

Martin drove to the institute and I leisurely cruised up to Düsseldorf to check in on Desperately Seeking Susanne. Martin's e-mail had stirred the place up.

"Why didn't we determine this ourselves?" Agent Orange was nagging as Keller, Stein, and the pretty-boy snot sipped at the acidic, burned coffee in their paper cups.

"Yes, why didn't you?" Stein hissed back at her.

"Why didn't anyone inform us that this Krämpel is dead?" Keller mumbled. If he had swallowed the coffee in his mouth first, before speaking, less would have landed on his shirt.

"Because you two dumbasses have been obsessed with Detective Kreidler from the get-go," the orange-headed émancipée crowed. "Your ridiculous envy of a colleague with an outstanding reputation was your biggest problem from the very start."

"There wasn't any evidence either on the cell phone or in her apartment that pointed to any strange events in the home," the pretty boy said, all snotty-like.

"Exactly," Agent Orange replied. "There was no evidence because there wasn't a laptop. But you guys also didn't look for it afterward."

"Neither did you," Stein replied.

"Wrong," Agent Orange explained. "And I not only looked, I also found it."

Now all the jaws fell open. "What did you find?"

"Not the laptop, but the cloud service Susanne Hauschild was using to save backup copies of her files."

"And what did she save?"

"We've put in to have the cloud service hand over the data, but with all the red tape, that's going to take several days. Meanwhile, some of our technical colleagues are trying to crack the password."

OK, then they would find exactly what Martin had sent them, although in a less scientific form. That didn't help Gregor any, so I left Düsseldorf and zoomed back down to Cologne.

Birgit was showing clear signs of impatience. She aimlessly waddled up and down through the apartment, picked up a book, set it down again, turned the radio on and off again, brewed some coffee but didn't drink it, and finally bit into a carrot like she wanted to punish it for something. Finally she reached a decision, struggled to get her feet into her shoes, grabbed her car keys, and left the apartment.

I followed her to the retirement home, where she ordered two slices of cake and watched Lila schlepp coffee and cake everywhere. Then Lila sat down with her, and she began to talk. She talked about a successful father who was never around, a cheerful mother who was the linchpin of the small family, always happy and satisfied until a miserable case of cancer she succumbed to five years ago. About an uncle who was killed by a junkie, and how her father hadn't laughed again since that time. Lila told Birgit about the ways she rebelled. Piercings, goth culture, punk stuff . . . I felt bad for the girl, and Birgit was a terrific listener, but all the chick chat was jibber-jabbering me into a coma. I tuned out, instead fishing for an idea that was flashing on and off in my head like a flashlight and keeping me from finding it. While I was zoning out, I lost track of my two coffee cats.

So I went to check in on Jenny and see what effect Martin's message had on her, but unfortunately it seemed like no effect at all. She was standing behind the chair at her desk, which was holding up Offermann, whose neck she was massaging.

"You don't need to worry," Jenny was saying when I flew in. "It's an appointment they set up for anyone who's fired his or her weapon on duty."

"But no one enjoys seeing the police psychologist, and I'm no exception."

Jenny kept kneading his pronounced neck muscles. "Will you ask for time off?"

"No way." Offermann sounded indignant, as though she'd asked him if he wanted to take early retirement. "I need work, not boredom. I have nothing to feel sorry about, but sitting at home and going through the events again and again in my mind isn't exactly my idea of fun."

"Well there's plenty of work," Jenny-Bunny confirmed. "I've got a new lead about the retirement home . . ."

Offermann reached up and put his hands on hers and held them tight. "Jenny, baby. Let it be. Don't make yourself unhappy on account of my obsessing."

Jenny froze and frowned. She pulled her hands back and looked at the clock. "You'd better get going; otherwise you'll be late for the psychologist."

Offermann dynamically leaped up, leaned down to Jenny, touched her nose, and whispered, "See you later, baby," and disappeared.

Jenny looked after him with an ice-cold glare.

What was her problem now?

Naturally I didn't get an answer to my question, but it was clear something was seething in Jenny-Bunny. She was seriously pissed off, the way she was at the cemetery when she interrupted Weiz's staged funeral. Her spine stretched tall, her eyes grew narrow, and her movements no longer reminded me of a rabbit scurrying to hide from a predator. Jenny-Bunny had suddenly mutated into Jenny the Tiger. Well . . . Jenny the Kitty, at least.

She sat down at her computer, read Martin's e-mail again carefully, picked up the manila folder with the Weiz file in it, and then she opened her Web browser. I watched her enter the term "Weiz Pharma" into the search field and call up Weiz's personal and business data, including all gossip column lies and news stories about his dead wife and daughter. None of this seemed that exciting, so I bailed.

When I tried to catch up again with Birgit and Lila at the home, I had to waft around a bit until I found them out in the parking lot. They loaded a big bag into the backseat of Birgit's convertible Beemer, got in, and buckled up.

"Where to?" Birgit asked.

"Home." Lila gave her an address.

"Is your father there?"

"I don't think so. He's most likely at work."

Birgit's giant belly could hardly fit in behind the steering wheel anymore, but she still managed to drive by sucking things in as much as she could. It would take at least twenty minutes to get to Lila's house, so I had time to work on capturing that evasive thought that kept flashing around in my brain like a piece of soap on the bottom of a bathtub.

Naturally I would have preferred for those two earthlings to stay put so I had time to straighten my brain out. But no. They kept weaving, and I had to pay at least some attention to bring up the rear.

Well, OK. I should have been paying full attention.

Because the flashlight in my memory blinked on, and I almost raced right through the post holding up a traffic light. Which wouldn't have been bad since I would have just zoomed through it, but those things are usually wired up all funky so my force field disturbs them, and then the whole intersection would have been screwed up for hours. That wouldn't have bothered me since I wouldn't even know about it, but whenever I smack into funky wiring, it can also mess with me and get the light in my head to flip off. And that would have been some hellishly bad news since the enlightenment that had just come to me took my breath away: Weiz!

THIRTY

"It's Weiz!" I yelled, still far away.

Martin stopped midsentence. He was in court, testifying as an expert witness in a murder case. His mouth hung agape. The air he had sucked in to speak his exhaustive answer departed his lungs uselessly. Both the lawyer and the judge seemed more annoyed the longer they waited for him to continue his answer.

"Dr. Gänsewein, would you please answer the question?" the lawyer probed after a few seconds.

"No!" Martin said loud and clear.

"No?" the lawyer replied, stunned.

"I-I beg your pardon, I didn't mean you," Martin stammered.

"Birgit is on her way to see him!" I yelled.

"No!" Martin yelled.

The lawyer, the judge, and everyone else in the courtroom stared at Martin incredulously.

"Your honor, I apologize, but I need to go." Martin leaped up from his seat and ran out of the courtroom. Twenty-four pairs of eyes followed his exit, partially horrified and partially amused. I stayed close to his side.

"Weiz Pharma is the key," I said. "The pills didn't have an active ingredient . . ."

"Those pills weren't from Weiz Pharma," Martin corrected me.

"I think they were! Weiz Pharma is held up as a rising star of privately held, family-run pharmaceutical companies, and out of its small make-to-order business it has spawned multiple companies the past few years that manufacture and market brand-name and generic pharmaceuticals they've developed in house. And his dead wife's name—hold on to your seat—was Melina!"

"The pills at the Sonnenschein Home . . ." Martin mumbled. A whole array of lights flipped on in his head at the same time. Obviously, because medicine-related topics are closer to his heart than to mine.

"My theory is that Paulina connected the dots between the deaths at the home and the pills from MelinaMed. After all, Mr. Hauschild emphasized several times that she had been a doctor before she moved to Germany."

"And then?"

"Uh . . ."

Yeah, I know what you're going to say now. That's not enough to explain the deaths of Paulina and Zuzubee, but I hadn't had anywhere near enough time to hammer out a reasonable theory, because Birgit couldn't stay put.

We left the building and hurried toward the parking lot. Martin turned his cell phone on and tried to call Birgit. The answer told us that the caller was not available. Shit!

"What now?" Martin asked desperately. "I need to get to her."

"By the time you drive to the other end of town in your trash-can car, the credits to this action flick will already be rolling."

Martin made a sound that sounded just like the howl of a wolf. A small, scared wolf. A wolf pup, more specifically.

Martin dialed one-one-zero, but I stopped him with a curt command: "How are you going to explain to emergency services that the highly esteemed lord of the estate to which you

283

are summoning the cops is the bad guy? He's widely known as a benefactor and philanthropist, but today somehow he's appearing in another role?"

The baby furball howled again, louder this time.

"Call Jenny and tell her to bring backup."

Martin dialed Jenny's number, and it rang about eight times before someone picked up.

"Cologne Police Department, Criminal Investigations. This is Detective Offermann."

I gave two thumbs up—virtually, of course. Offermann had returned from his psych session, was apparently back on duty, and of course he was even better than Jenny-Bunny. She had clued in that something was rotten in the house of Weiz, but, well . . . she was a woman. Offermann was a dude. Martin explained the situation to him, and Offermann said the words that someone like Martin wants to hear from law enforcement to feel safe again: "I'll take care of it."

Bastian Weiz almost fell out of his shoes when he saw Lila and Birgit standing on the porch.

"Did someone see you?" he asked his daughter as he rushed them both inside so roughly that they stumbled. Lila caught herself quickly, but Birgit's bonsai balloon put her off balance. She fell onto her hands and knees. Weiz roughly dragged her through the threshold and closed the door to the house.

"Urgh!" Birgit said, holding her belly.

"Papa, what are you doing?" Lila asked with panic in her voice.

"Come on, get up!" Weiz commanded.

Lila straightened her shoulders. "Papa, I want to know right now what's actually going on. What do you have to do with Paulina Pleve? And what—"

Weiz looked at Birgit, grabbed her gruffly under the arms, and heaved her up. Then he forced her into the living room.

"This wasn't a good idea, Lila."

"What?" Lila asked, her voice trembling.

"Coming here now of all times. And with a stranger."

Lila began to cry.

Birgit bent over and supported herself with her hands on her knees. "I'm sorry, folks, but I'm going to need to sit down," she gasped.

Weiz pushed her onto a sofa and sat his daughter down next to Birgit. Then he ran both hands over his face. "Who knows that you two are here? Come on, out with it!"

I flashed back over to Martin, who had finally made it to his trash can and was fumbling with the key.

"Forget the 2CV. Take a taxi. Now. Immediately," I ordered him.

He obeyed. He ran to the taxi stand in front of the courthouse and jumped into the back of the first cab in line.

"Express delivery," I said. "Tell him he'll get a twenty euro tip if he gets you there in five minutes."

Martin dutifully recited the instruction, the driver negotiated for twenty plus coverage of any fines, I gave Martin the address, and they pulled out.

I had no idea what was in store for Lila and Birgit at Weiz's. Was Weiz violent? Would he take his own daughter and a pregnant stranger as hostages to . . . uh . . . to do what? To skip off on his own? Without his daughter? Or would he hold Birgit hostage to beat it with his daughter? Or was he desperate and planning the sort of suicide where he wanted to take as many people with him as possible? Or did he have nothing to do with the whole situation, apart from the fact that his pills had been replaced at some point on the line with counterfeits? But what had happened to Paulina then? And who killed Zuzubee? And what did Yuri want from Krämpel . . . ? I just could not get any closer to the solution.

Did anyone have perspective on what was going on here? I didn't. That much was sure. Martin and Jenny either. Oh, but maybe there was someone on the trail of the connections because the case has to do with one of his employees. And because he was curious. And because he was on friendly terms with Birgit and, if I wasn't mistaken, with Katrin too. We needed any extra help we could get. Maybe I thought too highly of him and he couldn't or wouldn't help us, but asking couldn't make our situation any worse.

"Call Karpi," I demanded, giving Martin the number that Karpi had given Birgit in the puzzle.

Martin hesitated.

"He's our last chance," I said. "Go on. Call."

"But he threw us out in a very unfriendly manner," Martin began to lament.

I had to think for a second about what Martin was referring to, then I realized he was talking about his first and, to date, only meeting with Karpi, which had been about two weeks back. My God, if he knew that Karpi wasn't just a genuine gangster but had meanwhile become best friends with Birgit . . .

"I beg your pardon?" Martin said aloud.

"Huh?" the taxi driver asked.

"What did you do to Birgit?" Martin asked me in our usual noise-free communication style, although with a hysterical undertone.

"I saved her from death by boredom," I explained. "Now call Karpi."

"He'll have no idea who I am if I call him. After all, we saw each other only once, and he spoke primarily with Birgit," he objected.

"Tell him your name is 'Pajama Suit,' and then he'll know exactly who you are."

Martin gasped for breath, hesitated two or three more seconds, but gave up his resistance when I bellowed at him at the maximum mental volume I could muster.

Martin stammered the words I gave him into Karpi's ear. When he was done, Karpi silently hung up.

"You see? That gangster isn't interested one bit—" Martin complained as he dug with both hands into his seat to keep from being thrown around in the speeding taxi. The driver either had rallye experience or was a certified stunt man. The speeding fines were going to be astronomical.

THIRTY-ONE

"What is going on?" Lila whispered through her tears.

Weiz strode over to a table where the phone was. He dug for Jenny's business card in a drawer and dialed. It went straight to voice mail. "Hello, Detective Gerstenmüller. This is Bastian Weiz. My daughter is back at home, and I actually wanted to tell you the whole story, but . . . well. Another time." Then he hung up. He stood with his back to the sofa and whispered, "I'm not the man you take me for."

Lila sobbed more loudly. Weiz approached her and she jerked backward. Weiz stopped as though he'd run into a wall, and then a tear trickled down his cheek. "Lila, darling, you don't need to be afraid of me."

Lila Darling snuffled loudly and looked up at Birgit, who stared back at her with a pain-contorted face. "I don't have any idea what's going on here," Birgit managed to get out. "But if your father just called the cops, then I'm much less worried than I was before."

Weiz sank down into the armchair beside Lila and took a deep breath. "Why did you run away?"

He tried to take Lila's hand, but she turned away and pressed her hands between her knees.

"I overheard the conversation the night before I left."

Weiz turned ghost-pale. "I was afraid of that."

Lila trembled, but she held her tears back and her back straight. "So, what does it all mean?"

"I killed your uncle."

Lila turned whiter than her daddy, and Birgit tensed up and curled forward. Wait a second—what was this guy talking about? I was expecting a story about fake pills, Paulina, and Zuzubee, and here the guy was jibber-jabbing something about embarrassing relatives?

Weiz's voice interrupted my thoughts. "He had called me out to the pharmacy because he wanted to talk to me. I had a good idea what it was about, and I was right. He told me that our flu vaccine wasn't working, and it was also causing side effects in a lot of people. It was because of a contaminant in the raw materials we had sourced from Asia."

Birgit moaned, but I doubted it was over the story about Lila's uncle, because she was grabbing her bonsai balloon and didn't give the impression she was following the conversation anymore.

"I asked him to buy us some time before taking bureaucratic steps, because I was negotiating at the time with the bank about a new loan," Weiz continued. "The bank would have declined the loan if we had a product recall, because the company would have gone bankrupt. Your uncle didn't want to hear it, and we had a serious argument. He lunged for me, we wrestled with each other, and I lost my signet ring. I pulled myself away and pushed Stefan back, he stumbled, and fell over the stool . . . you know the rest."

Lila stared at her father, mouth agape and eyes wide.

Birgit had beads of sweat across her forehead, but she had evidently been listening. "I don't know the rest." She gasped between clenched teeth. "What happened then?"

"My brother-in-law broke his neck. I was taking his pulse when I heard the glass in the front door to the pharmacy break and crash. A junkie had kicked the glass in and triggered the silent alarm. He was looking for morphine and apparently already had an idea where to look, because he headed straight for the correct shelf. He didn't notice me. I disappeared out the back door and watched the police officer come from across the street. She found the guy with Stefan's wallet in his hand and his fingerprints on Stefan's throat."

"But . . . the junkie killed Uncle Stefan," Lila whispered.

"No," her father said. "When the junkie broke into the pharmacy, Stefan was already dead. The junkie just had the bad luck of being in the wrong place at the wrong time."

Birgit closed her eyes tight and moaned again. Neither Weiz nor Lila noticed her.

"But what does all of this have to do with Paulina?" Lila asked between sobs.

"Stop," Birgit said, making a time-out sign with her hands. "Could you please call me a taxi? I think the baby is coming."

"No one is calling a taxi here."

I knew the voice coming from off-stage, and of course it belonged to Offermann, who was leaning against the living-room door. He had both his hands deep in the pockets of his jacket.

Finally the cops get here, I thought, but then the whole situation suddenly seemed a little off to me. How had Offermann gotten in here? And why wasn't he acting professional, like, at all?

"H-how did you get in?" Weiz stammered.

Huh???

Offermann was laughing with contempt. "The code on your security system is your daughter's birthday, you idiot. One-two-three-four would have been harder to crack."

Wait, wait, wait, wait, I thought. *What's going down here?*

"That's the voice . . ." Lila whispered. Her face had gone pale as a corpse, and she pointed with a trembling finger at Offermann.

Offermann looked at the girl. "I should have known you were eavesdropping. Where in the hell have you been hiding, you piece of shit?"

"I need to get to the hospital," Birgit whispered.

"Lila didn't have anything to do with it," Weiz yelled.

"Of course Lila has something to do with it," Offermann hissed through bared teeth and barely suppressed rage. "She was eavesdropping on us when I told you I'd found the blackmailer and was going to shut her up."

I couldn't keep up anymore. Offermann and Weiz had talked about a blackmailer who Offermann was going to shut up? Did they mean our Paulina? But what did Offermann and Weiz have to do with each other. Why would the cop want to silence a blackmailer who was threatening the pill counter? And what was she blackmailing him over? Ineffective or counterfeit drugs? So, Paulina blackmails Weiz, who calls Offermann for help, who kills Paulina. Fucking hell.

Weiz looked at his daughter with tears in his eyes.

"He said it was a nurse at the Sonnenschein Home," Lila sobbed. "So I went there and tried to warn her."

"But you didn't warn her," Offermann said.

"I didn't know her name." I could barely make out Lila's words anymore. She was bawling hysterically now. "And then the police suddenly showed up and said Paulina was dead."

"Oh, God, Lila. Why didn't you come home?" Weiz asked, almost inaudibly.

"You were mixed up with the murderer!" Lila roared.

Birgit started to reach her hand out toward the completely unhinged girl, but instead she folded in half, cringing and panting.

"Hos-pi-tal," she gasped.

OK, the whole connection between Weiz and Offermann still wasn't clear to me, but I was going to have to think on that later. Now I needed something to happen, and fast, before Offermann staged a family tragedy and slaughtered everyone here—and before Birgit gave birth.

Where in the hell was Martin? And, more importantly, where were Karpi's troopers? Martin had informed Karpi that Birgit had fallen into a trap doing her research and needed to be rescued. He'd given him Weiz's address, but Karpi had hung up before Martin could even say bye. Was that a good or bad sign? If it was a good sign, then the rescue operation must be close.

Impatient, I flew out of the house—and couldn't believe my eyes.

THIRTY-TWO

Martin hadn't arrived yet, and there wasn't any other car on the street I expected help from, and looking left and right I saw no sign of SWAT approaching, either. But instead I noticed some movement just outside the house. Someone was fiddling around with the bathroom window. That someone had a "Fuck off, jerk-off" attitude that was extremely familiar, even though the short blonde hair wasn't quite yet. The person bumbling around with the bathroom window was Katrin.

German houses almost always have tilt-and-turn windows instead of lift-and-slide windows, and the bathroom window was tilted open. Katrin standing on an upside-down bucket in front of it, working on the window frame to get the pane of glass out. The crowbar she had in her hand gave a professional impression, and with a very quiet squeak, she pushed the window in slo-mo into the bathroom, where it would presumably shatter into a thousand pieces and wake the dead. But no! Katrin's reaction time had been honed from years playing volleyball. At the last second she caught the window, turned the pane of glass out of the last corner of the frame, angled it, and guided it out of the house with one hand. She set it quietly against the outside of the house.

She got down from the bucket and froze when she turned around.

Jenny was pointing her gun at Katrin.

"Katrin? You look . . . What are you doing here?" Jenny whispered perplexed.

"Shh!" Katrin said, her face desperate. "A hostage-taker is inside."

Jenny stopped short, carefully took a couple steps sideways toward the wall of the house, moved just around the front of the building, and then, camouflaged by an ugly bush with thick, shiny-green leaves, she took a brief, careful glimpse into the living room through the picture window in front.

"I don't see one," Jenny said.

"You see him, Jenny. It's Offermann."

Jenny turned pensive, maybe even a little resolute, the way she seemed before when Offermann had called her Jenny Baby earlier. But she didn't look like she was in disbelief or anything. "Do you have proof?"

Katrin nodded grimly. "Yes, but not here."

"I'm going in there now." Jenny's voice sounded unambiguously defiant.

Katrin lunged forward, knocked Jenny's pistol out of her hand, dived on it, and was back up on her legs faster than seemed possible.

And here I'd always thought volleyball was boring!

"What are you doing here anyway?" Katrin asked.

Jenny pouted. "Weiz left me a voice mail he wanted to explain everything to me now. When I got here, I noticed someone trying to break in through the bushes, but I didn't recognize you."

"Maybe you better stay out of it if you think Offermann's innocent," Katrin said harshly.

Jenny-Bunny didn't have any tears in her eyes; she had a sparkle I'd never seen there before. "I'm not a police-academy trainee, and I've had it up to here with people treating me like I am. So, if anyone should stay out of it here, it's the civilians. Give me my weapon!"

Katrin shook her head. "Not while you think Offermann is a good guy."

Jenny crossed her arms. "Convince me otherwise."

"When did Offermann start throwing himself at you? When you started on the Paulina Pleve case? He killed her and staged her death as a suicide. He followed and manipulated the investigation through you. He kept insisting you close the case as a suicide, am I right?"

Jenny was evidently not shocked by this interpretation of the facts.

"He's also to blame for Susanne Hauschild, and he planted the evidence against Gregor in her apartment. The coffee cup, for example."

OK, this time Jenny's eyes got bigger for a second, but then narrowed to slits. "Since when have you known all this?"

Something had happened to Jenny since I left police HQ. Offermann had pissed her off, and she had put two and two together herself. I don't think she had made it all the way to four yet, but she had gotten to three at least.

Meanwhile Katrin kept frantically, and quietly, talking. "It was clear to me from the get-go that Gregor had been framed, and that it had to be a colleague. Who else could have set up the crime scene so meticulously that all the evidence pointed at Gregor? And why wasn't Gregor defending himself? Well, he didn't know who he could trust. So Gregor asked me to sit tight and stay put, and I did at first. But then I lost patience. So I started asking around a little, and I can assure you: Offermann is the murderer."

Jenny turned red but then jutted out her jaw.

"Do you have proof?"

"Quite a bit."

Jenny-Bunny thought for several seconds. She didn't burst out in tears at the turn of events. Instead, she made a quick, decisive nod. "Give me my weapon back."

The gun changed owners, then the two of them hatched a plan together while I went back into the living room.

I had been gone only a few minutes, but the situation inside had fundamentally changed. Birgit was lying on the couch yelling, Lila was sitting next to her holding her hand, and Offermann was holding a gun to Weiz's head.

"The combination," Offermann ordered.

I wasn't interested in any combination; I was interested in Birgit. She looked like her last hour had come. White as the walls, wet with sweat, eyes huge and feverish. Not good.

Offermann and Weiz walked to the giant wood stove at the wall, where Weiz flipped two levers and the whole thing slid forward. Behind it was a large, cube-shaped recess in the wall. Weiz knelt in front and leaned into the niche, which was deep enough you could probably slide a bowling pin lengthwise into it.

Lila kept talking the whole time, reassuring Birgit, who called for Martin at regular intervals. I thought it was high time for the two Charlie's Angels outside to make their play to save the one inside. I imagined one of them, preferably Katrin, in knee-high black boots with stiletto heels hanging from a long rope as she crashed through the large glass sliding door and . . .

Something broke through the large glass sliding door in the dining room, but it wasn't Katrin on a rope. It was the ultimate suburban dream machine: a riding mower. Every Saturday, the big boys would mount those like a wooden horse, and, with a bottle of beer in hand, they would mow the lawn seven times up and down to spend the day with a feeling of freedom and adventure instead of going shopping with Honeykins. But no one was sitting on this one.

Nonetheless, Offermann turned to the lawn mower, moved his gun from Weiz's head pointed it at the clattering machine. And with that Weiz was out of the firing line.

Jenny jumped into the room, pointed her gun at Offermann, and yelled, "Put your weapon down!"

Offermann whirled around but didn't get far. A frying pan to the back of his head abruptly stopped his rotation. His eyes rolled back and he collapsed.

"Shit, that's not what we discussed," Jenny complained.

"I wasn't sure if you could shoot your lover," Katrin explained as she carefully shook out her right hand. "I think I sprained my wrist."

Lila had started shrieking when the glass had broken, and she hadn't stopped yet. Katrin walked to her and pulled her to her feet. Weiz staggered over and hugged his daughter. Katrin turned to Birgit.

"How are you?"

Birgit's answer was a piercing scream.

Jenny handcuffed Offermann, and just to make sure he wasn't going anywhere bound his feet with a jump rope that Lila had run to get from her room. Then Jenny went out into the front yard to call her colleagues.

Katrin, Weiz, and Lila took Birgit to Lila's room and tried to get her to lie down on the bed, but Birgit pointed at a wood stool and sat down instead. Katrin and Lila were trembling, Birgit was alternately panting and moaning, but Weiz was suddenly the embodiment of calm.

"Don't panic," he said. "A baby will come out one way or another. All of the hocus-pocus about childbirth is total hogwash. So just try to relax as much as you can; you need to play along only at the right moment. Your baby is directing everything, OK?"

Katrin turned paler and paler, but Birgit smiled at Weiz. "Ok-aaa-eee."

Weiz tasked Lila with fetching various items. Mineral water for Birgit, a couple of sheets, some towels, a tennis ball.

"Tennis ball?" Katrin asked.

"She can squeeze it instead of breaking someone's hand."

Katrin looked at the back of her hand where Birgit's fingers had left red marks. "Good idea."

Martin was finally getting out of the taxi and bounded awkwardly toward Jenny in the yard. He fell down but scrambled right back up and ran—to the extent you can describe Martin's frantic style of locomotion as running—to the front door. A few seconds later, Martin was sitting on the floor in front of Birgit, feeling her belly with both hands.

"How far apart are the contractions?"

Lila grabbed a pink stopwatch and checked the intervals.

"Hey, we're off to a fast start," Weiz said casually. "What kind of car do you have?"

"Deux Chevaux," Martin said, but Birgit screamed "Be-Em-Double-Yooouuuuuu!" with a contraction that looked particularly painful.

Weiz spread sheets out over the chair, the floor, and the bed. "Actually I don't think we have time for the hospital. Pick a spot you like best. And you can kneel on the floor if you like as well."

"I'm Birgit, by the way," Birgit whispered.

"Bastian," Weiz replied with a smile.

Birgit swallowed some water and asked Martin to help her undress.

"Would you prefer it if I go out?" Weiz asked.

Birgit shook her head. Katrin was now pale as chalk, and Lila was staring wide-eyed at Birgit.

"Now," Birgit whispered at her next contraction, and Martin, who was sitting on the floor in front of her chair, opened his mouth and eyes alike. His hands whipped forward, and he was holding a slimy ball in his hand.

Weiz sat beside him and told Birgit what was happening. "The head is out now. Now push just one more time . . ."

The head? That was the head? Eeew! It looked nasty. I had not wanted to be at the delivery, like, at all . . . a God-awful mess like that is not something you want to see unless absolutely necessary. But now . . . I stared fascinated at the scene below me. Birgit convulsed with pain once more, then there was a disgusting gooey sound, and suddenly a miniature creature was in Martin's hands.

"It's a girl," Martin said breathlessly. Birgit was still gasping for air like a sprinter after the hundred-meter, but she was all smiles.

There was a commotion in the doorway to Lila's room, and suddenly there were two paramedics standing there, staring.

"OK, we should cut the umbilical cord quickly. Who has the honor?" the tall paramedic asked, holding a scalpel out to the people in the room. No one leaped at the chance, so Martin nodded at the man. He carefully laid the gooey, writhing little being that displayed no feminine beauty whatsoever in Birgit's trembling open arms, and took the scalpel. He's familiar with slicing and cutting implements, obviously. The second paramedic took the baby out of Birgit's hands, gave it a good smack on its wrinkly ass, and was pleased with the squawking that instantly set in.

"Child abuse," Katrin muttered, the color not yet returned to her face. But then she began to weep.

Weiz helped Martin wrap the child in a bunch of towels, and, handing the child to Birgit, whispered, "Congratulations. You did great!"

Birgit was beaming with happiness, which was a serious feat given her frowzy appearance. Katrin managed to blubber out "a girl, a girl" between two sobs, and Lila stared fully hypnotized at the little bundle of person that was now lying on Birgit's belly and gradually calming down.

Martin's focus on the baby eased up for a split second during which he reproached me: "You've been lying to me the whole time."

I thought it better not to reply. I couldn't have said anything anyway. I was torn between the nausea caused by this glibbery, slimy something with glued-down strands of hair, a red nose, and threads of drool coming out its mouth who now shared my birthday and—I just need to say it now—an absolutely inappropriate level of emotion.

"Sonja," Martin said quietly.

Birgit stopped short and turned red. "Uh, Martin . . ."

"Yes?"

Well, here comes the confession about the deal where she hawked the kid's name to Karpi.

"Nothing," she said quietly.

Good decision. Harsh reality would catch up with the little family soon enough. After all, fate had been merciful: a Katharina was a hundred times better than an Anatol.

THIRTY-THREE

Transcript: Jürgen Gernot

Question: "Why did you kidnap Till Krämpel?"

Gernot: "I thought he was the person Paulina was trying to blackmail."

"Blackmail? How did you come to think that Ms. Pleve was trying to blackmail someone?"

"She told me. She said she was onto some kind of scandal with the drugs at the retirement home. I said she should go to the police, but she wanted to get rich instead."

"And you didn't know whom she was trying to blackmail?"

"No. I thought it was someone from the home."

"So you tried to convince her to file a complaint with the police?"

"Yes. But she didn't want to. I ended the relationship. I don't want anything to do with criminal activities—or with a blackmailer."

"And after she died, you thought your girlfriend had been blackmailing Till Krämpel and that he had then killed her?"

"Exactly."

"But that's not correct."

"No. He didn't have anything to do with it at all."

"Why then did you shoot him?"

"I didn't! The cop who stormed into the lodge killed Krämpel. And then he shot at me."

Transcript: Gregor Kreidler

Question: "Detective Kreidler, why didn't you say anything in your defense?"

Kreidler: "I had been warned: 'Keep quiet; remember Katrin.' I took that warning to heart."

"But you could have sped up the investigation considerably by making a statement."

"I didn't give one shit about your investigation. It was about the safety of my girlfriend."

"How did your key fob end up in Ms. Hauschild's apartment, actually?"

"It was broken. The eye that I used to attach it to my keychain had ripped through. Susanne offered to have a friend of hers repair the plate, which is why I gave it to her."

"And the coffee cup?"

"I had taken it with me from my apartment to the office weeks ago. Offermann must have taken it from my desk and planted it in Susanne's apartment."

"You should have told us all of that."

"My colleagues could have figured out a great deal of that all on their own."

"There is a possibility you will be charged with interfering with a police investigation."

"No problem," Gregor said. "Then I will file a disciplinary complaint with Internal Affairs for failure to exercise due diligence."

"Yes, well, fortunately everything turned out OK."

The subsequent noise was not transcribed into the record, but I heard it when it came out of Gregor's nose. Fearlessness combined with complete and utter disgust.

Transcript: Katrin Zange

Question: "Dr. Zange, why didn't you come to the police?"

Zange: "Are you joking? Paulina Pleve and Susanne Hauschild's murderer is a cop. And the geniuses up in Düsseldorf put Detective Kreidler in jail and neglected all other evidence. My confidence in Criminal Investigations was zero."

"How did you realize that Offermann murdered Paulina Pleve and Susanne Hauschild?"

"He's a partner in MelinaMed and thus significantly invested in its profitability."

"What's illegal about that?"

"*Nothing.* But where would Offermann have come by a half million euros to buy his shares of the company?"

"Well, where did he come by the money?"

"He didn't have the money at all. The owner, Bastian Weiz, transferred the shares to him. In other words: a gift. And that was just one month after Detective Offermann had handled the murder of Bastian Weiz's brother-in-law."

"You could have come to the police with this information."

"I could have. But I didn't want to."

"Instead you broke into a house . . ."

"Mr. Weiz has not filed charges about that."

"You interfered in a police investigation—"

"Nonsense."

"And you struck Andreas Offermann with a pan. He has a severe concussion."

"My sympathy has its limits."

"Detective Offermann's attorney is considering a lawsuit against you and Detective Gerstenmüller for assault."

"Detective Offermann's attorney can kiss my ass."

Transcript: Bastian Weiz

Question: "What happened the night after your brother-in-law died?"

Weiz: "I drove home in a panic. About two hours later, the doorbell rang. Andy was at the door."

"Andy?"

"Andreas Offermann."

"You knew him?"

"We used to be in the same tennis club and played on the club team. The poor devil hardly had money for a racket, but he had unbelievable natural talent."

"So what happened after Offermann rang your doorbell that night?"

"He said, 'I know what you did tonight.' He was grinning. As though he were just poking a little fun. But I knew him well enough to know that he wanted something. He had that greedy look in his eyes, like before an important match. He wanted to win. At any price."

"And what did you do?"

"I invited him in, and we went to my study. He silently set two things out on the table: my signet ring and a police badge."

"And then you reached an agreement."

"Yes. He offered to keep me out of the investigation if I paid him accordingly. I laughed at him. My company was nearly bankrupt."

"But somehow you managed to come to an agreement."

"I explained the problem about the inferior raw materials that had led to the argument with my brother-in-law. He thought about it for a few minutes and proposed making cheap raw materials the basis of the business. That would result in equal sales but four times the profit."

"Which you paid to him."

"Yes."

"Why did you agree to this deal?"

"To stay out of prison, of course. My daughter was already half an orphan. Should I have left her all by herself?"

Transcript: Lieselotte Berger

Question: "You're quite certain that you saw this man on the day your neighbor, Ms. Hauschild, was murdered in her apartment?"

(Note: Mrs. Berger studies the photo of Andreas Offermann.)

Berger: "Quite certain."

"Why didn't you say anything about this before?"

"You asked only about the other man. The one who rang Ms. Hauschild's buzzer."

"And this man here? He didn't ring?"

"No. I thought he was here for the young woman who had moved into the penthouse apartment that day."

THIRTY-FOUR

July 14, one day after Gregor's release

"We're eternally grateful," Katrin said as she hugged Karpi, who blushed like a virgin in the men's sauna. The fat jellyfish was wearing light blue today, and with his red cheeks he looked like a neon sign outside a gay club in Miami Beach.

"If you hadn't been there for Birgit and sent me to Weiz . . ."

Karpi cleared his throat and devoted himself to his Technicolor drink at the club's bar. This was the first time I'd seen him upstairs in his bouncy castle instead of in the basement of his bunker, and he seemed far less like a criminal in this environment. "You're welcome, *Liebelein*."

The way the term of affection in Cologne's dialect rolled off his tongue sounded like a lion roaring a lullaby, but Katrin and Gregor both smiled wide.

"How did you catch on so quickly to what was happening?" Katrin asked.

Karpi emptied his glass and ordered another drink with a grunting sound. The bartender who had been serving the blonde girls and gold-chained wannabe gangsters at the other end of the bar scurried up and got Karpi a refill. Then he fist-bumped his boss, nodded at him, and went back to the kindergarten crew.

"You do me too great an honor, Beautiful. I was simply and absolutely sure that Gregor was innocent. So it was clear someone had framed him, fairly professionally. And the fact that Gregor wasn't saying anything told me that he wasn't sure whom he could trust anymore. Which is why I was so pleased when Birgit suddenly showed up here."

"And you encouraged me to act like I had written Gregor off," Katrin added.

"To keep you safe," Karpi confirmed with a nod.

"But when Martin called you, you already knew Offermann was the murderer, yes?" Katrin asked.

"After the shoot-out in the Sauerland, I put Offermann under the microscope a bit. It's rare that a cop from Cologne finds himself in a hunting lodge in the Sauerland with one man who's dead and another who's as good as dead. I learned that he had been a gifted tennis player until he developed a serious injury, that he was a successful police officer, and that he was living rather large. So I took a closer look at his accounts, where I saw large sums of money coming in from a company called MelinaMed. I was surprised he had such highly lucrative shares in a pharmaceutical company, but nothing pointed to him being the murderer."

"Until the day he showed up at Weiz's to silence him once and for all . . . ?" Gregor asked.

I had to grin. Gregor had heard the whole story from Martin and Katrin, but he just couldn't believe it. Or he didn't want to. Or at least, he wanted confirmation directly from Karpi that Martin had called up one of the city's best-known criminals to get the mother of his child out of the clutches of a policeman. Whereupon he dispatched a secret weapon—code name, Katrin.

"This Martin called me and said Birgit was at the home of someone named Weiz and she was in danger there and that I had to do something to save her. Which set off warning bells in my head: I had read the name Weiz in connection with that pharmaceutical company Offermann was invested in. Also, he and Weiz had been on the same tennis team, but I didn't think there was anything suspicious about that, so I didn't probe further into Weiz. I did that only after I got the call from your treasured friend, Martin. And that's when I stumbled across the story about Weiz's brother-in-law."

"The break-in at the pharmacy," Gregor said. "But the junkie confessed at the time."

"Of course. But he died from an overdose before the trial. And the transfer of the shares in MelinaMed to Offermann didn't close until a month after the pharmacist died."

Gregor nodded slowly, realizing that Criminal Investigations could and should have found this information as well.

"That's how you get from one piece of information to the next," Karpi continued. "Contacts, finances, real estate, strange murder cases, and so on. Suddenly the picture was quite clear. So I called Katrin and quickly told her the whole story."

"But you must have known she would set out and put herself in harm's way," Gregor said with a grumble.

Katrin rolled her eyes.

"Of course," Karpi said. "But what would you have done in my place?"

"Why did Susanne come here that Wednesday before she was murdered?" Katrin asked.

That was a cool maneuver to distract them, because she had already fought with Gregor for hours about him sitting in jail and keeping quiet to protect her, leaving her nothing better to do than hunt Offermann down herself. Katrin was sick of the topic.

Karpi laughed. "She wanted to buy research. No idea how she knew about my little side business. Perhaps from that brat whose grandma lived next door."

"Buy research?" Katrin asked. "Side business? Did I miss something?"

Gregor and Karpi grinned at each other.

"Karpi hacks computers," Gregor said. "Professionally." Katrin's jaw fell open.

"All above board," Karpi added. "We are hired by victims of cybercrime. We look for security vulnerabilities, document weak points, and patch the holes."

"You're competing with the Chaos Computer Club?" Katrin asked, referring to Europe's largest hacker association, which is based in Hamburg.

Karpi nodded. "There's no competition. I'm high up in the club myself, just anonymously."

I wondered how someone with a stage presence like Karpi's could do anything anonymously, but he presumably never made appearances in person. And he didn't need to be in a computer club.

"The kids who earn their pocket money here think my business is totally illegal. They would never join the club otherwise, because it's quite well established now and even a little stuffy. What the kids are into is how it kisses the bounds of legality, and even takes a step to the other side. But that's how I keep them under control."

"Still, it *is* child labor," Katrin mumbled.

"You wouldn't believe how clever those little shits are nowadays. Lots of them are in the fast lane speeding way past our in-house pros. We learn tricks from them they'd never tell if they knew what side I was playing for. They show off everything they know, and each one of them wants to be the biggest gangster. So they spend all this time coming up with Internet worms and the like, but no sooner have they thought one up than we've neutralized it for our clients."

"So you're not a criminal at all?" Katrin whispered.

"Disappointed?" Karpi asked.

Katrin smiled wide again. "I'm afraid I must decline to comment."

THIRTY-FIVE

July 24, twelve days after The Birth

Katrin, Gregor, Martin, and Birgit were sitting in the kitchen filling up on noodles. The main if not only thing Birgit had been eating since she'd outsourced the kid, in fact, was noodles. She had a lot of catching up to do, she claimed, even though she'd just spent nine months alternately eating and sleeping. But I wasn't worried about her. Yes, she was still a little pudgy, but she wasn't fat-fat, and I suspected that the noodles were somehow bypassing Birgit's stomach and intestines anyway, diverting directly to the mammary glands. As for Sonja Katharina, the stinky little bullhorn, she knocked back milk like a Hummer knocks back gas. And naturally everything that went in at the top came out at the bottom, so Martin and Birgit had metamorphosed into world-champion diaper changers. Every time they opened one of those poo-nami pouches, I panicked and bolted out into the wild blue yonder.

But right now I was with the whole group. It was the first time since Sonja was born that everybody was sitting around the same table, and I didn't want to miss it, although it looked for a while like such get-togethers might be a thing of the past.

"That you have a criminal hacker as a friend and that he uses child laborers is something I do not think is all right, no matter how much he may have helped in this case," Moral Martin was blathering on disapprovingly at Gregor.

"Karpi isn't a criminal," Katrin corrected him. "It's just that the kids can't find that out, which is why he pretends he is."

"And Weiz is in jail?" Birgit asked. She was also a card-holding member of the Karpi Fan Club, which irritated Martin enormously.

"No." Gregor grabbed the last noodle from the bowl. Birgit stood up and put a pot of water on the stovetop. My God, did she need more fodder?

"He's out on his own recognizance because there's no danger of flight or suppression of evidence," Gregor said. "And with some luck he'll get a suspended sentence. The deaths at the home won't be prosecuted as murder, after all, but manslaughter, and he's cooperated fully with the authorities."

"How did Paulina Pleve get wise to Weiz?" Birgit asked. She was practically slobbering into the boiling pot of noodles, she was lusting for the next batch so badly.

"She had noticed the strange cluster of deaths at the retirement home, and by comparing patient data she evidently figured out that an unusually large number of patients were dying when their old medications were swapped out with versions produced by MelinaMed."

"And how was Susanne connected to it?"

Gregor sighed. "Offermann had been keeping an eye on Jenny and me after Paulina Pleve was murdered to keep up-to-date on the investigation. That's the same reason he starting making the moves on Jenny. He must have noticed Susanne talking to me during one of his snooping operations. Maybe he already knew at that point that she was on to the cluster of deaths, but maybe he only got interested in her after he realized she and I knew each other."

"And by framing you as Susanne's murderer, he'd be rid of you both," Birgit concluded.

"Exactly."

"Did Offermann actually admit to any of that?" Birgit asked.

"He's been quiet as a tombstone," Gregor grumbled.

Three pairs of eyes looked at Gregor.

"Yes, I know. I kept my mouth shut too. Even so, Offermann's silence pisses me off. We all know what he did, but the question is whether we can really prove that without any holes. We found DNA evidence of him at Paulina's and at Susanne's, but that doesn't prove murder."

"And Susanne's laptop . . . ?" Martin asked.

"Never turned up."

No one said anything for a moment. Katrin stroked Gregor's back, Martin scraped the last remnants of tomato sauce from his plate, and Birgit stared ravenously into the pot of noodles.

Gregor was motionless for a moment, staring off into space.

"When did Offermann become corrupt and criminal?" Martin asked.

Gregor sighed. "Weiz thinks Offermann developed a taste for an expensive lifestyle when he was at the tennis club, and he figured out ways to enjoy a higher standing of living. We're researching all the cases now that he was an investigator on. A whole series of them look quite suspicious now. But worse yet . . . we stumbled across a horrible bit of news . . ."

Katrin rested her hand on Gregor's arm.

"It looks like Offermann also killed my cousin's daughter because she caught him during a drug deal. But I doubt we can ever prove it."

The noodles were good, as Birgit demonstrated by noisily vacuuming one from the pot into her mouth and carefully chewing it. She poured off the water and took the pot to the table.

At that moment the doorbell rang.

Martin left the kitchen and returned a moment later with a thick, padded envelope in his hand. Birgit's name was on it. She set down her silverware and opened the package. A bundle of banknotes fell out along with a greeting card with only one word written on it: Katharina.

"What's this?" Martin asked.

Birgit turned beet red. "Um, I think the money's from Karpi."

"Not again, that—" Martin began.

"Small, unused, unmarked bills, not consecutively numbered," Gregor announced after taking the bundle from Birgit. "You can accept it with a clear conscience."

"We're returning it," Martin said, taking the money from Gregor.

"Out of the question," Birgit said. "One does not refuse a gift at the birth of one's child. It brings bad luck. The money is for Katharina, and we will invest it for her." She took the money back and stormed out of the room.

"You have no chance against two women," Gregor said with a grin.

"But you still have me on your side, so it's a draw," I yelled at Martin.

As Birgit walked back in, Martin's sigh made them all laugh.

EPILOGUE

"Martin?" Birgit whispered one night under the anti-electrosmog net, after Sonja Katharina was finally snoring now that the obligatory dairy operations were done. "Who is Pascha?"

"No!" I roared. "Don't tell her!"

I still hadn't decided if I was more worried about my frustration over Birgit not knowing or about my fear of how she would react.

Martin said nothing for a moment, and I wished he could hear me, but the net was tightly shut, and I couldn't get in there with him.

"Well, it's a long story."

"Much too long for a bedtime story if Birgit's eyes are already drooping," I yelled.

"But you'll tell it to me at some point?" Birgit whispered.

"Promise," Martin whispered back.

I stayed until Birgit had fallen asleep, and then I followed the flashing blue lights that raced past the bedroom window.

ACKNOWLEDGMENTS

In this latest case I am once again in the debt of Dr. Frank Glenewinkel, who generously shares his expertise in forensic medicine with me so that Martin at least comes across with commanding knowledge of his profession. Klaus Dönecke at the Düsseldorf Police Department is much more professional and much nicer than his fictitious colleagues, and Ludger Rath at the Upper Sauerland County Police is no less impressive. Markus Kröll at the Kreidler Motorcycle Interest Group in Altenstadt, Hessen, sent me his own VIN plate as a sample and gave me a helping hand picking a model. In addition, I would like to thank Stephan Immen, spokesperson for the German Federal Department of Motor Vehicles, for providing a correction to the traceability of VIN plates; and Petra Sommerhäuser, director of the Korschenbroich Senior Home, for her insight into administrative issues. Mechthild Wintgens enlightened me on the weal and woe of the final few weeks of pregnancy. I would also like to thank Joe Bausch for his book *KNAST* (*Jail*), which gave me a few points of inspiration for Gregor's involuntary sojourn at the "state guest house." Administrative Director Charlotte Najes at the Düsseldorf Detention Center added further details, especially about pretrial detention. Any inaccurate portrayals are my own fault—they are either unintentional errors for which I ask forgiveness or deliberate variations for dramatic effect.

Jutta Profijt

ABOUT THE AUTHOR

Jutta Profijt has worked as a project manager in exports, as a freelance lecturer in business English and business French, and as an examiner for the German Chamber of Commerce and Industry. Her novel *Morgue Drawer Four* was nominated for the 2010 Friedrich Glauser Prize for best crime novel, and her series featuring Pascha, the cocky ghost detective, now includes five books. In addition to crime fiction, Profijt also writes more cheerful fare. Both her Morgue Drawer series and other novels have been translated into English. Profijt currently writes full time in the hinterlands of Germany's Lower Rhine region.

ABOUT THE TRANSLATOR

 Erik J. Macki worked as a cherry orchard tour guide, copy editor, Web developer, and German and French teacher before settling into his translation career. This was probably inevitable, as he has collected grammars, dictionaries, and language-learning books since childhood—and to this day is not above diagramming sentences when duty so calls. A former resident of Cologne and Münster, Germany, and of Tours, France, he did his graduate work in Germanics and comparative syntax. He now translates books for adults and children full-time, including works by Kerstin Gier, Mirjam Pressler, Jutta Profijt, and Sara Blædel, among others. He works from his home in Seattle, where he lives with his family and their black Lab, Zephyr.